TIMELESS
WESTERN
COLLECTION

A Wyoming Summer

TIMELESS
WESTERN
COLLECTION

A Wyoming Summer

CARLA KELLY
CHRISTINE STERLING
HEATHER B. MOORE

Mirror Press

Interior Design by Cora Johnson
Edited by Meghan Hoesch and Lorie Humpherys, and *The Widow of Daybreak* edited by Carolyn Leggo, Amy Petrowich, and Amber Downey
Cover design by Rachael Anderson
Cover Image Credit: Arcangel, Magdalena Russocka

A Wyoming Summer is a Timeless Romance Anthology® book.

Timeless Romance Anthology® is a registered trademark of Mirror Press, LLC

Published by Mirror Press, LLC

ISBN: 978-1-952611-32-2

Timeless Western Collections
Calico Ball
Mercer's Belles
Big Sky
A Wyoming Summer

Timeless Georgian Collections
Her Country Gentleman
A Lady's Wager
A Midnight Masquerade

Timeless Regency Collections
Autumn Masquerade
A Midwinter Ball
Spring in Hyde Park
Summer House Party
A Country Christmas
A Season in London
A Holiday in Bath
Falling for a Duke
A Night in Grosvenor Square
Road to Gretna Green
Wedding Wagers
An Evening at Almack's
A Week in Brighton
To Love a Governess
Widows of Somerset
A Christmas Promise
A Seaside Summer
The Inns of Devonshire
To Kiss a Wallflower

Timeless Victorian Collections

TABLE OF CONTENTS

Ellen Found

Carla Kelly

In loving memory of Virginia Kent, dear friend and reader—

the best part of writing are the people I meet.

One

NINETEEN YEARS OLD. AFTER A short lifetime of wanting little because she had nothing, Ellie Found decided she wanted more.

There it was, an ad in the *Butte Inter Mountain*. She moved the smelly fish head aside, supper for Plato the monster cat. "'For the adventurous only,'" she read out loud, then read in silence about the Yellowstone Park Association needing a kitchen girl for the crew building a hotel near Old Faithful. "'Room and board, thirty dollars a month,'" she read.

She needed a change from the Mercury Street Café. A month ago, Mr. Linson fired Addie Jackson. Ellie couldn't help overhearing. "You sassed me once too often. Get out."

Addie was gone by noon, telling Ellie, "Leave this dump." She lowered her voice. "Don't trust 'em."

Ellie didn't.

Addie Jackson was replaced by a cook who smoked constantly, the ash from her cigarette ending up in many a meal. Revolted, Ellie still found it fascinating how ash looked like pepper in the scrambled eggs. The cook never spoke. All she did was roll another cigarette and point to the next task.

"I can't stay here," Ellie muttered as she scraped a carrot. "Get a plan, Ellen Found."

She tore out the ad and wrapped the fish head for Plato, the demon cat who barged into her life in a snowstorm and never left. Last year, when he limped toward her in the alley, she found a friend. As Ellie stared, he'd raised his afflicted paw. "Don't scratch me," she said. He yowled when she yanked out a thorn, then licked her hand and followed her into her miserable room under the Mercury Street Café.

She'd shared her dinner of soup and bread with him, explaining that he would eat when she did, and it might not be what he wanted. He curled up beside her on her cot, apparently willing to take the good with the bad, same as she did.

That was last year.

"Goodnight, Mr. Linson," she said, hoping her boss's slimy son wasn't around. He frightened her too.

"Don't be late tomorrow," Linson said. She was never late, a lesson learned from the nuns of St. Catherine's, who ran an orphanage and taught her to work hard and remember her lowly place.

Plato waited politely for her in the alley. She let him out every morning to do whatever a cat who looked like him did, but he always came back.

After a feast—for Plato—of fish head, and stew and stale toast for her, Ellie reread the ad, her eyes lingering over thirty dollars a month, plus room and board. She kept reading. "'Work guaranteed until June 1904, when Old Faithful Inn opens. Continued employment possible.'"

Her letter went in the corner mailbox after breakfast. She found a stamp in the drawer under the cash register. While Linson argued with his son in the back, she addressed the envelope: *Harry Child, Yellowstone Park Association, Bozeman, Montana.*

Ellie knew better than to use the Mercury Street Café as a return address. She darted across the street to the Miners Emporium. The owner always smiled at her, so she did not fear him.

"May I use your address for this job application?" she asked, after a glance behind. She had never seen him inside the Mercury Street Café, so she knew he was wise.

He took the letter. "If a reply comes, I'll get it to you."

Ten days later, a bum palmed off a note into her hand. When Mr. Linson retreated, muttering, to his office, she hurried to the emporium. "Good luck," the merchant said, handing her a letter.

"'Dear Miss Found,'" she read later, "'We are considering several applicants. Be in my office Monday, 1 p.m., Babcock Building, corner of Babcock and Timmons.'"

Others? Was this a yes, or as near as? Was she going? *Yes*, she told herself. *I'll get that job.*

Ellie debated all weekend whether to say anything to Mr. Linson. She decided against it. Better to simply steal away.

Plato waited for her in his usual place that Sunday night. For a moment she debated whether to take him along, then knew she must. He was her only friend.

An earlier renter had left a shoddy carpetbag. She stuffed her belongings inside, including Plato. "You're not going to like this," she told him. "It's an adventure. Curl up on my clothes." In went his water bowl, and her toothbrush, hairbrush, and comb. "I don't own much, do I?" she asked. "Neither do you, Plato."

She kept her life savings—fifteen dollars—in her corset. She put six dollars of that in her pocket, knowing she needed tickets to the Northern Pacific Rail Road, then a little more to Bozeman.

Ellie closed her door quietly on the Mercury Street Café. At the depot, she spent one dollar and fifteen cents for the short line ticket. "That'll be another two dollars and fifty cents when you get there," the clerk told her. Three dollars and sixty-five cents gone so soon. She stared at her money, willing it not to shrink more.

She curled into a dark corner in the depot. The clerk ignored her. This was Butte; he had seen other hard cases.

"We're going to get that job, Plato," she said. "Butte, I have had enough of you."

TWO

THE NPRR WAS LATE THAT morning, and she didn't know Bozeman. She asked an older man at the depot for directions. "Four blocks over, miss," he said, and tipped his hat. Painfully aware she was late, Ellie ran the four blocks, then down the hall to find *Harry W. Child* on door eight. She hurried inside.

A pretty lady waited, dressed impeccably, her polished shoes peeking out from under a stylish skirt. Two men sat there, one an older fellow, deep into Bozeman's *Avant-Courier*. The younger man carried a clipboard and an officious air—the interviewer, obviously.

"Miss Found?"

"Yes, sir."

He scrutinized his timepiece, and her heart sank. *I snuck out of Butte, and I don't know Bozeman*, she wanted to say.

"Glad you could make it," he said.

The other candidate already looked smug. Ellie took a deep breath. "Thank you for this opportunity."

"Please wait outside," he said to the lady. "This won't take long." He barely glanced at Ellie. "Will it?"

Ellie knew he had already decided. She thought of her nine years working in Butte since the age of ten, with fifteen dollars, a moldy cat, and wariness to show for it. She had nothing to lose. "All I ask for is a chance." Ellie waited for the older man to leave, but he gave her a glance that took in everything from her bare head—a hat on her wages? Hah!—to broken shoes.

Ellie considered. She knew the job wasn't hers. *I will use this interview as a lesson for future interviews*, she thought. No one said she could, but she sat down.

"Found is an odd name," the interviewer commented.

"My mother was a lady of the line in Butte, who died at my birth," she said, her head high. "Her name was Ellen, last name unknown. The nuns found me, so that's my name."

The interviewer made a note on his clipboard. "This isn't much of a work history," he said, glaring at the two jobs she'd listed. Calmly, Ellie told him about working for free in the Copper King Mansion, starting when she was ten, then kitchen work in the Mercury Street Café.

"No such place, and I know Butte," the interviewer said. Newspaper Man coughed discreetly.

"It's there and it's not a good place," Ellie said. "When I saw your advertisement, I knew I could do better." This wasn't getting her the job, but the chair was comfortable.

"You cook?"

"Yes."

Plato started to purr. The man stared at the carpetbag. "There's a cat in there?"

"Yes."

"No cats in Yellowstone Park," he said in triumph. "Good day, Miss, uh, Found."

Not so fast, mister. "Plato is a mouse killer," she said firmly. "Don't tell me Yellowstone Park has no mice." She folded her hands in her lap, needing a chance where there was none, knowing that every deck of cards in the universe was stacked against her when all she wanted was to work in a safe place.

The man frowned at his clipboard. His expression neutral, Newspaper Man leaned over, wrote something, and raised one eyebrow.

The interviewer nodded as his face reddened. "Maybe we need a cat."

Ellie glanced at the older man, almost encouraged. She decided to act as though *she* had the job, and not that lady with the wonderful shoes. "Plato is amazing. Mice walk around Butte in fear and trembling."

The older man smiled, so she plunged on. "When he's full, he leaves me the extras." She didn't add there were hungry days when she almost considered Plato's generosity.

"Plato?" the interviewer asked. "Where would *you* have heard of Plato?"

The older man frowned, whether at her presumption or the interviewer's rudeness, she could not tell. "I dusted the books in the Copper King's library," she explained. "I opened *The Republic* and liked the name."

The interviewer looked toward the door, maybe wishing she would take the hint and leave. Newspaper Man left the room, and Ellie heard low voices. Clearly, he was giving the lady outside the good news of her hire. He returned and nodded to the interviewer.

The interviewer stared at his clipboard. "It won't work. You're too pretty. The crew will hang around the kitchen, and time is of the essence on this project. Sorry."

Ellie stared, amazed and a little flattered. Why not set the man straight? "You want my cat, but *I* won't do?" She took Plato out of the carpetbag and set him down. "I dare you to take two steps toward me. No man is going to hang around any kitchen where *I* work."

Plato flattened his ears and hissed when the interviewer stepped forward. Her hero crouched low, his eyes never leaving his prey. Plato's hindquarters twitched and his tail lashed back and forth. The interviewer leaped back, holding his clipboard in front of him.

"Stop, Plato!" She rubbed behind Plato's ears in that favorite spot and returned him to her carpetbag. "Let's go." She stood up.

"Not so fast, Miss Found." Newspaper Man glared at the interviewer. "We're hiring her, and Plato too."

"*Me*? You are?"

"Heavens, yes," the man said. "I'm Harry Child, president of the Yellowstone Park Company, and you're working for me."

"But that lady . . ."

"I sent her on her way." He turned to the interviewer, who stared back. "Hopkins, not one job seeker out of ten will tell you the truth. That's all we have heard from Miss Found."

"But . . ."

"That other woman? Don't you know when someone's lying?" He turned to Ellie. "Well? Are you in?"

Ellie nodded, too shy to speak.

"Room, board, and thirty dollars a month." He laughed. "And five dollars for Plato, plus kitchen scraps. Welcome to Yellowstone Park."

Ellie signed a contract for the winter. "Sir, how long is a season?"

"As long as I say it is," he replied. "Now, head over to Hotel Bozeman."

"We can stay in the depot," Ellie assured him. "I

wouldn't want to . . ." *Spend any more of my money,* she thought. *Suppose a season is really short?*

Mr. Child held up one finger. "Miss Found, let us come to a right understanding. *All* my hires stay there." He glanced at the interviewer, who seemed to wilt before Ellie's eyes. "Hopkins, I'll handle this." The door closed quietly.

Mr. Child handed her a voucher for a room and meals. "The Bozeman is around the corner. Settle in and be ready for an early start."

She hesitated; he noticed. "Yes?"

"Why didn't you hire that lady? She was dressed so nicely, and I know what I look like." Might as well be honest. "I told Mr. Hopkins I was a found baby and he wasn't impressed."

"Mr. Hopkins is a new hire, too, and he lacks experience."

"Yes, but—"

"I've eaten in a few Mercury Street Cafés. I hire determined people wanting to do better." He touched the contract. "I saw your determination."

She nodded, too overcome to speak because he was right.

"Alice Knight sings at the Bonanza Casino. I, uh, planted her to teach Hopkins something about hiring people." He chuckled. "And maybe learn to look inside people, and not just at nice clothes."

"I wish I had better clothes," Ellie admitted.

"No worry. Mrs. Child is creating uniforms for the Old Faithful Inn staff. She'll have something soon. It comes with the job."

"All I want is a chance."

"You have one."

9

Three

I can't discard this journal. Gwen might want to read it someday to know more about her dear mother. Also, I want to write about this construction, as Mr. Child's lead carpenter. We've been building the Old Faithful hotel since June. This was my chance to retrieve Gwen from Clare's sister in Helena. She didn't relinquish my child willingly, but Gwen is mine. Gwen has attached herself to Ellen Found, a quiet woman Mr. Child hired to assist Mrs. Quincy in the kitchen. She has a fearsome cat and a sweet smile. (Hers, not the cat's.)

THREE DAYS LATER, TRAVELING IN a yellow tourist stagecoach from Mr. Child's transportation company, Ellie arrived at the construction site. They spent one night at a hotel in Gardiner, and another night at a soldiers' station inside Yellowstone Park. Even better, Ellie made an acquaintance.

Two acquaintances. She noticed the man and child in The Bozeman's lobby after breakfast. Mr. Child knew them, so she assumed he was one of the workers. That was that, at first.

It was a short walk to the depot from The Bozeman. To her delight, Ellie found an empty seat that contained a discarded newspaper. The porter offered to take her carpetbag, but stepped back when he heard Plato's rumbling growl from within.

She admired the scenery as they clacked along, reveling in unheard-of leisure, then opened the newspaper. She was deep in an article titled "American Renegade Killed. Desperate Fighting in Small Boat with Filipinos" when someone cleared his throat and Plato hissed.

"Oh, Plato," she said. There stood the man with the little girl. "Yes, sir?"

He had wonderful blue eyes and a close-cut beard as dark brown as his hair. "Pardon me, but my daughter needs to use the ladies' room. I'd rather she didn't go alone. I am Charles Penrose."

"Pleased to meet you, sir." She had heard that lilting accent before, reminding her of miners who came to the Mercury Street Café on Tuesdays when they served pasties. "I'm happy to help," she said, even though a train's lavatory was a mystery to her. "Where is it?"

He pointed to the front of the car. *I hope it's free*, Ellie thought.

"This is Gwener," he said. "*Gwener* is Cornish for Friday, her birth day. I call her Gwen." He gave his daughter a gentle push. "Go along, Gwen. The nice lady will help you."

The nice lady did. The two of them navigated the swaying car to a door with *Ladies* in gilt lettering. Inside was a small room with a sink and a cloth-roller bar. The other room contained the toilet.

Gwen came out promptly enough, her eyes wide. "Miss, you can see the tracks below!" Her words had a pleasant lilt, but it was not as pronounced as her father's.

11

Ellie pointed to a sign. "'Passengers will please refrain from flushing when the train is not in motion,'" she read. Gwen giggled.

Ellie steadied Gwen as she returned to her seat. Ellie put away the newspaper and admired early snow on mountain peaks, far better than a dingy café in a mining town. She fed breakfast scraps to Plato, hunter of mice and scourge of people. *You're all I have*, she thought, then looked ahead to see Gwen smiling at her.

She usually never put herself forward, but Ellie beckoned to the child, who talked with her father, then made her way cautiously toward Ellie.

Plato went back into his carpetbag. Ellie patted the seat and Gwen joined her. "You have a cat? I like cats. Is he shy?"

"Hard to say."

Gwen handed Ellie a book. "Da said you might read to me. I can read, but isn't it fun to be read to?"

Ellie had no idea, but she nodded. "*Rebecca of Sunnybrook Farm.*"

"Da gives me a book on birthdays and Christmas," Gwen explained. "What do you get on your birthday?"

"A year older," Ellie said, amused.

"No presents?" Gwen's eyes were wide with surprise.

"No." Ellie admired the cover, wondering how some people had so much, and others so little. "Where are you in the book?"

"I'm on chapter four. Again." She leaned closer. "Da has read this book over and over and is about to bop me on the head with it."

Ellie laughed. "I've never read it, so I won't bop your head."

Ellie read out loud to Gardiner, Montana, then on into the next day when Mr. Child directed his six workers plus

Gwen onto one stagecoach, with two freight wagons following. "Park visitors use such coaches in the summer," he said, directing his remarks to his new hires.

"Crowded like whelks in a basket," Mr. Penrose said to Ellie as they sat down, his daughter on his lap. He pointed to the stone arch just outside Gardiner. "'For the benefit and enjoyment of the people,'" he read. "People are already calling it the Roosevelt Arch. The president himself dedicated it last spring, when he visited the park."

Ellie looked skeptically at the scenery, which was less than impressive. Mr. Penrose must have noticed her expression. "Not too dramatic, is it? Wait 'til you see the geyser basin at Old Faithful."

Mr. Child motioned to him. "Let's have a meeting now, Charles. Move up."

"Coming, Mr. Child," he said. "May I leave Gwen with you?"

"Certainly. We have a book." She couldn't resist. "*Rebecca of Sunnybrook Farm*. You may have heard of it."

He rolled his eyes.

The builders conferred all morning in the four front rows. Lunch came from hampers, which Ellie organized because she decided to start earning her salary now. She helped with dinner as well, eaten at the log cabin soldiers' station beside the Gibbon River. The men grabbed fishing poles and joined the soldiers at the river, where they caught dinner.

Ellie and Gwen set the table inside the station. Soon potatoes were frying into crispy, salted rounds. The corporal tasted one. "Miss, come back often."

She protested, but they all helped with the dishes. Ellie walked with Gwen down to the Gibbon River after dishes, while Mr. Penrose watched. "Don't stray," he cautioned.

"Bears are chunking up for winter, and you'd be a tempting morsel."

Ellie laughed at that. "It's no joke," he said seriously.

Very well, then. Conversation. Conversation. "What is this inn like?" she asked.

"It's huge. The foundation is massive, concrete layered over with rhyolite, a volcanic rock found here. The first two floors are lodgepole pine with the bark still on. Mr. Reamer wants it rustic, bringing the outside inside." He rubbed his hands together. "The walls are up and sturdy, and we're almost done shingling the roof. Oh, the roof. Amazing."

"It'll be done by next summer?" she asked, feeling dubious, and she hadn't even seen it.

"It has to be." He nodded toward Mr. Child, who walked with Mr. Reamer, the architect. "He'll lose his shirt to the Northern Pacific if it isn't. At least we can work indoors for the winter. You'll never believe the cold."

"I know cold," she said quietly, thinking of her unheated room under the Mercury Street Café.

He gave her an appraising glance. "I believe you. You'll earn every penny of your salary."

"I intend to." She sensed kindness in this capable man who loved his daughter. "Same as you."

Four

October 12, 1903. I'm glad Gwen is with me. We'll do fine in this double log cabin, one of several built earlier as a possible hotel. Gwen is happy with Mrs. McTavish, who lives in the other half with her husband and son. She will watch Gwen while I work. It's a good arrangement. Gwen told me she wants to share a place with Miss Found.

THEY ARRIVED AT WHAT MR. Child called the Upper Geyser Basin ahead of nightfall. Ellie squinted into the gloom, seeing modest, crude buildings, all of them dwarfed by the behemoth, unfinished monster that must be the inn.

She had opened the carpetbag to give Plato some air. Before she closed it, he sniffed, then growled. "It's sulfur," she whispered to him. "Get used to it."

"Do you always talk to your cat?" Gwen asked.

How to explain Plato to this child who had probably never felt the burden of loneliness or the reality that there was no human to help her? "He understands me."

Gwen nodded, accepting her answer as a child would. She joined her father, following him in the dark toward a log cabin. Ellie realized that she had never inquired where she would be staying. All she'd wanted was out of Butte.

Mr. Child pointed toward a larger building. The new hires moved that way. When Mr. Child looked her way, she asked, "Where do I go?"

"This way. Mind your steps."

She trailed after her employer. The path was slick with snow turning into ice. She saw small shacks and larger ones and something that looked like a machine shop. She sniffed the air and smelled freshly planed boards as they passed a larger structure.

"Take my arm."

They made their way up shallow steps into a cavern. She looked up, squinting to see how tall the room was. She saw no end to it, not in the gloom of early evening. Imagine the place at midnight.

"This, Miss Found, is the lobby. It rises seventy feet or so. There are three floors, with rooms branching off from the main hall." She heard his sigh. "There's much to do."

"At least it's not snowing inside," she said finally, which made Mr. Child laugh and tease, "That's the best you can come up with?"

If he could joke, so could she, something she hadn't attempted before, not with someone who had power to hire and fire. "It was short notice." He chuckled, which she found gratifying.

"This was the big push during summer and autumn, to enclose this monster so we can finish the interior when snow falls." He gestured toward a massive stone structure. "This fireplace has four sides and four hearths." He gestured broadly. "It will be a great place to congregate."

"I imagine so," she said, hoping she didn't sound too dubious.

He lowered his voice. "I should warn you about Mrs. Quincy."

Oh dear, Ellie thought. *Please don't let the cook be a silent smoker.*

"My charming wife is a fine woman, but she has her moments. Don't we all? Adelaide decided she wanted a French chef, so Mrs. Quincy finds herself *here* instead of in our kitchen back home. She isn't particularly pleased."

Ellie reasoned that this could be worse. She stayed close on his heels, afraid that the darkness would swallow her. Ahead she saw lights under a closed door and smelled food cooking. The familiarity calmed her.

"Here it is," he said. "Mrs. Quincy will be fair, but she'd rather be back in our home kitchen."

Mr. Child opened the door to the finest kitchen ever, with the same rustic look of the dark lobby. There were two Majestic brand ranges, both bigger than the poor excuse in the Mercury Street Café; shelves with white china cups and plates; tables and benches; wooden bins probably holding flour and sugar; a coffee-bean grinder; two sinks; bags of carrots and potatoes and tins of tomatoes, beans, and corn. Ellie sighed with relief. She knew kitchens.

A woman not much taller than Ellie stopped stirring a pot of what was probably stew and turned around, wiping hair curled by the heat off her forehead. She frowned.

Don't complain yet, Ellie thought. *Get to know me.* "I'm Ellie Found," she said. "I come with a mouser."

The frown disappeared. "Very well, then," the cook said. "Close the door after you on the way out, Mr. Child. Tell your ill-begotten crew that we'll eat in half an hour."

The door closed. Ellie had the distinct impression Mr. Child was happy to leave. "Come over here," Mrs. Quincy said. "Let me see you better."

Ellie did as directed and set down her carpetbag. Through lowered eyelids, Ellie did her own appraisal. Mrs. Quincy looked like someone who had never suffered a fool gladly in her life.

"You're too pretty and the men will hang around," she said.

"I am here to cook, same as you," Ellie said, surprising herself. Hadn't Mr. Child said to be firm? The job was hers, after all. "No one ever said I was pretty either."

"You don't own a mirror?"

Ellie shook her head. Maybe mirrors were mortal sins at St. Catherine's. "I don't own anything," she said. "I have another dress and an apron. That's it."

"No one takes care of you," Mrs. Quincy said, her tone not so forbidding.

Ellie shrugged. "I'm an orphan."

"Is this your work dress?"

Oh, dear. Ellie's chin went up. "It's my best dress." Something compelled her to stick out her foot. "These are my only shoes, Mrs. Quincy. But I can prep and cook, and you won't be disappointed."

"You're forthright," Mrs. Quincy told her, but without the accusing tone this time.

"I never was, before I answered Mr. Child's ad," Ellie said. "May I let out my cat? I think he's the real reason Mr. Child tipped the balance in my favor."

"He's in your carpetbag? You may." Mrs. Quincy indicated a closed door. "That's your room. When the inn is done, it will be used for food storage. I suppose your cat will come and go as he pleases. They do that, don't they?"

Ellie picked up her bag and opened the door. She couldn't help her gasp of delight at seeing a bed already made, with a patchwork quilt and a pillow. There was a bureau with a mirror and a stand for a washbowl, complete with towels. "I've never seen anything like this," she said to Mrs. Quincy, who had followed her. "This is all for *me*?"

"I have the room next to yours. I'd call this a bit of a come down."

"Ma'am?"

"I was *the* cook in the Childs' residence in Helena," she said. Her voice hardened. "I cook plain food, and Mrs. Child wanted a French chef. I have been reassigned to outer darkness here."

If this was Mrs. Quincy's idea of outer darkness, she had obviously never set foot on Mercury Street in Butte. "It's a nice room," Ellie said cautiously.

"Our rooms are Mrs. Child's experiment to decide what bedroom furniture and coverlets will look best in a wilderness environment. She thinks rich folks want rusticity."

"It's the nicest room I have ever seen," Ellie said simply. She saw hooks for all the clothing she didn't own, and a shoe rack for her one pair of shoes. One drawer in the bureau would suffice for her possessions. She could pull out the bottom drawer for Plato, who, like most cats, preferred hidden spaces.

"Does your cat like meat scraps?" she heard from the doorway as she lifted Plato from the carpetbag.

"He eats what I eat," Ellie said, then took another chance. "That was the condition of our association." She felt the need for this woman to understand her, if they were going to work together. "I took a thorn out of his paw and he wouldn't go away."

Mrs. Quincy smiled at that. "Set him down and follow me," she said. "I'll need you to scrape and chop more carrots for the stew. Potatoes too. Maybe an onion. We didn't know how many more workers Mr. Child would dredge up."

Ellie set Plato on the bed. Mrs. Quincy returned to the cooking range for another stir and taste. Ellie got carrots from a sack and looked for a knife. Mrs. Quincy made a shooing gesture. "Don't dawdle! They'll be here before we know it!"

"I never dawdle," Ellie said. "More potatoes and onions?"

"Yes, and when you're done . . ." Mrs. Quincy looked Ellie over again. "How're your biscuits? I've been giving these miscreants pilot bread and they're sick of it."

"None finer," Ellie said firmly, well aware that this was a test, one she intended to pass. "Just point me to the baking powder."

Five

She talks to her cat. She's shy around men. Shingling done. Now a banquet. I ask myself if Ellen Found is making a difference, but how can that be? She's just kitchen help. I think she is more.

THE WORKERS FILED INTO THE kitchen in thirty minutes, dutifully lining up by the serving table. No one looked excited or happy. The new arrivals hung back, so Ellie drew on all her bravery and gestured them in with a smile. Everyone made a wide berth around Plato, who stood by her and hissed.

Several of the men sniffed the air and exchanged glances. *I've got you*, she thought as she brought out a massive bowl mounded with hot biscuits. Mrs. Quincy slapped down the butter and a bowl of strawberry jam.

"Miss, put them on the table instead," someone said. "It's easier." He gave Mrs. Quincy a cautious glance.

"Good idea," Ellie said. A minute later the biscuits were on the tables where the men sat. She put two more pans of biscuits in the Majestic and started around with the coffee while Mrs. Quincy watched.

Ellie looked for Mr. Penrose and Gwen, then remembered that they lived somewhere else and probably didn't eat here. She lost sight of Plato. She eyed the Regulator on the wall and took out the next batch of biscuits when it was time. A red-haired man transferred them to the table, pan and all.

Mr. Child watched his crew with real satisfaction, then found a place. He tapped his mug, stood up, and indicated Ellie and Mrs. Quincy. "We're in good hands, men," he said simply.

They're just ordinary biscuits, she wanted to tell them. *I can make them in my sleep.* She dipped a sudden curtsy, enjoying unexpected applause.

"No one goes hungry here," Mr. Child informed the newcomers, and in saying that, he relieved Ellie's heart as well. He snagged a biscuit as the bowl went by. "Tomorrow, we'll finish the roof because we have enough shingles now." He smiled at the good-natured groans. "We'll be working inside, then. Fire up the Majestics early, Miss Found. We'll warm those nails."

Ellie leaned toward Mrs. Quincy. "Warm the nails? Why?"

"They're working outside on the roof. Warm nails keep their hands from freezing."

She stood by one Majestic and felt Plato rubbing around her ankles. "It's your turn," she said, adding more meat to his bowl, although he never minded carrots. She watched him hunker down and eat, knowing there was stew for her too, probably as much as she wanted. She opened the door to her room a crack, to make sure it wasn't a mirage. Nope.

After the last worker filed out, Ellie filled one sink with hot water from the Majestic's boiler. The dishes were already stacked on the serving table. Ellie saw the sag in the older woman's shoulders. "I can do these," Ellie told her. "You look tired."

That earned her a sharp look, then a reluctant nod. "Drain them on the serving table. It's oatmeal and applesauce tomorrow morning. I'm soaking the dried applies over there." Mrs. Quincy hesitated, then spoke. "Could there be biscuits again?"

"Yes'm."

"Be up by four-thirty to lay the fires. I won't be much later."

Mrs. Quincy went to her room. Ellie found rough sacking to spread on the serving table and put the washed crockery there to drain. She looked for Plato and found him by the slightly open door into the lobby, where he had already accumulated a pile of mouse carcasses. "Impressive," she said. "You're earning your keep."

"Gwen's right," she heard from the dark. "You do talk to your cat."

"Mr. Penrose! You startled me!"

Mr. Penrose held up his hands and a burlap sack in defense. "I come in peace with a bag of nails." He set the nails by one of the Majestics and set a metal sheet on top. "Pour these on the sheet. I'll bring more during the day. We'll have the roof over the *porte cochère* done tomorrow."

"I'll remember, Mr. Penrose."

"Call me Charles," he said. She nodded, certain she would do no such thing.

"I came for another reason too, Miss Found." She had no reason to back up, but she did. "Maybe you'd like to see why this inn is important."

"Well, I . . ."

"Come outside," he said. "It's just about that time. No worries. This was Gwen's idea, but she's asleep."

He held the massive iron-studded door open, and she shivered. Hopefully this wouldn't take too long, whatever it was.

They stood under the sweep of the *porte cochère* that would, by summer, shelter stagecoaches dropping off park visitors. "Over there."

She saw a plume of steam rising off a higher mound she had noticed when the stagecoach stopped. It was cold enough to see her breath, but *this* steam must be the breath of the gods of the underworld.

"Old Faithful erupts about every fifty-five minutes," he said. "Feel that?"

Ellie felt a rumble beneath her thin-soled shoes. The steam rose higher, then fell, then rose up again and then higher. She held her breath at the solitary majesty of this amazing sight, something that had probably played out, unseen, for more time than she could imagine. Just when she thought it must be done, the steam sank and then rose higher.

"Some of the soldiers tell the visitors that it's set to go off between nine in the morning and six at night," he said.

"Hopefully no one believes them!"

"Only the gullible."

She watched as Old Faithful rose once more, sank until only puffs of steam remained, then stopped. For a moment she forgot she was cold, worried about Mrs. Quincy, hoping this job would last, and embarrassed to think that her work dress was a disgrace, but she had nothing else. *Stop*, she told herself. *Enjoy this.*

Mr. Penrose said nothing to break the spell. He walked her back inside the cavern of the lobby, stopping at Plato's stash of dead mice. "Impressive."

"Plato never fails," she said, wondering at anyone's attention, aware that for the first time in her life, someone wanted to chat, not to order her about, but share an experience.

After he left, she regarded all the bowls drying on sacking and the cutlery jumbled together, an unwelcome, early-morning task. This was work on a larger scale than anything at the Mercury Street Café.

Here's the thing, she thought, after a glance at Mrs. Quincy's door. *I can't shingle a roof, but I can make a difference.*

She dried the bowls, then placed them around the two long tables, along with knives and spoons beside each bowl, a place for each man, so they didn't have to line up like, well, orphans. She filled the sugar bowls and placed those at appropriate intervals. The coffee mugs went down next as the Regulator's hands inched toward ten thirty.

The table was as nice as she could make it, even without napkins. She nodded in satisfaction, content to wake up in the morning to the pleasant fiction that during the night, someone had been kind enough—cared enough—to do all this for her as a welcome surprise.

It was a durable gift she had given herself since those earliest days in the Copper King Mansion when, as a child of ten, she already knew she would be the only person looking out for her. It was her daily gift to herself, and it felt fine in Yellowstone Park.

By seven o'clock, oatmeal, coffee and biscuits warmed themselves on one Majestic, with applesauce and canned milk and sugar on the table. Nails basked in welcome heat on sheet-metal trays on both ranges.

She had opened her door at five o'clock, and saw the tables set and ready. "Thank you, whoever you are," she said softly and began the day cheerfully, laying the fires and grinding coffee beans. She also prepared herself for more work than she was used to, because no one deliberately came to the Mercury Street Café for breakfast. It was the day's slowest meal.

The workers eating stew last night assured her she would be busy, but for the first time in her life, she understood the difference between work and drudgery. She was now part of this enterprise of building a hotel.

Mrs. Quincy noticed the tables. She walked around, seeing the order. "Ellie, you needn't go to all this trouble."

"I know," Ellie replied, hoping Mrs. Quincy would understand. "Mr. Child said last night how busy these men are. Let's make things easy for them in the mornings." She picked up the nearest bowl. "They can go to the range for their oatmeal, but everything else is on the table in easy reach. It will save time. I couldn't find any napkins."

"That's almost too much gentility for these ruffians," Mrs. Quincy said, but her voice was milder. "I doubt we have napkins. What are their sleeves for?"

"We can do better. Maybe there is a spare sheet somewhere? This is a hotel, after all," she added, which brought genuine laughter from her boss and gave her heart. "Some of the biscuits are warming, and two more pans are almost ready. If you can locate more canned milk . . ."

Everything was ready by the time Ellie heard the first boots stamping in the concrete drive. "Come in, come in," Mrs. Quincy commanded. "Take a bowl from the table and dip out your oatmeal. Plenty of biscuits too." She put her hands on her hips. "Don't stare!" She glanced at Ellie. "We decided to make things better for you."

The men went about breakfast quietly, chatting with their neighbors, holding out their mugs for more coffee when Ellie came around, never failing to thank her. When they finished, the carpenters stacked their bowls, mugs, and utensils by the sink.

"Never seen 'em do that," Mrs. Quincy whispered.

Ellie watched them each pick up a metal cup she had noticed earlier. Gloves on, they put hot nails into the cups, ran a cord through the lip of the cup, and tied them around their waists over their outercoats. Other men poured more nails onto the heated sheet as someone added a log to the Majestic.

Mr. Penrose came in after breakfast with his nail cup. "We can't wear thick gloves or we'd never be able to use a hammer well. Nobody gets frostbite with thinner gloves and heated nails."

"That's clever," she said. "Who thought that up?"

"I did."

Ellie wanted to thank him again for last night's glimpse of Old Faithful, but there was Mrs. Quincy. Better just wash dishes.

"Ellie, one more thing."

She wiped her hands on her apron. "Yes, sir?"

"My crew said they came in here to see everything already on the table. It means a lot to all of us. Thank you."

She could have mumbled her thanks and gone back to washing mugs. She couldn't, not after the wonder of Old Faithful by moonlight last night, and the kindness of the man beside her.

"You've been kind to me, Mr. Penrose," she said, "you and Gwen both. And Mr. Child too. I'll do my best work here."

"I don't doubt it," he said and joined his crew.

Mr. Child came in for coffee after the dishes were done. "Charles Penrose told me what you did this morning."

"I like things to be orderly," she said, hoping she didn't sound silly, and remembered her request, hoping it didn't sound silly either. "Mr. Child, do you have a spare bedsheet? I want to cut it up and make napkins."

27

"I have a better idea," he told her. "Come with me."

Ellie followed Mr. Child into the massive cavern that would become the lobby someday. He looked through one crate and another, then pulled out tablecloths and napkins already folded and separated into stacks by the dozen.

"Use these, starting tonight. Mr. Blackstock, a vice president from the Northern Pacific, is coming to dinner." His gesture took in the vast unfinished room. "The railroad is funding this venture. I didn't think we could do anything fancy, but . . ."

Ellie heard what he was trying to say. She saw the audacity all around her of a project unlike any other, in a place suited for the unusual. "You would like a banquet tonight," she said simply. "Maybe a glimpse of what we . . ." The enterprise grabbed her and caught hold. She held out her arms for the tablecloths and napkins. "What we can show the public this summer."

"You have it," he said. "The soldiers are bringing elk roasts for tonight. What can you do to make it special?"

"A cake," she said with no hesitation. "Mashed potatoes. Gravy. Canned vegetables, but that can't be helped. Rolls."

"You're on, Miss Found." He started for the big doors. She could hear men stamping around on the roof over the entrance. "Six o'clock?"

She wondered how Mrs. Quincy would appreciate taking orders from her. "Yes, sir."

Six it was. The hardest part was informing Mrs. Quincy what she and their boss had agreed to. To her surprise, Mrs. Quincy merely nodded. "I'll do the meat and gravy," she said.

"I'll do rolls and a cake," Ellie added.

"Wonderful."

What had happened? It was as though a light switch— none of which were here in the hotel yet—had turned on, and her advice mattered. Ellie looked at Mrs. Quincy for explanation. What she saw was an older woman, a tired one, maybe someone who had served her own apprenticeship in a Mercury Street Café somewhere, only it had turned her suspicious and maybe bitter. And sad about being replaced by a French cook in an elegant house. *I think I understand you, Mrs. Quincy*, Ellie thought.

So the day went. Lunch for the crew was a hurried affair eaten on the porch, potted meat and pilot bread sandwiches and plenty of hot coffee. Gwen came by in the middle of the afternoon to check up on her father, which meant Ellie took a break and joined her beyond the porch to step outside and watch the carpenters, some of whom were shingling outer walls, too.

Gwen pointed to the pinnacle, with its flat surface and railing. "Papa is up there, where he watches." She blew a kiss. Far above, Mr. Penrose touched his cheek where the "kiss" landed. "You could blow him a kiss," Gwen said. "He wouldn't mind."

Oh no. Ellie invited Gwen inside to help roll yeasty doughballs and stuff them three at a time into muffin tins. "Cloverleaf rolls," Ellie explained. No need to let anyone know that she had never made anything this elegant for the Mercury Street Café, where Mr. Linson would have berated her for wasting time on bums.

The shingling was done by four o'clock, just as the cake—Ellie's first, but no one needed to know that—came out of the oven and the first batch of rolls went in. She looked around, pleased to hear Mr. Penrose compliment his daughter on the symmetry of her doughballs.

Gwen sidled closer to Ellie. "Can we butter him one or two?"

"If he behaves," she teased. "Perhaps he can tell me something about this . . . monster, if he has a moment to spare."

"You'll hear more tonight from the architect himself," he said as Gwen handed him a cloverleaf roll. "Other ruffians, as Mrs. Quincy likes to call us, have been framing the other levels, the hotel rooms." She saw the pride as his gaze took in the men lounging on the porch, some smoking, others downing more coffee, all of them done for the day, which was quickly turning to dusk. "Soon you'll see amazing scaffolding going up inside. We'll get it done."

He indicated the small man with gold-rimmed glasses who stood at the entrance to the lobby, a clipboard under his arm. "Mr. Reamer is in charge. See? He has a clipboard."

She thought about clipboard efficiency, as she iced the sheet cake after Mr. Penrose left. "No, Plato, I have never made a cake before, and I don't have a clipboard," she told her cat, who lounged between the warmth of both Majestic ranges. "But I can read a cookbook, and you can't."

Plato didn't seem to give the matter much thought. He rolled onto his back as if to announce, *I am full of mice.* "Don't concern yourself," she added, then laughed when Mrs. Quincy regarded her. "Yes, ma'am, I talk to my cat. He's my friend."

"I'd say that Mr. Penrose and his daughter are your friends."

She could blush and deny and keep her head down, but why? Something was changing in her. Maybe she could blame it on geysers. "I hope they are my friends." And why not? "You too, Mrs. Quincy."

Six

Great banquet. Ellen Found is even more of an asset than Mr. Child realized when he hired her. She has a quiet way of taking charge. I doubt she is aware of it, but I am.

"THEY TUCKED IN THEIR SHIRTTAILS," Mrs. Quincy whispered to Ellie. "Even One-Eyed Wilson."

The builders congregated in the dining room, sneaking peeks at the mounds of mashed potatoes, gravy with no lumps, boring canned peas, stewed tomatoes with chunks of bread, and rolls glistening with butter. To her surprise, Mr. Penrose and Gwen were among the guests.

Brought by soldiers from Fort Yellowstone, the elk roast took up considerable real estate on the next table. Excellent. Mr. Child wanted elk, and here it was. Somehow even the heavy China plates and bowls looked elegant.

The door opened and Mr. Child and Mr. Blackstock, his railroad guest, entered, swiping at the snow on their overcoats. Mr. Child was joined by Rob Reamer, the architect, who looked at the tables and nodded as if this sort of thing happened every day.

Mr. Child took the arm of a commanding-looking woman wearing a hat too frivolous for a snowy day. Mrs. Quincy whispered, "Mrs. Adelaide Child herself, the law-dee-daw lady who threw me over for a French chef."

"Her loss," Ellie whispered back. "Let's serve dinner."

Mrs. Quincy had argued for a separate table for the dignitaries, but Ellie had quietly and kindly overruled her. To her relief, she was right, watching with satisfaction to see the railroad executive in animated conversation with the one-eyed roofer. The architect appeared in deep conversation with a German in charge of steam boilers, soon to provide electricity.

She wasn't prepared for Mr. Child to gesture *her* over. Mrs. Quincy gave her a prod in the back, and she found herself under the scrutiny of *the* Mrs. Child.

"This is the resourceful miss who is adventurous," Mr. Child told his wife. "She is also responsible for tablecloths for my workers' breakfast." He smiled. "I hear they were suitably impressed!"

"Do you do that every morning?" Mrs. Child asked. To Ellie's relief, she sounded genuinely interested.

"Yes, ma'am," Ellie replied. "To me, it's a . . . a rehearsal of what this hotel will look like in June."

Silence. Worried, Ellie glanced at Mr. Child and saw his approval. "Keep doing this," he said. "We need to understand what a great enterprise looks like." He turned his attention to the serving table. "Do I see *cake?*"

"You do, sir," Ellie said. She understood cake, but she had never attempted piping on little rosettes before, done with a pastry bag made of rolled, stiff paper. Maybe no one would look too closely at the writing.

Mrs. Child came closer. Ellie held her breath, hoping it would survive the scrutiny of someone like Mrs. Child, who had a French chef.

"'Old Faithful Inn,'" Mrs. Child read. "You should have piped on our geyser."

"All I had was red food coloring," Ellie said and couldn't help a smile. "It would have looked like a burst artery."

Everyone laughed, a good-hearted, we're-in-this-together sound. The cake slices went around, and all was well.

"Better look out, Ellen," Mr. Penrose said when he picked up two plates. "Mrs. Child might nab you for her mansion in Helena."

"I won't go," she said, her face warm. "I like it here where I have . . ." She looked at him, admiring his blue eyes and frank face. "Friends."

"Count me among them," he said.

To Ellie's surprise, when the meal was over, everyone except the guests cleared the table. She and Mrs. Quincy headed for the kitchen, but Mr. Child stopped them. "That will keep. Please join us. Mr. Penrose, there's an empty chair next to you."

She sat, too shy to look at the boss carpenter, but happy to smile at Gwen. Mr. Penrose leaned closer. "Bravo, Miss Found. *You* are an event planner, obviously."

"No . . . I . . ."

"Papa is right," Gwen said. "I wouldn't argue."

"I won't," she whispered, stifling her laughter.

"Mr. Reamer, the floor is yours," Mr. Child said.

The architect pushed his glasses higher on his nose. He turned to an easel and put up an artist's rendition of the inn at Old Faithful. He took his listeners through dismal years of poor lodging—one was actually called the "Shack Hotel"—and bad food at one of the world's most amazing places.

"Mr. Blackstock, earlier impresarios didn't dream big enough," he said, addressing the railroad executive. "What we have in Yellowstone are forests and geysers and hot pots and utter magnificence."

"Otter magnificence," one of the workers called out. "I saw some in August!"

It was the perfect, spontaneous touch. Everyone laughed and suddenly seemed to own the project. Ellie felt it inside her. Mr. Reamer relaxed; he must have felt it, too. "What I am doing with this . . ."—he gestured toward the dark cavern beyond the dining room—"otter magnificence"—more laughter—"is bringing the outdoors indoors."

More renderings appeared, one showing fanciful woodwork made of twisted lodgepole pines that in other projects might have been discarded. "Let the forest speak, I say," Mr. Reamer told his audience. He raised his pointer toward the ceiling in the next room. "Whimsical dormer windows here and there will mimic the play of sunlight in our wonderland."

Mr. Reamer continued, after a dramatic pause. "No one will come to this inn, experience our hospitality, and leave without an appreciation of what we have to offer the world. Yes, the world." He paused again for dramatic effect, then pulled out the final rendering, a completed hotel. "Old Faithful Inn will set the standard for all national park lodging. Thank you."

He sat down. Mr. Blackstock broke the silence, pulling out a check and waving it. "Will this help?" he asked. "The Northern Pacific Railroad believes in you!"

Everyone rose and applauded. Mr. Penrose put Gwen to his shoulder and stood. The child looked around with sleepy eyes, then nestled against her father again. Ellie felt the loveliness of a moment only she witnessed. All other eyes were on Mr. Child and the railroad executive, as he handed over the check that would complete the project.

"June first!" Mr. Blackstock proclaimed.

That was everyone's signal to leave the powerful men alone to talk. Mr. Penrose walked among the workers who followed him into the kitchen, rolled up their sleeves, and started on the dishes.

Mr. Penrose looked around. "Is there somewhere I can put Gwen?"

Ellie opened the door to her room. "She'll be fine here."

"Posh digs, Miss Found," he teased, looking around in appreciation. "I like it."

"I've never lived anywhere so wonderful in my life."

Maybe she was too fervent. Mr. Penrose gave her such a look, the sort of look she knew she would remember forever. He set his child down and Ellie covered her with a light blanket. "You're right," he said. "It's a nice room."

"You can't imagine," Ellie told him.

"Maybe I can. Kindly call me Charles." He smiled. "So I can call you Ellen."

"Everyone calls me Ellie."

He shrugged. "I like Ellen."

The dishes were soon done. With a red-haired roofer's help, Ellen turned over two mostly clean tablecloths and set the breakfast table. "I wish it could be something besides oatmeal," she told Red Hair.

"Convince ol' Harry Child to get us some laying hens," he said. "I'm a tenant farmer from County Cork." Ellen smiled at his wonderful accent.

"Add a pig or two," chimed in One-Eyed Wilson. He nudged the other man. "We have enough shanty Irish working here not to mind a pig in the bunkhouse!" Red Hair glared at him.

"I can convince ol' Harry."

Ellen turned to see Mrs. Child, who raised her eyebrows as the strong men cowered. The two men quietly melted into the gang finishing the cleanup.

"Let me see your room," Mrs. Child said. She made a face. "The men's bunkhouse is a disaster! They scattered like rats when I came in."

Mr. Child joined her. "They weren't expecting you, Adelaide. And you forgot to knock."

Ellen kept a straight face only through years of being a servant who, she had been informed by the copper king's wife, was never to be seen *or* heard. "This way, Mrs. Child," she said, and put a finger to her lips. "There is a sleeping child."

She opened the door to see Mr. Penr—Charles—picking up his still-sleeping daughter. "Thanks for the loan of your room," he whispered.

Mr. Child and Charles conversed quietly in the doorway while Mrs. Child surveyed the room. She jiggled the mattress. "Firm, but not too firm." Mrs. Child pointed to the hooks in the wall, where Ellen's other dress, the sadder one, hung. "You should hang up all your dresses."

"This is all I have," Ellen said, head up but cringing inside.

Mrs. Child turned to her husband. "Harry, I have a wonderful idea."

"Yes, my dear?"

"I've decided to speed up my plans for hotel uniforms."

"Yes, my dear."

"Ellie will be my model. I'll be here tomorrow with my tape measure," she announced, then followed her husband and a grinning Charles Penrose out the room.

Mrs. Quincy joined her. "'Yes, my dear,'" she teased. "In case you wondered who wears the pants in that family." Her voice hardened. "I only wish she had been nicer to me."

"Maybe she regrets it."

"Do you give everyone the benefit of the doubt?" Mrs. Quincy asked as she opened the door to her own room.

Do I? There's no harm in that, she thought. *It's all I want.* "I suppose I do," she replied.

She searched for Plato and found him crouched over another mouse carcass in the pitch-dark lobby. "I saved some crispy elk pieces for you."

"Any for me? I like crispy bits too."

Funny how she already recognized his voice. "Mr. Penrose—"

"Charles."

Hands on hips. "Mr. Penrose, you're too quiet!"

"I learned that after Gwen was born," he said. "Let sleeping children lie. She's in her bed, and I come at Mrs. Child's request. Well, perhaps her command."

"Look out for Plato."

Plato hissed. "Is it men he doesn't like, or is it everyone except you?"

"Everyone," she said, enjoying the mild banter. "What does the lady want?"

"I am to measure your foot for shoes."

"I . . . suppose she couldn't help seeing . . . I could use some good shoes." It was true. Why protest? Everyone knew it, including this man with kind eyes.

"Take off your shoe and stand on the paper."

She did as he said and stepped on the sheet. He grasped her ankle and outlined her foot. "Mrs. Child is observant," she said, keeping her voice light, wanting to cut the odd tension.

"Not her," he said quietly. "Me."

The nuns had warned her about predatory men years ago. But as she stood there, one shoe on, one off, Ellen knew this man was no predator. She knew that she had fallen among friends.

"Thank you, Mr. Penrose."

"Charles," he reminded her. "You'll have shoes. Winters

are cold here." He nodded toward the door, perhaps wanting to change the subject. "Feel that rumble?"

She followed him outside to the porch, rubbing her shoulders against the cold, to watch Old Faithful erupt.

Ellen watched, thinking of cold men on a steep roof. "Thank goodness the roof is done."

"We'll finish the inside this winter." He sniffed the cold air. "Not a minute too soon." He nodded to her as if she mattered. "Goodnight, Ellen. You will have shoes."

Seven

*Morning coffee with Ellen. Can I tell you, dear journal, how
nice that is? I had almost forgotten.*

THE SHOES ARRIVED THREE WEEKS later, along with uniforms.
Since she was cutting up onions, her tears needed no
explanation.

"Try them on now." Mrs. Quincy looked around. "Be
sure to close your door! The builders are indoors and drop in
at all hours for coffee and whatever else they can scrounge."

What a change three weeks had brought. Mr. Schmitz's
"Vee vill haff electricity" came true. Three steam boilers,
brought earlier in August, were encased in their own
building behind the inn, voraciously scarfing down all the
lodgepole pines that woodcutters produced. The steam
powered the generators and produced electricity. Power
tools and lifts went into action.

Inside the lobby, more scaffolding went up, which
entertained Plato mightily. Now he could climb the scaffolding and threaten carpenters nailing narrow split logs high

above the floor, covering the ceiling to match the walls below.

Now she had dresses. Ellen's cautious mind had told her that Mrs. Child didn't really mean it, but here they were, wrapped in brown paper.

She spread the two outfits on her bed, dresses sewn to her specifications alone. Sensible black brogans came from the box, plus six pairs of stockings. "I have never had six of anything, Mrs. Child," she murmured.

Which outfit first? Practical to the end, she pulled on the no-nonsense dark blue muslin, with its long sleeves and buttons at the wrist so she could tug them to elbow-length while working.

She buttoned up the front, pleased how well the bodice fit. The brown paper also held two petticoats. Wordless, she held them against her face. She was too shy to open a smaller package that might, just might, be what she wore under her petticoat. She tore off a corner and put her finger inside. Was this *silk*?

The other proposed uniform was a brown skirt and a green and white checked shirtwaist. She slipped on one of the two new petticoats first, then buttoned up the shirtwaist. The skirt brushed the top of her new shoes. She smoothed it over her hips, enjoying the feel of good material. Next came an apron, looking more like a pinafore, frilled along the bib. She patted the pocket and gasped as she pulled out a lacy brassiere.

Mrs. Quincy had to see this. She opened her door and tucked the brassiere behind her back quickly because two roofers from the highest portion of the interior roof had come for more heated nails. They grinned at her; maybe she hadn't hidden the brassiere in time.

Back it went into her pocket, just as Charles Penrose came inside for nails.

Ellen amazed herself by twirling around for him, stopping when he applauded.

He held out his tin cup for nails. "Shoes, too?"

Ellen raised her skirt to show him.

"I'm relieved," he teased. "Now you can run fast and not become a meal for bears bulking up for hibernation."

"Charles!" she exclaimed, and he laughed. "I . . . I think the blue dress is for daily wear, and the brown skirt and shirtwaist is for special events, which I don't need now. Should I return the skirt and shirtwaist, Mrs. Quincy?"

"Not on your tintype," her kitchen boss said firmly. "You are now the owner of two new dresses."

Well-dressed and enjoying it, Ellen unpacked crates of canned food, as welcome to her as the venison and moose meat now hanging in the temporary meat locker, a washroom locked and cold, safe from bears still nosing about, wondering where to hibernate.

As the days passed, Ellen began to look forward to Charles Penrose every morning before breakfast. "You make good coffee, and I don't," he said.

If she started earlier on the biscuits, she had time to sit with him. While he sipped and relaxed, Ellen started asking him what he planned for the day, which seemed to please him. "You're interested in everything," he told her one morning.

"Does that make me nosy?"

"It makes you smart," he replied, which gratified her more than the neat rows of canned beans, corn, carrots, and tomatoes.

You have a fine smile, Mr. Penrose, she thought, after he nodded to her and returned to his quarters to ready Gwen for her day next door with the McTavishes.

She wished Charles would bring Gwen by for supper,

then reminded herself that they ate with the McTavishes. She wanted to tell him how nice the mezzanine looked—and how much safer it was—now that the railings were in place. She reminded herself that he had a life outside of Old Faithful Inn.

He didn't come the next morning. She walked from the dining room to the lobby's entrance, assuring herself that she wasn't looking for Charles Penrose. Just curious. That was all.

There he stood, looking out at the geyser field in front of the hotel. "Mr. Penrose?" she asked, uncertain. "I made you some biscuits." She hoped that wasn't brazen. "Is something wrong?"

"I need a favor," he said, "if you think you can."

Well, that is a novelty, she decided as they walked inside. Usually, people told her what to do. No one asked.

"It's this: Mrs. McTavish is expecting another child and the post surgeon from Fort Yellowstone says she needs to leave right now. She has pleurisy that will only get worse as winter moves in."

"Poor lady. Her husband is your chief assistant, isn't he?"

"Aye. Jim tendered his resignation last night. What a blow. Well, a double blow. I've lost my right-hand man and the lady who watches my daughter."

She knew what he needed, and she knew her answer. "Charles, Mrs. Quincy and I can watch Gwen right here." She decided not to imagine what her boss might *really* think. "She can help us in the kitchen."

She saw the relief in his expressive eyes. "When did *you* start peeling potatoes?" he asked, making a little joke of his concern.

She understood. "I was ten. We were taught to earn our

keep young." *And remember our place and never make a wave*, she reminded herself. *Gwen will never need those lessons.* "See? Problem solved."

Sensing there was more, she waited for him to speak. "My wife, Clare, died two years ago when Gwen was four."

"So young," she said.

"Both of them." He eyed the Regulator on the wall. "Got a minute?"

"I'll stop the clock's hands if I have to. Tell me." He needed to talk and she wanted to listen.

"Clare's sister in Helena invited me to move in with her and her husband, and we did. I never have trouble finding work. I answered that same ad you did and started work here last May. Mr. Child put me in charge of the carpenters, and I answer directly to Mr. Reamer."

"I knew you had a lot of responsibility."

"Trouble came when I told Amanda I was taking Gwen along, too. She told me I was crazy to do that and an unfit parent."

"Which you are neither."

"Thanks," he said with a brief smile. "Amanda has no children. She pleaded with me to leave Gwen with her. I can't. Gwen is mine. Mine and Clare's. It's hard though. Can you clear it with Mrs. Quincy?"

Ellen knew she had no power or standing. What was she thinking? "I will," she said firmly. "We'll do fine."

Where was her courage coming from? Maybe from the quiet man with heavy responsibilities and a small child. *I like this man*, she thought. The feeling was novel, and she wanted it to linger.

She had another thought. "I wish we could offer Gwen wages. Women need money of their own. At least, I always wanted that."

She felt he was measuring her in that same way she had seen him stare at a board before he started to saw. "How about you offer Gwen one dollar a week, which I will slip to you on the sly?"

"Done," she said. "Bring her over. See how easy that was?"

She meant it as a joke. He appraised her again, serious. "A mere thank-you is inadequate."

If Mrs. Quincy had objections when Ellen approached her about it, she stifled them. "We can use her help," was Ellen's clinching argument.

"I believe we can, Ellie," was all she said. "You're in charge of her."

Gwen and her father came over after breakfast when Mr. Reamer gave the crew his daily list of projects. Charles helped Gwen off with her coat, kissed her cheek, and went about his business for the day.

"We have a lot of potatoes," Ellen said, kneeling down. She found a potato peeler. "Let me show you how to peel them."

The child nodded. "I'll miss Mrs. McTavish and her little boy," she said, taking the peeler and looking it over.

"They'll be better off in a warmer climate, and she won't cough so much."

Ellen sat her down at the table and brought over a bowl of scrubbed potatoes. "We'll work together," she told the child. She glanced at Mrs. Quincy, who, to her surprise, watched them with an expression she might be tempted to call tender, were this anyone but Mrs. Quincy.

This turned into a day of surprises. Charles had said his daughter still liked a nap. After lunch, when Gwen started tugging on her eyelashes, Ellen took Gwen to her room, removed her shoes, and covered her with a blanket. When she came back later to check, Plato had curled up with Gwen.

"Good for you, Plato," she whispered. "Every lady needs a bodyguard."

Gwen made sure her father had an extra serving of mashed potatoes that night. "I mashed these," she announced.

He hugged her. "Never better." He smiled at Ellen. "Thank you. I know Gwen is in good hands."

She saw how tired he was, how tired they all were. Until the newly built fireplace was ready, the lobby was still going to be cold. Even working indoors was no proof against Yellowstone in the winter.

He helped Gwen with her coat. "We'll be eating here now, since the McTavishes are gone. I'm no cook."

"He isn't," Gwen agreed.

Ellen walked with them through the dark lobby. Charles stopped when his daughter stooped down to pet Plato, who had come up silently beside the child. "Uh . . . careful."

"He's my friend," Gwen said.

Charles held out his hand slowly. Plato sniffed but did not hiss, and turned away. "He'll be your friend too, Papa," Gwen assured him. "I know it. Give him time."

Give me time too, Ellen thought.

Eight

Life and death can turn on a dime. I owe Ellen more than I can ever repay. More later.

GWEN PENROSE PROVED A WELCOME addition to the "kitchen staff," as her father described them. When the cook scoffed, he wagged a finger at her. "Mrs. Quincy, when I work with one other carpenter, it's the two of us. When I add another, it's a crew. Staff sounds nicer for ladies."

Ellen could tell when Mrs. Quincy was amused by how hard she tried not to show it. "You might as well add Plato to the staff," she replied, which made Gwen nod seriously.

With the men working inside the inn, the whole building reverberated with noise that Mr. Reamer stated was music to his ears. "June is coming, so the louder, the better," the architect announced after breakfast one morning.

Interested, Ellen stood in the kitchen doorway as Charles Penrose took everyone through the day's tasks. The architect was there too, sketching designs and plans on the underside of leftover shingles. When he finished, the shingles went into the kitchen ranges.

"By the end of next week, every room on each floor will be roughed in," Charles told her as they finished their morning coffee. "We'll close the big doors off the second-floor mezzanine and finish those rooms after the lobby is done."

As if aware of the need, winter held itself at bay, teasing with snow flurries and an overnight addition of a few inches, easily swept away from the porch and off machinery. Plato remained ever vigilant, perhaps mindful in his cat brain that cold weather meant mice were seeking warmer shelter too.

"You're getting a bit of a belly on you," she told him one night, as she prepared to blow out the light in her glorious bedroom. Plato assumed his usual place, curled up by her feet. He still ignored the men who trooped in and out of "his" hotel, hammering and sawing, but he didn't hiss at them. *Even alley cats can change*, Ellen thought. *Maybe someday he'll let Mr. Penrose pet him.*

She felt herself changing, too. At the Mercury Street Café, her usual morning routine was a quick swipe at her hair and then an old shoestring to pull it back. If she could fix Gwen's hair into French braids every morning, she could do hers, too.

She didn't think anyone noticed, but Charles Penrose did. She saw it in his eyes, which pleased her more than words. Corporal Dan Reeves of the Old Faithful soldier station noticed too. One morning he gave her a string of Indian seed beads. "You could weave these in," was all he said, but it warmed her heart for a week.

On orders from Major Pitcher, acting superintendent at Fort Yellowstone, Dan and his three privates took over a corner of the hastily built boardinghouse, closer than their regular soldiers' station. Mr. Reamer made note of the addition. "They're here to protect us from bears and poachers," he announced one morning after breakfast.

47

Maybe it was the good coffee and biscuits. Maybe it was the tablecloths, or even the warmth from the two Majestic ranges. No one rushed off in silence anymore. "Things are different now," Mrs. Quincy said, and Ellen heard no irritation.

"Plato, we have landed in a good place," she announced one night as he turned around a few times on his woolen square that Gwen had given him and plumped down on her bed.

Ellen sighed with contentment, thinking of the chaotic order around them as twisted tree limbs, cast-offs of lodgepole pines, filled in the spaces below the handrails on the stairways up from the lobby. "Nature is naturally chaotic," Mr. Reamer said one morning. "Visitors want the rustic experience. Here it is."

Other chaos came home one morning when, elbow-deep in bread dough, Ellen heard shouts and carpenters running. She looked around, but there was Plato, slumbering between the warm Majestics, not guilty of a single hiss.

Followed by Gwen, she opened the glass-paned door between the lobby and the dining room when someone shouted, "Hey, bear! Hey, bear!"

She slammed the door, her arms tight around Gwen, as a bear charged down the hall, picked up speed, and raced across the lobby to the open front door. He was a blur followed by men with brooms, who slammed the door after him and laughed nervously.

"We found him all snug in his bed for a warm winter's nap in one of the rooms at the end of this hall," a carpenter said and pointed when she opened the dining room door just a crack this time.

Charles Penrose came on the run. He pulled all the men off the lobby to shore up the wall where the determined bear had worried open a spot to crawl through. "Let's go around again, men," he said. "Let's be certain. I'll sleep better when every bear is denned up away from here."

For a week Ellen opened that door cautiously, which made One-Eyed Wilson laugh at her. "It wasn't a big bear," he assured her.

"He looked huge," Ellen said, with all the dignity she could muster.

Maybe the bear *wasn't* so big. She took the crew's good-natured ribbing in stride, but welcomed every degree that the thermometer dropped, driving bears away to their winter-time sleep, once they had eaten everything in sight.

"Maybe I'm a goof," she told Gwen a week later as she bundled up the child for their walk to the log cabin where she and her father "batched it," as Corporal Reeves said.

Charles had asked if Gwen could stay with her until seven, because he had a meeting with Mr. George Wellington Colfitt, blacksmith from Livingston, who had braved the cold and snowy roads with two iron workers to bring his own plans for a makeshift forge here.

She assured Charles she could walk Gwen to his cabin, not so many steps from the back entrance. "I'll walk you back," he said.

She wanted to tell him that wasn't necessary. All he had to do was stand in the open doorway and watch until she was inside the lobby again. Still, it was a nice gesture.

She handed Gwen a packet of meat and cheese from the supper that Charles had skipped. "You know, just to tide him over until breakfast."

By now, she knew her way in daylight or gloom, but something was off in the lobby. She stopped and sniffed, wrinkling her nose against an unfamiliar odor, wondering about that meat and cheese.

The bear came at them from behind, snuffling, moving fast, and chunky from eating everything in sight. She stopped, its outline barely visible because of a sliver of moonlight from the randomly placed dormer windows overhead, the ones calculated to bring the outdoors indoors. The outdoors indoors . . .

She grabbed Gwen, but there was nowhere to go. The bear, much closer, came between them and the dining room door. The outside door looked farther and farther away as the seconds passed. They were stuck. The bear kept moving.

"Toss him the meat packet," Ellen whispered to Gwen.

Misunderstanding her, Gwen threw the packet as hard as she could into the bear's face. It reared up, roared, and charged.

Gwen screamed and screamed as Ellen snatched her up and backed toward the stairs. She knew she couldn't outrun an angry bear up the stairs, but they were suddenly desperate, two people out of their element in bear world.

She grabbed Gwen tighter and darted under the stairs instead. Kneeling, she shoved Gwen against the bottom step, forcing her as far in as she could go, and crawled after her. Cramped into the tight space, she threw her arms around Gwen and covered her with her own body.

To her horror, the bear crawled after them. Thank God he was too big, too bulked up for winter. He growled and swiped at Ellen's back, ripping through her dress and scoring her shoulder. As blood dripped from her shoulder, she cried out in pain and tried to make herself smaller.

The bear wouldn't stop. Blood meant food. He swiped at her skirt and managed to hook a claw in it. He tugged as Ellen clung to Gwen and tried to wrap her arms around the bottom rung. She sobbed as the bear inched her out farther. To let go and save Gwen? She had no choice.

Through the bear's deep breathing and Gwen's screams, Ellen heard Plato growl—Plato, who had vanished after supper to gnaw on mice somewhere. *No, Plato, no*, she thought as the bear tugged at her skirt.

The fiercest tomcat who ever roamed the mean streets of Butte growled and hissed. She had heard him warn away stray dogs and hiss at carpenters. This was different. This was the sound of life or death, and she knew it.

The bear grunted, then roared in pain. Looking behind her, Ellen saw Plato leap on the bear's head and claw at its eyes, an impossible task for a cat too small to fight a bear, a cat possessing nothing but puny claws and a heart so big that even the lobby couldn't contain it. "Plato, run," she whispered. "Please. *Please.*"

With a roar that echoed off the distant ceiling, the bear grabbed her cat, chomped down, and flung what remained against a far wall. Tears streamed down her face as Ellen clapped her hand over Gwen's mouth and held her tight against her body.

She waited for the bear to grab at her again. When it didn't, she looked over her shoulder at the beast to see it rubbing its eyes where Plato had clawed and bit. The bear whimpered, distracted, unsure.

After years and years, she heard the back door slam open. She watched, dull with pain of the heart worse than the claw marks on her back, as Corporal Reeves went to one knee, took deliberate aim, and fired. The noise reverberated in the huge room and her ears rang. He fired again and once more until the bear lay still.

Ellen felt herself pulled gently from that too-small space. Some primitive reflex made her cling tenaciously to the little girl, even though the more rational part of her brain assured her the ordeal was over. Someone carefully pried her fingers from Gwen, then kissed her hand.

"Ellen, my debt to you is eternal," she heard before she closed her eyes and wept.

Nine

Ellen Found is resilient, but such loss! I have only a glimmer of how sad she is. What can I do?

SHE WOKE UP MERE MINUTES later, clawing and scratching to hang on to Gwen, who was clasped tight in her father's arms. Corporal Reeves held her in a sitting position as Mrs. Quincy, her face white and her eyes huge, dabbed at her back with a dishcloth.

Lanterns and men filled the space close to the stairs, and it was light enough for her to really see the bear. Just an ordinary bear, but a big one, a bear looking for one last meal before the long winter's sleep.

Ellen looked harder against the distant wall. She sobbed when she saw the ridiculously small bundle of fur and bones that had taken on a behemoth in the Old Faithful Inn lobby. "Please, someone get Plato. Please."

One of the privates followed her shaking finger. He knelt, then called to another soldier, who went into the dining room and returned with a dish towel. Carefully he wrapped it around the little body and carried Plato to Ellen, who held out her arms.

"He's still alive," the private said. "Not for long."

Time, merciful time, stood still long enough for her to cradle the demon cat of Butte and smooth down his torn and bleeding fur. "Plato, you should've run the other way," she whispered to her friend, her only friend ever. She had helped him out of his pain in the alley, and he returned the favor moments ago by distracting a monster many times his size and saving two lives. "You thought you were a mountain lion, little buddy," she said. "And here we were at last, with enough food to eat and a safe place to sleep."

Mr. Penrose made a little sound when she said that, or maybe it was Corporal Reeves.

She wept over her dying cat, smoothing his fur. Plato put a delicate paw on her wrist finally, as if to say, "That'll do, my lady friend. I'm all right now. You're here." To her stunned amazement, he started to purr and then he died. She marveled that such a small body could hold something as enormous as death, then fainted.

Ellen woke in her own room, wearing her flannel nightgown with most of the flannel gone, her left shoulder throbbing and wrapped in a bandage. His face a study in agony, Charles Penrose sat on her bed, his daughter asleep in his arms but crying out at intervals.

From habit, Ellen looked toward her feet, but there was no Plato, only his wool square. Charles's eyes must have followed hers. "I wrapped him in a towel," he said, his voice strained. "I have a carved wooden box in my quarters. I will bury him in a good place."

"Please put in Gwen's wool square," she said. "He liked to sleep on it."

"I will."

He didn't leave, not even when Mrs. Quincy came into her room with something sweet and chocolatey, something Ellen saw the children in the Copper King house drink, but which she was not allowed. She took a sip and another, knowing that Plato would have liked it, too. She took tiny solace remembering that for dinner that night, there had been plenty of stewed tomatoes and break chunks, something Plato loved.

"My shoulder?" she asked, not sure who would answer and not wanting to think that Mr. Penrose had to get her out of the tattered dress. Her back felt on fire.

"There was one deep scratch."

"Who fixed my shoulder?"

"The one-eyed man, name of Fred Wilson, and Mrs. Quincy helped. He's a good carpenter and maybe a better taxidermist. Miss Found, you have a neat row of stitches as nice as anything I've ever seen. He does good work."

She shook her head at that and felt an absurd urge to smile, maybe even laugh. Charles watched her. "Ellen, he said it was the best row of stiches he ever put in anything." He patted her hand, and she realized he was holding it. "He said you were museum quality."

She laughed, just a small laugh, a tentative one, the sort of laugh that maybe a person tries out who is wondering why she is even alive. She looked at the sleeping child in her father's arms. "You hold her tight tonight," she said, not meaning to sound so adamant. "For as long as she needs you." *Who will hold me?* remained unspoken. Her only friend was gone.

"I had better leave," Charles said.

"Where is . . ." She couldn't even say his name.

"Plato's in the room where we hang meat," Mrs. Quincy said.

"I'll do what you want and bury him tomorrow," Charles told her. "I know a good place." He walked to the door, his arms tight around Gwen, and stood there a long moment. "I am truly in your debt." He tried to say more but shook his head instead and left.

Mrs. Quincy stood by her bed, the torn dress over her arm. "Mrs. Child is going to be so disappointed in me," Ellen said. "I wish I had been wearing my old dress."

Her eyes intense, her boss plumped down on the bed. "Ellen Found, Mrs. Child is going to be so relieved—as we are—that you had a champion defending you! Don't you dare worry about your dress. I can sew the tear, and you'll wear it again."

And not think about Plato? she asked herself. She nodded, feeling the tug of gravity on her eyelids. Was it even possible to sleep after the terror of this evening? She knew when she closed her eyes, maybe every time she closed her eyes, she would see that enormous bear rising on its hind legs. Maybe she would feel its hot breath on her neck as she struggled to make herself small under the stairs and keep Gwen covered with her body. Or maybe she would just sleep, which was what happened.

More than once, though, she woke in tears during the night, feeling for Plato, who liked to migrate north from her feet to curl up next to her shoulder in cold weather. She thought she heard him purr, which sent her back to tears and then to sleep.

Through it all, she was aware that Mrs. Quincy never left her, but sat on the floor beside her bed, her hand on Ellen's good arm. She even hummed once, a tune Ellen had heard one night passing a honky-tonk on Mercury Street. "Sweetest little fella, everybody knows . . ." She wiped Ellen's eyes when she cried and said, "Shh, shh, shh," softly.

Morning came as it always did. Ellen was aware that Mrs. Quincy had left, and she heard low voices, then the rattling of wood into the Majestics. Breakfast was going to come as it always did, no matter how dead Plato was or how her shoulder ached. She reminded herself that she was earning thirty dollars a month and sat up.

Her entire body ached, from the tousled hair on her head to her toenails. She moved her arm tentatively, pleased to discover that she could even move it. It pained her greatly, so what did a little more exertion matter? There was a table to set and biscuits to mix, and no one else was earning thirty dollars a month to do her chores.

She decided not to look at the foot of her bed, because it was empty. She didn't know Charles Penrose well, but she was certain he would do what he said for Plato, then search every inch of those half-finished rooms down each hall on the first floor with extra-strong boards and longer nails to keep out bears seeking warmth for the winter ahead.

Ellen groaned and slid out of bed, going to her knees because she had no strength. This would never do. She hauled herself up and sat on her bed until the room stopped whirling. Through grit she didn't know she possessed, she pulled on a petticoat and her best old dress, not wishing to wear the remaining checked shirtwaist and brown skirt and stain it with her blood.

Reaching up to brush her hair was more than she could manage, so she smoothed the ends down with her fingers and tied a shoestring around it. She opened the door and stared into the kitchen, where Mrs. Quincy was making biscuits. A glance beyond into the dining room showed the usual tablecloths on two tables and bowls and spoons, everything in place.

Charles Penrose brought out the coffee mugs and set

them around as she watched. He smiled at her. "Mrs. Quincy doesn't trust me with biscuits, and she figured I wouldn't harm anything if I set the tables." He nodded toward two other men. "I have help."

As she leaned against the kitchen door, he came around the table and put an arm around her waist, guiding her to a table. "Mrs. Quincy told me that you wouldn't lie still. I didn't think you would either, but you can sit down and watch us this morning."

Knowing better than to spar with someone whom she didn't think would appreciate an argument, Ellen did as he said. She gasped when she heard a scraping sound from the lobby, and his hand went to her good shoulder. "No fears! They're setting up the hydraulic lift closer to the fireplace to finish the roof." His voice turned serious, hard, even. "Right now we're going through all the rooms. When we find where this bear came in, we'll batten it down and nail the door shut until spring."

"Where . . ." She couldn't say his name.

"You know that little overhang of windows by the kitchen's back door? It was a great place, secluded too, because we know Plato. He won't be crowded there."

She nodded.

"I put Gwen's wool square in my box like you wanted, and I wrapped him in another towel." He took a deep breath. "I did one thing more. I wanted to pet him just once, and I did."

He seemed to gather himself together, doing his own reliving of last night's terror. "Gwen told me to tell you not to worry. He'll be warm."

Ellen covered her face with her hands until the moment passed. "Where is Gwen? You shouldn't leave her alone."

"I didn't. Corporal Reeves is in my room. I'll bring Gwen here when she wakes up." He gave her that appraising look she was already familiar with. "We would all feel better if you would lie down."

"That wouldn't earn me my thirty dollars a month," she replied, touched at his concern.

The appraising look turned into something more intense. She felt the warmth of his hand on her shoulder. "You have gone above and beyond earning your thirty dollars this month," he assured her. "I can never put a price on what you did last night."

"I would do it again."

"I know you would." Over her protest—a feeble one— he picked her up and carried her into her room, setting her down on her bed. He looked around and found her hairbrush. He brushed her hair, gentle strokes that soothed her more than anything else possibly could. How did he know?

He seemed to sense her question. "When Clare became agitated about something or other, this always seemed to help." He said it apologetically.

"It does," she said. "No one's ever done this, but it does."

Her eyes closed as she felt herself relax, well aware that in her short lifetime of constantly doing for others, someone—out of kindness or gratitude for his daughter's life, or maybe even because he missed doing this for his wife—was doing something solely for her.

In a few minutes she heard the carpenters, mechanics, and men who fed the hungry generators troop inside for breakfast. She tried to move, to do her job.

"No," Charles said softly. He tied her neat hair back with the shoestring, swung her feet onto the bed, removed her shoes, and covered her with a blanket. "Sleep now."

Before she opened her eyes later, she sensed the presence of someone in the room. For a moment, she hoped it was Charles Penrose.

Mrs. Quincy sat there with a dress across her lap. She stroked the fabric gently, smoothing out wrinkles, and brushing away some speck that Ellen couldn't see. She patted the dress as if someone wore it, then looked up. "Here."

Ellen raised herself on her good arm. Mrs. Quincy helped her sit up, then draped the dress across Ellen's lap. "I took in the hem, so it should fit. She was taller."

Ellen admired the pretty thing, with eyelet lace at the sleeves and a ruffle around the bottom. It was a dress from an earlier time, but not so distant that she hadn't mooned over something like it in a Monkey Ward catalog. "Where did . . ."

"I had a daughter once," the cook said, then left the room quietly.

Ellen stared after her, then touched the dress. *What if I get it dirty working in a kitchen?* warred with, *She wants me to have this. She cares.*

Ellen stared at the ceiling as a great realization settled in. *I doubt there is anyone here who has not suffered a loss*, she thought. *I doubt I am the only child of dubious parentage here. Others are poor, too. Mr. Penrose's wife is dead. One-Eyed Wilson has only one eye, for goodness' sake.*

She thought about Plato, dead after a heroic attempt to protect her, because that's what friends did. She lay there and took a quiet census in her heart.

Corporal Reeves shot the bear. One-Eyed Wilson stitched her shoulder together. Gwen gave Plato a wool square. Mrs. Quincy hemmed her daughter's dress for her. Charles Penrose brushed her hair.

She closed her eyes, thinking through the fear, the pain,

the sorrow, and dared to imagine that maybe, just maybe, she had more friends than she knew. What to do with this startling revelation?

I must be a friend, she told herself. *It begins now.*

Ten

Dear Journal, remind me not to think only men are brave and stalwart. I am in debt forever to someone more brave and stalwart than whole armies.

SHE FELT WELL ENOUGH AFTER an afternoon nap to put on Mrs. Quincy's gift to her, and it fit. Her shoulder ached, but she could bear the pain. She touched her hair that Charles had brushed so thoroughly. It needed nothing.

Mrs. Quincy was opening cans of green beans in the kitchen. Her eyes seemed to soften as she looked at Ellen in her daughter's dress. She pulled out a chair beside her.

Ellen sat down carefully, fearing any movement that might add more pain. She thought of her resolve and forged ahead. "What was your daughter's name?"

The motion of the can opener stopped. *Maybe I was wrong*, Ellen thought. But no. "Verity. Her . . . her father was a New Englander."

"What a beautiful name."

"Yes. Diphtheria took her."

The cook opened another can, then another. "A year later, typhoid took Mr. Quincy, and I moved West."

Mrs. Quincy rested her hand on Ellen's good shoulder, a light touch. "I'm sorry for your losses," Ellen said. She realized she had not known a kind touch before Charles Penrose and now Mrs. Quincy, unless she chose to count Plato's gentle paw on her wrist last night as he surrendered. She chose kindness.

"It was a hard time," Mrs. Quincy said simply. "Everyone knows hard times."

Ellen understood. Others suffered too, but no one spoke of it. She had waited all her life for her luck to turn, and in a moment without warning, it turned. She bowed her head against the emotion.

Mrs. Quincy pressed down on her good shoulder. "Are you all right?"

"I am," Ellen said, and she was. "I am. How can I help now?"

"Will you be able to stir the gravy while I mash potatoes?"

She did, and no one went hungry. Ellen's worst moment came when, with an apologetic glance, Mrs. Quincy opened the Majestic oven and one of the stronger men pulled out a large pan of roasted bear. Ellen watched as Corporal Reeves carved it and the carpenters served it. As she cautiously took a bite and then another, she felt only triumph. They were eating *the* bear and it seemed right. Drat that bear, but it tasted good.

"Miss Found!"

Ellen turned at the familiar voice and held out her arms. She stifled her pain as Gwen threw herself into her arms and clung to her. In another moment they were holding each other close as Charles Penrose knelt by her chair and somehow held them both. She stroked the child's hair, murmuring words that weren't words as she realized how much she loved Gwen.

"You'll be here in the morning to help me?" she asked when Gwen burrowed as close as last night under the stairs but without the terror. Ellen fingered her soft hair, which smelled of her father's aftershave. "Mrs. Quincy opened an apple barrel, and we're making pie tomorrow."

"I'll be here," Gwen assured her. She put her hands on Ellen's face, drawing her closer. "I found a silk flower for Plato."

"Will you show me where your father buried him?"

Hand in hand, when all Ellen wanted to do was lie down again, they walked out the back door, where Corporal Reeves stood watch, rifle in hand. He nodded to them.

"Miss Found, I telephoned Major Pitcher," he said. "He is sending down two more privates to stand guard here until the bears are denned up. We'll patrol the inn."

She saw him in her mind, kneeling and taking careful aim in the middle of roars and screaming to shoot a bear and save their lives. She held out her hand and he took it. "Thank you seems inadequate."

"I wish I had been quicker." He let go of her hand and pointed. "Here he is."

In the light from the kitchen, Ellen saw the small mound under the window overhang, a spot no tourist was likely to notice. Only she would remember he was not a showy cat and required no praise, just a scratch behind the ears and whatever the night's menu happened to be, from salmon bits to green beans cooked in bacon fat. And he had saved two lives.

She admired Gwen's rose and looked closer. "Mr. Penrose put the board there," Corporal Reeves explained. He read out loud, "'Plato, 1903. He had a brave heart and was loved.' Mr. Penrose said there will be a headstone later."

"This will do," she said, her heart full. She looked again. "Gwen, is this your lucky magpie feather?"

The child nodded. "If you hold it right, there are green lights."

"Plato never could catch a bird," Ellen said. She felt a tidal wave of grief. "Thank you, Corporal."

She heard the capable man's shyness, followed by a quiet sort of pride. "That's sergeant now. When I called Major Pitcher, he told me that my overdue promotion came through."

"Congratulations, Sergeant Reeves." She kissed his cheek. "That's from me and Gwen."

He took it in stride with a grin. "If you're going to kiss me," he joked, "maybe you'd better call me Tom."

"That's your name?" she asked.

"No, it's Dan," he said with a straight face, then laughed. "Call me Dan."

"Oh, you!" She laughed and it felt good.

Gwen tugged on his sleeve. When he bent down, she kissed his other cheek.

Charles waited for them in the kitchen. He took Ellen aside. "If I can do anything for you, let me," he said, for her ears only.

"Be my friend," she said impulsively. "I'm a little low on friends now."

"No, you're not," he replied. "Not at all."

Eleven

Christmas soon. The bears are denned up, thank God, and our extra guards have returned to Fort Yellowstone, leaving only Sergeant Reeves, a new corporal, and the two privates. Ellen misses Plato. She and Gwen still hesitate when they enter the dark lobby, but she has lost her wary look. She calls me Charles now, and Sergeant Reeves is Dan. One-Eyed Wilson is Mr. Wilson because she defers to age. She is so pretty.

TO EVERYONE'S RELIEF, REAL SNOW came at last, snow that meant bears were hibernating. To Mrs. Quincy's delight, Sergeant Reeves and his men shot three wild turkeys for Thanksgiving.

The magical moment for the lobby came after Thanksgiving dinner when the massive fireplace, with its four hearths, was lit for the first time. "Rumor is the Childs are coming for Thanksgiving," Charles told her.

The Childs arrived at the inn the day after Thanksgiving, accompanying the freight wagons on skids, a four-day journey as the snow deepened.

"I am impressed," Mrs. Quincy said, when the Childs came into the lobby, laughing and shaking off snow, accompanied by the architect. "I didn't think Mrs. High-and-Mighty would want to spend Thanksgiving away from her French chef."

Ellen listened for bitterness, but she didn't hear it. "I wouldn't think Thanksgiving had too many French pilgrims," she teased.

It was a small joke, but Mrs. Quincy laughed. "There's leftover ground turkey. We can call it *les hashe*."

Les hashe it was, flavorful and accompanied by biscuits smothered in turkey gravy. Ellen heard Mr. Reamer ask Harry Child, "We weren't sure you were coming. How did you manage it?"

Mrs. Child waved away any difficulties. "Harry and I climbed into the freight wagon four days ago. Call us stowaways! We hunkered down in a pile of blankets intended for the rooms here."

"We wanted to be here," Mr. Child said simply. "You are all working magic."

"I'm certain your French chef was disappointed he couldn't cook for you," Mrs. Quincy said, her voice perfectly bland.

Was Mrs. Child touched by that same bit of Yellowstone magic that Ellen had been feeling despite everything? How else to credit what happened then? Maybe Ellen didn't really know Mrs. Child, except through her boss's jaundiced view.

"Mrs. Quincy, I was perfectly wrong about a French chef," Adelaide Child said, mincing nary a word. "He left in a huff a month ago when all I did was say I'd like bacon and scrambled eggs for dinner, you know, the way you make them."

Stunned silence. Mrs. Quincy stared at her former employer.

"You should have seen his hissy fit," Mrs. Child told her. "I hear he's working for some copper king in Butte now." She took Mrs. Quincy's hand. "I was wrong, and I apologize. Would you come back and cook for us?"

"I'll think about it," Mrs. Quincy said after she got her breath. "But now, I do have hash, if you don't mind a little solitary splendor in the dining room."

"That would be delightful," Mrs. Child said. "First, though, I want to sit by the fireplace."

Everyone gathered in the lobby, the warmth of the fire reaching into dark corners. It was Ellen's turn to give Mrs. Quincy a little prod in the doorway to get her moving. "I can't believe my ears," her boss whispered to her. "She wants me back."

Ellen squeezed Mrs. Quincy's hand. "Don't leave us." It sounded bold and brave to Ellen, but she meant it. Her answer was a squeeze back.

Even with the warmth and light, Ellen felt a momentary fear of the bear. To her relief, it was now a catching of breath before taking that first step. Gwen moved closer to her. She put her arm around the child even as Charles did the same. Their hands met and he smiled. "No fears, you two," he admonished gently. "You're safe. The bears have gone to bed for the winter." He leaned closer to Ellen, his daughter between them. "You'll feel peaceful someday."

His hand was warm on hers. She nodded, too shy to speak. She thought about him later after everyone admired the fireplace, chatted about what lay ahead, and left the building, the Childs to share the photography studio with Mr. Reamer. The glowing coals from the hearths had winked out, and the massive red door, with its iron straps, was closed but not locked. Everyone's goodnights followed a predictable, bravura appearance by Old Faithful. "It never gets old," Mrs. Child said.

Lying in bed, her feet warm, Ellen contemplated how much of that peace came from Charles Penrose, the quiet, capable carpenter and father to a child becoming such a part of her life. What better time to consider the matter of father and daughter, here in bed with the luxury of time to think.

Aided by Mrs. Quincy a week earlier, Charles had done something that Ellen knew she would never forget, no matter how many years passed. When her shoulder still ached, and she grieved the yawning void left by Plato's death, she went to bed one night to discover a hot water bottle wrapped in a towel between the sheets in precisely the place where Plato used to sleep.

As her feet warmed and her heart softened, she knew the gentle blessing of unexpected kindness. She couldn't recall a time when anyone had been so thoughtful. How kind of Mrs. Quincy.

She told her so that morning, and Mrs. Quincy shook her head, her eyes lively. "I'd love to take credit, Ellen, but that goes to Mr. Penrose. He thought you might find it comforting."

"I do," Ellen replied after a moment of amazement. "Charles Penrose?"

Mrs. Quincy continued to amaze her. "I believe he is looking out for you."

"I think he will always be grateful that I . . . I . . . well, you know, kept his daughter safe." She shivered, the memory too real.

"It's more than that," Mrs. Quincy replied. "More." She clapped her hands and broke the spell, but Ellen sensed no harshness. "Let's get busy! Breakfast isn't going to make itself."

Ellen could have said nothing. Maybe the Ellie Found who was raised on sufferance wouldn't have. Things were different now. She waited until after breakfast when the architect gave his instructions for the day's work and Charles Penrose made the assignments, then brought his daughter into the kitchen.

Ellen patted Gwen and gave her a gentle nudge. "Mrs. Quincy needs you to help her carry some Carnation cans from the shelves over there," she said, hoping that Mrs. Quincy would understand she wanted a quiet moment with the tall carpenter.

To her delight, Mrs. Quincy didn't hesitate. "Follow me, Gwen," she said, after a slight raise of her eyebrow that spoke louder than words ever could. Ellen had an ally.

With an ache, Ellen realized that she knew nothing about addressing kindness. She took a deep breath and a chance, the same as when she answered the advertisement a few months ago. "Charles, thank you for the hot water bottle," she said, her hands clasped together to keep them from shaking. "It made me a whole lot less sad."

"Oh, I . . ."

Could it be that Mr. Penrose didn't know what to say either? Ellen felt herself relax, happy to know she wasn't the only shy person. "You were kind," she told him. "I needed that."

To her delight, he seemed to relax too. He glanced at his daughter, busy with Carnation cans, and came closer, keeping his voice low. "After my wife died"—she saw sudden sadness cross his face—"I did that for myself." He hesitated, then must have understood that since he had gone this far, he might as well forge on. "Clare liked to put her cold feet on my legs."

No matter her inexperience, Ellen knew this was a charged, intimate moment, a contained man's attempt that she understood: Loneliness is worse than almost anything.

She spoke quietly to him alone, as if the room were empty. "I didn't feel lonely."

"Mrs. Quincy said she would make sure you had it every night."

"I hope you didn't use your only hot water bottle."

"I have another one. That one's yours now."

Such a memory. Mrs. Quincy had not forgotten the water bottle tonight. "Stay here at Old Faithful, Mrs. Quincy," Ellen said softly. "We need you . . . I need you . . . here at the inn. Mrs. Child can wait. Please?"

Besides themselves, Mrs. Child had brought along burlap sacks of onions and carrots, and even celery. The next day Harry Child had Charles's crew unload a heavy cache from Mr. Colfitt, ironworker extraordinaire. Straining and sweating, even in below-zero weather, the freighter hauled in crates of Colfitt's best efforts, including iron bands crafted to Mr. Reamer's specifications to wrap around the inn's stone front desk.

Even more remarkable were the electric lights shaped like candles. Charles held one up, turning it to catch the early-morning sun, at least what there was of it.

"Four crates of these, with more to come," he said. "Our electrician arrives in March to wire this whole building. You'll see these everywhere in the lobby and halls."

"Winking little stars among our lodgepole pines," Ellen said, enchanted. "How does Mr. Reamer do it?"

"He has a vision of what can be."

So do I, Ellen thought much later, warming her toes against the hot water bottle after a long day's work. It was still her more-modest vision of wanting something more, but what? Her life had trained her to expect nothing, so the matter required some thought.

Warm from the water bottle, tired from the work, safe with her door closed, and free finally from an aching shoulder, Ellen closed her eyes. Before she slept, she wondered what Charles was going to do with the little iron fish that she saw Mr. Colfitt hand him. Perhaps he had requested it from Mr. Colfitt for his daughter because Christmas was coming. A fish?

She was still thinking of the pretty thing next morning when she opened the back door of the kitchen that led to the massive bear-proof garbage cans, ready to dump in breakfast scraps.

As always, she looked down at Plato's grave, which lately had become a repository of magpie feathers, a shell or two from someone, even a sardine can that made her smile.

There rested the iron fish.

Twelve

I admire Sergeant Dan Reeves. He's careful with his men, and he is fair, if firm. He is a peerless horseman, something I am not. He's equally adept on skis. We trust his judgment. Lately, though, I wish he could find another diversion besides Ellen Found. How is it that Ellen grows more lovely by the day? For a man of at least a little experience with women, I know nothing.

CHRISTMAS CAME, AND FOR THE first time in Ellen's life it meant something besides serving clam chowder—Mr. Linson's one concession to the holiday—to sad-eyed men who had nowhere else to go except the Mercury Street Café.

She wouldn't have told anyone about that, but for some reason, Sergeant Reeves had instituted a nightly walk among the geysers of the upper basin that fronted the inn. It usually began with a view of Old Faithful from the newly completed second-floor porch, with its overhang of roof that kept off the snow.

Provided the weather cooperated, she bundled up in her shabby coat. It didn't look so bad in the dark. Sergeant

Reeves—Dan—knew where to walk safely among the geysers and hot pots, and he kept a firm hand on her arm.

He wasn't a talkative man during the day—what she saw of him and his patrol—but the dark made him voluble. He told her about growing up on a farm in Connecticut, a state so far away that she could barely imagine it. "I wanted something more adventurous, and I joined the army," he said. He had more recently finished a tour of duty in the Philippines, and she learned about the insurrectionist Moros, humidity that did wretched things to wounds, and jungle fevers.

"Do I talk too much?" he asked one night.

She assured him he did not. "No. All I ever knew before Yellowstone was Butte, Montana," she said. "I hope you've never been there."

He laughed at that. Nights like this, she found it easy not to think of Butte. Plato was seldom far from her thoughts, but they had mellowed, as Charles Penrose had earlier suggested that they would. "I won't say grief vanishes, but it changes, or so I have discovered," was all Charles said about the matter. She knew he meant more than he could express, and she honored that.

"We won't forget Christmas," Mrs. Quincy said one morning. She said it with considerable finality. "I will requisition a suitable tree. Shouldn't be hard to find one."

It wasn't. Ellen asked Dan Reeves to locate a tree, but not a big one. By the week after Thanksgiving, there it was, modestly resting under the *porte cochère*. Decorations proved to be no problem either, and they came from a surprising source: One-Eyed Wilson, a.k.a. Mr. Fred Wilson. "I've been collecting them for years," he told Mrs. Quincy. "Never had a tree before, but I've been hopeful." And that was all he said as he gave Mrs. Quincy his carefully wrapped box.

Presents. Ellen had eight dollars left from her life savings, but she knew there was money percolating now in a Bozeman bank, thanks to her thirty dollars a month. She knew what to get Gwen, who confided in her one morning as they diced potatoes that her papa wrote in a journal every night before he slept. "I wish I had a journal," she said. "Think what I could write, now that I can write a little."

A search for paper in a room containing items stashed for the inn turned up ledgers and a massive book likely intended for the front desk and registration of visitors, come summer. *I daren't use that*, Ellen told herself and continued her search.

She found plain sheets of thick paper between bed linens, for some reason. Twenty sheets easily folded into forty. She knew Mr. Wilson had thick black thread because he had used it on her shoulder. "I'll do it for Gwen," he said.

She debated whether the paper was useful to the inn, finally assuaging her conscience by leaving a dollar and a note among the sheets. The journal became a thing of beauty, carefully stitched down the middle by Mr. Wilson, with Gwen's name in elaborate script, Ellen's contribution.

Mrs. Quincy became a fellow conspirator. "If I had yarn, I would knit mittens for Dan and Charles," Ellen told her boss over breadmaking. The next morning, hanging on her doorknob was a man's sweater with a note attached. *Unravel this*, she read. *Should be enough for mittens.*

Did she even dare ask Mrs. Quincy if this belonged to her late husband? She dared, or almost did. Her "Is this . . ." was enough for a nod. "I shouldn't," Ellen said and tried to hand it back. Mrs. Quincy pressed it into Ellen's hands. "I have his letters and a stickpin," she said. "Put it to good use."

What about Mrs. Quincy? She could tell the constant racket of saws and hammers in the hotel, plus the power drills, taxed the woman. There were long evenings when the cook stood at the large window in the lobby, staring at the deepening snow beyond the overhang of the porch. Ellen consulted with Mr. Wilson, who spent more and more of his time in the kitchen "helping out," as he put it or "mooching for cookies," as Mrs. Quincy said. No matter. The cook never seemed inclined to shoo him away.

"She needs something to cheer her up," Ellen told him.

Mr. Wilson gave the matter some thought. A week before Christmas, when she was knitting mittens in her room at a furious pace, he knocked, identified himself, stuck his arm in, and held out a carved wren no taller than three inches. "I made this," he told her when she opened the door wider, sounding shy and proud at the same time, not like an older gent of some years and one eye, lost in a mysterious time and place.

"Beautiful." Ellen touched the upturned tail. "Maybe she'll think spring is coming."

"My mother did, when I carved my first wren for her."

Do we all have secret lives? Ellen asked herself, humbled by this one-eyed man who had stitched her back together.

She returned to her room and came back with two dollars. He shook his head. "Between you and me, missy, I wanted to give Vera something. You can give it to her. Maybe tell her I made it, if you want to."

Vera, is it? Ellen thought, delighted. "I can do that," she told him. Vera.

Ellen's gift to everyone was a cake on Christmas Eve, but not just any cake. This one was four layers of chocolate goodness, chocolate because Gwen confided that her father loved chocolate. All Ellen had was cocoa, also "liberated" from pantry supplies clearly labeled *Not for use before summer.* She put another of her vanishing dollars by the cocoa tin and a note.

In a democratic vein, as in, "All in favor say aye," everyone agreed that the big dinner would be Christmas Eve, whereupon there would be silence and sleeping in on Christmas Day, which Mr. Child, via telegram, had declared would be a day off with pay. "Leftovers will be generous," Mrs. Quincy assured them. "Ellen and I deserve a day off, too."

The banging and drilling and sawing continued through the afternoon as Ellen and Mrs. Quincy cooked, ably assisted by Gwen, who confided to Ellen that she had a tidy stack of one-dollar bills, her salary for helping. "I wish I could spend them somewhere," she told Ellen after her nap. "I wanted to get Papa a new cravat. He's not very stylish," she added, which made Ellen laugh.

"It'll keep, my dear. Here's a sheet of paper. Draw him what you want to give him."

Gwen flashed her a smile, reminding Ellen how much she looked like her father, who, for some reason, wasn't smiling so much. Maybe Christmas did that to some people. Mrs. Quincy continued to gaze out the window and rub her arms. As for her, Ellen could barely contain herself. Christmas in the Copper King house just meant more work. In the Mercury Street Café, it meant sad people with nowhere to go. This was better.

At six o'clock, all drills and sawing stopped. Someone lit two hearths of the massive fireplace this time, which made Gwen clap her hands. Ellen watched her from the dining room as she sat in one of the new wicker chairs, her feet not touching the floor, chairs intended for grown-up summer visitors. Gwen's fear of the lobby had vanished, but then Gwen had not felt the claw on her shoulder. *Thank goodness for that*, Ellen thought.

Probably against orders—but who was there to

object?—Ellen and Mrs. Quincy dug around in the kitchen crates and favored the crew with Blue Willow dishes this time. "No one will know," her boss said. She put her hands on her hips. "Besides, they're just rough men."

Ellen smiled to herself, amused that Mrs. Quincy still thought of herself as a woman hardened through tough times. She had seen the way she tucked Gwen in for a nap when Ellen was too busy, or the extra cookies that came Mr. Wilson's way. *Are we all changing?* she asked herself.

Mr. Reamer didn't always join them for dinner, but this was different. There were no railroad financiers to impress on Christmas Eve, only the men and two women and a girl doing the work that would turn this hulk of a building into a magical place. In his quiet way, he stood and tapped on his glass when the wondrous dinner of elk and turkey and mounds of mashed potatoes and chocolate cake was a pleasant memory.

"Thank you for what you are doing," he said simply. "We would probably all rather be somewhere else this holiday, raising a toast with loved ones, but here we are."

Ellen looked around, amazed at the lump in her throat. There was nowhere she would rather be than right here, right now. She glanced at Charles, who was looking at her, and then down at his daughter. There sat Sergeant Reeves with his men. She blushed when he winked.

"I wish you a Merry Christmas, gentlemen," Mr. Reamer continued. He nodded to Ellen, Mrs. Quincy, and Gwen. "And the ladies, of course." He chuckled. "I know it's hard to contemplate right now in this stage of construction, but someday millions of people will pass through these doors. We will be remembered in the wood, the stone, our electric candlesticks"—everyone laughed—"and our rustic hospitality. To quote the inimitable Tiny Tim, 'God bless us, everyone!'"

Everyone applauded. Charles Penrose raised his hand and gave a nod in the architect's direction. "Sir, we have an early Christmas present for you."

He motioned to the architect, then picked up Gwen and carried her at the head of his crew into the lobby. Several of the men carrying lanterns led the way. They stopped in front of one of the guest rooms, one with an iron "1" on the door, part of the pile of numbers Mr. Colfitt had sent ahead. He opened the door and gestured.

"Here you are, Mr. Reamer, a portion of the magic. We wanted to complete one room."

"Oh my," Ellen whispered as she took in the iron bedstead and the mattress, two chairs with cushions, a rustic bureau, and a washstand with a cream-colored pitcher and bowl. The curtains at the window, with its many small panes, looked suspiciously like a gathered sheet. Underfoot was a rag rug.

"Just one hundred and thirty-nine rooms to go!" Mr. Wilson said to laughter.

Gradually, the men moved away, chatting in small groups, heading toward their own rustic boardinghouse, destined to be torn down when the project ended, and they moved on to other jobs.

Mr. Reamer cleaned his glasses thoughtfully, carefully, as he did everything. "Thank you for this Christmas surprise, Charles," he said. "It means more than I can say. Bless you all, and good night."

Thirteen

What a paltry present I gave Ellen Found. Maybe I can redeem myself in the spring, if ever I can get to a store. What would be the perfect gift for her?

"STAY A BIT," ELLEN SAID to Charles and Gwen. "I have something for you."

She had never received a present of any kind in her life, but here was One-Eyed—no, Fred Wilson—smiling at her, obviously curious to know how Mrs. Quincy would react to his carving.

Sergeant Reeves started to follow his men, but Ellen told him to wait too, hoping he wouldn't be teased later by this little group he commanded. Not for nothing had she stayed up nearly all night, knitting like fury to finish the mittens.

Charles whispered to Gwen and patted her shoulder, then shrugged on his overcoat and hurried after the two privates Sergeant Reeves sent on ahead. "I'll be right back."

Mrs. Quincy turned her attention to the tree, a modest lodgepole pine that knew better than to compete with the potential majesty of the unfinished lobby. Mr. Wilson's ornaments were positively perfect.

Ellen went to her room for her presents, which now seemed so paltry. What was she thinking? She picked up the presents wrapped in brown paper, the only thing available, and set them beside the tree.

Mrs. Quincy already sat in the step-down area around the fireplace, Mr. Wilson beside her. Ellen noticed for the first time that he must have stood closer to his razor than usual, and she didn't know he owned a white shirt.

Here she was, wearing the brown skirt and gingham shirtwaist because this was a special occasion. The contrast couldn't have been greater between tonight's feast and last year's hurried cheese and crackers and the sad men with nowhere to go on Christmas Eve except the Mercury Street Café. She was well-fed and wearing a new dress. Her shoulder barely pained her. If there was never to be a better Christmas Eve than this one, it was enough.

"I think my father's been hiding a book for me," Gwen whispered to Ellen when she joined her by the fireplace.

"I hope it's one you'll let me read to you," Ellen said.

Sure enough, Charles returned with a book-shaped present, also done up in brown paper. Sergeant Reeves sat beside her. "I wanted to get you something," he whispered, his eyes on Charles, "but I couldn't even get past Fort Yellowstone this winter, let alone Gardiner. Maybe a bouquet of sagebrush when the snow melts a little?" All she could do was blush and smile. It was more than enough.

Charles added a log to the fireplace and joined them after dropping his present by the tree. "It's so little," he murmured.

"Books are everything," she reminded him.

This event was her idea, so everyone looked at her. Ellen

stood up, heart in her mouth, as she realized *she* had engineered this, from the tree on down. She glanced at Mr. Wilson, her fellow conspirator, who nodded his encouragement.

Everyone also knew her circumstances. She took a deep breath. "I never had a tree, and I never had a Christmas Eve dinner." She smiled at Gwen, on sure ground now with the friendly child who had first sat with her on the train, and whose life she'd saved. Her heart swelled with an odd feeling of commitment or camaraderie. Maybe it was love. She didn't know, but it was Christmas Eve in a wonderful place she could never have imagined only months ago.

"Gwen told me that her father writes in a journal," she said. She handed her present to the wide-eyed child. "Mr. Wilson and I did this, Gwen. Merry Christmas."

With the studied efficiency of someone who had opened many a present, Gwen carefully removed the yarn bow made from the final row of yarn on that old sweater from Mrs. Quincy. Gwen opened the journal and turned the blank pages Mr. Wilson had stitched together. "Papa, we can both write each night, can't we?"

"We can, my dearest," he said, with a long look at Ellen that made her stomach settle lower in her lap. He handed Gwen his present, which proved to be *The Tailor of Gloucester.* She pointed to the word. "Gloucester," Charles said. "I know how you liked *Peter Rabbit.* This is by the same author."

She hugged her father and Ellen, and after a moment's shyness, Mr. Wilson, who rubbed his remaining eye and mumbled something about dust.

Such a moment. Ellen had never seen presents exchanged, and she knew she would remember the good feeling forever. But here was Mr. Wilson nudging her. "No, I think you should present it to her," she said, handing him the package. "I knew Mr. Wilson likes to carve," she said to them all, "and I asked him for something for you that reminded him of spring, Mrs. Quincy."

Her boss gasped and shook her head, but Mr. Wilson wasn't about to back down, now that he had the courage. Vera Quincy's fingers shook as she unwrapped the carved wren, that perky little bird that was long gone to warmer climates as winter reigned.

"We . . . we both wanted to cheer you a little," Ellen said.

Mrs. Quincy dabbed at her eyes but made no comment about dust. "I'll set this wren where we can all see it. Spring is still a long way off."

Ellen picked up the two remaining packages, handing the first one to Dan Reeves. She decided in that moment and forever after to say what she meant. "This is from Gwen and me. Thank you for having a steady aim that . . . that night."

"Anyone with a rifle would have done what I did," he said.

"But you were there, and you did it." She touched her heart. "I will never forget."

He swallowed several times, then took out the mittens and put them on. "I have regulation gloves, but it can get pretty cold out in the weather," he said simply. "This'll help." He kissed her cheek.

She handed the other package to Charles. "Your gloves have gotten a bit raggedy from all those heated nails," she told him. She wanted to laugh, but the mood in the room was strange to her. "You have one hundred and thirty-nine other rooms to finish down cold corridors."

Everyone laughed, maybe willing to forget frigid days for a few hours. Mrs. Quincy hurried into the kitchen and came back with more cookies. "Divide these," she ordered.

"Ellen and I will bake more tomorrow for the rest of the crew. Thank you all, and good night."

"One moment."

From her apron Ellen took the envelope Mr. Reamer had handed her earlier and gave it to Mrs. Quincy. "This is from Mrs. Child to you, Mrs. Quincy."

"Oh no!"

"Go on," she coaxed. "Look what she wrote on the back."

Mrs. Quincy turned over the letter slowly, as if fearing what she would see. "A Christmas surprise?"

Mrs. Child isn't unkind, Ellen thought. "It can't be that bad."

"If I must." Mrs. Quincy opened the envelope and read the letter. Her expression changed. "I never in my life . . ." Mrs. Quincy sat down. "She's officially offering me my job back. I guess she *was* right about the French chef."

The others applauded, but no one looked happy, especially Mr. Wilson. Mrs. Quincy fanned herself with the letter. "I have until spring to think about it. I might stay."

Ellen glanced at Mr. Wilson. *This could be an interesting spring,* she thought.

"It's been a good day," Mr. Wilson said as he and Charles doused the fires. Sergeant Reeves gave Ellen a small salute. As he left the lobby, she heard him whistling "Good King Wenceslas."

She took Mr. Wilson's arm and escorted him to the door. "Thank you, Mr. Wilson. The wren was perfect."

"Thank *you.* I've been wanting to do something nice for her." He chuckled. "Guess I needed a nudge."

She waved goodnight to the Penroses and followed Mrs. Quincy into the kitchen. The dishes were done, and plates were ready for tomorrow's pancakes and bacon, a rare treat, but it was Christmas Day, after all. There were ample leftovers for the day, so it would be like a little kitchen vacation for them.

Mrs. Quincy hugged her and went to her room, leaving Ellen to douse the lights. Ellen left one lantern burning and went to the back door, happy for a small moment with Plato. She looked down at the snow-covered mound of the bravest cat in the universe.

"Ellen, do you have a moment?"

Startled, she turned around to see Charles Penrose standing inside the kitchen. She hurried inside, hoping he wouldn't think her a fool for mooning over Plato.

"I have something for you. I wanted you to have this without an audience." He held out an envelope.

A present. Her name in firm lettering. *I will keep this envelope forever*, she thought. She opened it. Seeds. Charles came closer.

"Every autumn, Clare shook seeds out of her summer flowers," he said, his voice low, even with no one else around to hear. "She never was able to plant these, and I've hung on to them for two years."

"I can't . . ." she began.

He raised his hand. "You can, please. When spring comes, plant them on Plato's grave. Goodnight, and Happy Christmas."

Ellen wished she could tell him that no one had ever done a nicer thing for her, but he would probably scoff at that. "I will save some of the seeds. You and Gwen can plant them later, somewhere else."

"If you'd like." He drew her close for a surprising moment. "Thank you again for my daughter's life. Words can be inadequate, even for a Cornishman."

"It's just that . . ." How to explain this? "I wish I could have done better for Plato."

85

"If we could delve into the feline mind, I think Plato would say you did very well by him."

"I wish I felt worthy of that much devotion," she admitted, surprising herself. "Who am I, after all? My mother—"

"You never knew her."

"But she was—"

"And you are you," he said firmly. "I have something to say."

She wondered at this quiet, capable man who usually kept his thoughts to himself. Why was he going to this trouble for her?

"When I was eight, my father came out of the Dalcoath tin mine and said we were going to America," he told her. "He never said what happened in the pit to cause such a decision. We came to America and managed well enough."

"You had family. I have no one," she reminded him. "No one now."

"Are you so certain? My father worked with wood. He taught me everything I know and use today. The way I see it, you are your own teacher. Never discount that."

"I have nothing!" she said, trying to remind him, the stubborn man.

He put his finger to her lips. "Most of us require teachers. You taught yourself kindness and bravery. You taught *yourself.* Think on that."

She stayed a long time in the kitchen, holding the envelope to her cheek.

Fourteen

Did I say too much? Was I too impulsive? We're working too hard, but we must. The electricians have created their magic. Ellen Found is also lovely by electric light. The plumbers are going to spoil us soon with indoor plumbing. I remember how nice it was when Clare scrubbed my back in the tub. I miss that. I miss a lot of things.

EVERYONE BUCKLED DOWN EVEN MORE after Christmas. January saw the welcome addition of Mr. Colfitt, who set up his temporary forge and shop practically by the inn's back door. He also brought with him more electric candlesticks and an amazing five-foot iron clock that Mr. Reamer had designed for the fireplace.

After surveying the situation and muttering to himself, Mr. Colfitt forged an iron ladder-bridge from the second floor landing out to the massive fireplace. Ellen watched two brave souls inch across, affix the massive clock to the fireplace, and set it ticking. "Someone has to wind that monster once a week," Charles said over coffee the next morning. "Not me!"

Charles made no mention of their Christmas Eve conversation. He didn't avoid her, but he remained his usual, quiet self. Ellen considered the matter as she grieved for Plato, wishing she could have . . . what? "He chose to stay with me for two years," she told herself late one night. "He didn't have to, but he did. I should let this rest." She slept better after that.

Next came the inn's electrification. Mr. Reamer called them artificers, those two fellows from Bozeman who, with Mr. Colfitt, wired the electric candlesticks throughout the lobby, down halls, and into guest rooms, where the carpenters hammered and sawed.

For a quiet man, Mr. Reamer had a dramatic flair. At nightfall in mid-February he announced over dinner that now was the time. "Gentlemen and ladies, join me in the lobby."

Everyone watched as the architect and his electricians moved to the wall behind the front desk and Mr. Reamer flicked the switch. Each electric candlestick seemed to light itself by magic. Gwen clapped her hands.

Ellen stared in wonder. She looked around at tired faces that didn't seem so tired. Maybe it was a trick of light after all these months of gloom and snow. She decided it was pride in the work, a commitment to a unique building in the wilderness and its pinpoints of light.

These electric beauties couldn't flicker like ordinary candles. Their steady light shone on lodgepole pine walls and oddly shaped, lacquered branches twisting under the handrails. She took a good look at the small landing near the pinnacle of the roof where Mr. Reamer said a string quartet would perform during dinner and dancing. The crew already called it the Crow's Nest.

She knew Plato would have enjoyed such a perch.

Lately, she could think calmly of him, sorrow replaced by good memories and gratitude without relentless grief. Maybe Charles Penrose was right.

"There is nothing like this anywhere," the architect said, recalling her to the moment. "June first, my friends," he told them. "We are making history."

Plumbers came the next week, bundled up in freight wagons on skids. With electric lights, the carpenters worked even later hours on room after room. Ellen saw the toll it took on Charles Penrose, the man she enjoyed seeing every morning for coffee. Now he carried a drowsy Gwen into Ellen's room, where she patted Ellen's pillow and returned to slumber.

"Your face is too thin," she told Charles one morning. Electric lights made it harder to hide exhaustion. "Being in charge can't be easy."

He smiled at that, which helped her heart, that odd organ that lately seemed to govern more than her wary brain. Why else did she want to tuck his muffler tighter into his overcoat?

"I'll survive," he assured her one morning. "Sit down. You're too busy. Just sit with me."

She sat, hoping he would say more. She pushed forward a plate of Mrs. Quincy's doughnuts. He took one, nodding his appreciation. *Say more*, she thought, then thought the impossible: *I want to know you better.*

Maybe he was feeling expansive. Maybe more at ease. Maybe it was the doughnuts. He leaned back in his chair. "Clare would do that—bustle about until I grabbed her and sat her down. We didn't usually say much. It was enough to just . . . just . . . *be*. Try it."

One morning he asked her about Mrs. Quincy. "She seems different these days," he said, then gave her a broad smile, as he used to before the work began to wear him out. "May I give the credit to Fred Wilson?"

She nodded, pleased that'd he noticed. "She doesn't stare out the window so much," Ellen confided. "She makes ever so many doughnuts. She won't admit they're for Mr. Wilson, but I know better."

Then came the morning when his guard must have been down. "The fellows tell me that Sergeant Reeves always seems to find something to do here when he isn't on patrol."

"He does," she agreed, wondering what to make of this widower, this tentative man.

"He's a good fellow with a promising future in the army," he said. She listened for animosity but heard only words carefully chosen.

"He has plans," she said, choosing carefully too, because she liked Dan Reeves.

"Do his plans include you?" he blurted out another morning.

"He hasn't said so," she replied, wanting to shake him a little, or maybe a lot, because she realized that somewhere between the envelope of seeds and iron fish, something had happened to her. And so she sat with the tentative widower who touched her mind and heart.

She taught Gwen to make biscuits, and how to French braid her own hair. "After all, when this project is done, you'll be moving to another place with your father," she said, which broke her heart in ways she hadn't reckoned on.

Mr. Reamer asked her and Mrs. Quincy to increase their chores to include sweeping out the finished rooms and wiping them down. "That last freight sled brought in iron bedsteads and bedding," he told her. "The chairs and bureaus are here too. Time to furnish the rooms."

Mrs. Quincy asked her to work with Gwen. "I work

better alone," she assured Ellen, who wasn't even slightly fooled. Mr. Wilson always managed to show up to sweep and mop too. She heard them laughing together down the hall and felt a twinge of envy.

"Does he like Mrs. Quincy?" Gwen asked her once when it was almost warm enough to open a window. "She doesn't seem to grumble as much."

Ellen kissed the top of her head.

"I am observant," Gwen told her. She plumped herself down on a bed. "Papa doesn't write so much in his journal. He stares at the pages, then shakes his head and closes it."

"Do you write in yours?" Ellen asked, powerfully wanting to have a look at Charles Penrose's journal.

"Aye." She leaned closer. "Papa is hoping to get another assignment here in the park. A place called Lake. Are you staying here?"

"I hope to."

"Come with us to Lake," Gwen said. "You'll be too far away here. I . . . I asked my father if you could come with us."

Ellen heard the urgency and sat down beside the little one. She held her close. "What did he say?"

"He kissed my cheek like you kissed my head. I am getting nowhere with him!"

I know the feeling, Ellen thought.

The days began to lengthen as snow moved from endless powder to wet, heavy flakes that signaled a change of season. Already some of the workers had left for other jobs. The only thing that made her happy about that were their bashful thanks to her for good food, something she never heard at the Mercury Street Café.

Sergeant Reeves came by more often after supper. The exhaustion of cold patrols on skis and frustrating searches for poachers who robbed Yellowstone for their own enrichment had left its mark. As worn down as he was, she knew he would show up after dishes were done to walk with her in the geyser basin.

The snow never stayed long there, vanquished by the everlasting warmth of fumaroles, hot pots, and geysers. As impressive as they were, none of them rivaled nearby Old Faithful, which showed itself at a regular fifty-five minutes, but life, she knew, was seldom spectacular.

"Think of the tourists coming in June," Dan said one evening as they strolled. "They'll ooh and aah, but for my money, I like this basin."

They paused to watch Old Faithful erupt. Who wouldn't? As they watched, she told the sergeant her plan. "I've applied for a position as front desk clerk here."

"You'll get it." He turned to her. "You're the kind of pretty girl Mr. Child wants to see in his hotel."

"Thanks, Dan." Goodness. Better make a joke. "I should have put my hair up months ago," she told him. "Every girl likes a compliment."

"It's more than that, Ellen," he said, more serious now than she had seen him. "You have kind eyes and a good heart, and it shows."

He had kissed her before on the cheek, but this was different. This was a serious kiss on the lips, her first ever. "Been wanting to do that," he whispered when his lips still nearly touched hers.

She strolled with him, shy and pleased. She knew Dan Reeves was a good man with honorable intentions, the sort of man she could never have found anywhere near the Mercury Street Café. In her short lifetime of wanting little because she had next to nothing, she had wanted more. That wanting had brought her to Old Faithful Inn.

To her chagrin, she still wanted more.

Fifteen

What do I do? I'm thirty-two years old, and I'm thinking like twenty again. I'll be ~~damned~~ darned if the sap rises in places besides pine trees.

AFTER ONLY A FEW BLOCKS, Charles knew Ellen was right about Butte. It was a no-account town with more bars and brothels than churches. He gave Butte the benefit of the doubt at the depot. He had been around enough depots to know that things looked better after a few blocks. Not in Butte.

He was only supposed to go to Bozeman to inspect and purchase a new power saw, except that the salesman didn't know his Bozemans from his Buttes. "You'll find what you want in Butte," he said with no apology. Ah well. The day was warm, and he was amenable to a little longer with nothing to do, a rare novelty. A telegram to Mr. Reamer easily explained a few more days away.

More than that, he wanted to think. He'd said nothing to Ellen—it was hardly his business—but he had seen Sergeant Reeves kiss her at the upper basin last week.

At least it wasn't a long kiss. Maybe a business trip with time on the train would give him the courage to admit to himself what he had known for some time: he was in love with Ellen Found.

He knew he could rationalize the powerful emotion that played merry hell with his peace of mind. Gwen needed a mother. A man was entitled to another wife to make his way easy in life.

It was time he admitted to himself that Gwen had not once entered into his desire to marry Ellen. He wanted Ellen as much as he had wanted Clare Hayden, and for the same reasons. He missed the pleasure of married life, from the simplicity of sharing a pillow and talking about life plans, to the complexity of loving a woman because he had urges that weren't going away.

He smiled to himself as he walked along streets dirty with black snow found in mining towns like Butte. He was thirty-two years old but as frisky as a colt.

He stopped in front of a shop window to stare at himself in the reflection. He knew he was a handsome man. Clare used to get tight-lipped when women stared at him and flirted. He pleaded innocence because he didn't care as long as Clare found him attractive. He could easily have enjoyed a lifetime with her, but fate had shuffled their cards.

Now he found a promising future in Yellowstone. A recent letter from Harry Child stated there was work to be done finishing the remodel at Lake Hotel as soon as Old Faithful Inn was completed, and was he interested? Aye he was. And could it also involve Ellen?

What prevented him from being the man kissing Ellen? Did he need some cosmic approval to marry again, have more children with likely an excellent mother, and grow old with someone besides his first love?

He stared at his reflection, which had turned glum and stupidly pathetic. "I want a wife," he told his wavy image. "It's no crime."

He'd started contemplating remarriage a year ago when the raw hurt of Clare's lingering death from a failing heart had turned to a dull ache and then to tender memories of a woman he loved who died too soon. He decided he should look for a wife like the one he had lost.

Then why Ellen? From her dark looks and olive skin, she possessed none of Clare's rosy complexion or her majestic height and truly elegant features. Ellen was small and energetic, with wonderful brown eyes and black hair. With that energy came a quiet nature at odds with the fervor of her labors. Perhaps he could trace that to a child trained from youth to be seen and not heard, a child of low origin that was somehow her fault. Ellen was a person on her own from youth.

She was also the bravest person Charles knew, someone who did not lose her head in a crisis, someone ready to sacrifice herself for another. He doubted he had that much courage and prayed it would never be tested. He could tell Ellen loved his daughter. Did Ellen love him too?

Enough of this; he was here on business. Charles purchased the power saw to replace the saw and bits worn out with chewing into lodgepole pine. He handed over the cheque from Harry Child and received a receipt and guarantee that it would arrive in Gardiner, Montana, in two weeks. Done.

He didn't want to stay another moment in Butte. He already had a ticket for tomorrow's first train to Bozeman, but that was tomorrow. *I wonder...* he thought, then turned back to the clerk. "Where is the Mercury Street Café?" he asked.

The clerk stared at him, maybe seeing a capable man wearing a good overcoat, and wondering why on earth . . . "It's not a place for gents like you," the clerk said tentatively.

"I know someone who worked there, and I was wondering . . ." Charles saw the smirk. "No, not *that* sort of person."

"I'm relieved to say it burned to the ground two weeks ago."

Insufferable prig, Charles thought, then, "*Really?* I'd still like to see it."

The clerk pointed. "Two blocks that way, then three more north." He stifled a laugh. "Nasty place. Glad it's gone."

Two blocks took Charles into an even worse part of town, where women wearing nothing but wrappers and smiles leaned out windows. One whistled at him and made a vulgar comment about the swing to his walk. He blushed at the unwanted attention. Clare had mentioned that swing herself, but not while leaning out a window.

There it was, a blackened heap giving new meaning to the word "eyesore." He breathed in the stink of burned wood and old grease that had probably been trapped in drains since the town's founding. Someone had hung a sign, "Too bad, so sad."

A merchant stood in the doorway across the street; Charles joined him. "I used to know someone who worked here," he said, wondering if he should admit that he knew *anyone* associated with the café. "A kind woman with a mean cat."

"Meanest cat that ever lived," the man said with a laugh. "I hear she snuck out at midnight a few months ago, cat and all."

"She did. You knew her?"

"She bought soap and tooth powder from me. She asked

to use my address as a return address for a job she wanted. She got the job?"

"A good job," Charles said, then nodded at the eyesore. "What happened?"

"Ol' Linson had a cook who smoked. Near as anyone can figure, she dropped ashes on a pile of newspapers, and whoosh!"

"That bad?"

"That bad. The old rip flicked her final ash. Linson left town the next morning, and good riddance." He paused, then peddled back a bit. "Hopefully you're not related to him."

"Not I."

"Good." His face took on a wistful expression. "That little lady who got away . . . she was a pretty thing with kind eyes, but oh, that cat."

Charles almost told the merchant how Plato the demon cat saved his daughter's life and the life of that pretty thing, but that meant more questions. He nodded his goodbye and strolled down the street.

Making sure he wasn't being watched, he found his way to the alley. The burn smell was even stronger, along with alley odors best left unidentified. He paused before a door hanging off its hinges. In his mind's eye, he saw a woman of courage and determination living there, sharing her skimpy meals with a cat.

He looked inside to see a precarious ceiling sagging and a rotting floor. The bed was no more than a cot, and there was a three-legged table and one stool. Pages from magazines were still tacked to the walls, photographs of mountains and streams, and a lady in a frilly dress. With a pang, he wondered if Ellen had tacked the picture there, her homage to a mother she never knew, a lady of the line, but her mother despite all.

"Family's what you make it, dear lady," he said.

Where now? He didn't want to pass those ogling harpies again, so he walked up the alley. He slowed, knowing he was being followed. He tightened his grip on his carpetbag and turned around.

It was a cat. No, a kitten, ambling along, maybe following him, maybe not. Who knew with cats? He watched, amused, as it pounced on a leaf, tried to eat it, then found a prize. He looked closer as the kitten wriggled its backside, then pounced on a cricket that had somehow survived into winter. It ate with some relish, then looked around for more.

"Tight times, little buddy," Charles said softly.

He had always been a careful man, measuring twice before cutting once, taking good care of his wife and daughter, and then his daughter. He kept his saws sharp, and he hammered nails straight and true. He left little to chance, because that was how buildings fell down and chairs collapsed.

In an impulsive gesture he could only credit to a longing to make a pretty lady happy again, he knelt. "How about you come with me . . . uh . . . Socrates?"

Without a hiss or a backward glance, the little morsel made no objection when Charles deposited it in his overcoat pocket. To his surprise, he felt an outsized purr against his hip. He stopped at an emporium near what looked like the least-scabrous hotel in town and bought several cans of Carnation, a can opener, and some sardine tins.

"You're changing residence, Socrates," he said the next morning as the kitten, its belly full of milk and sardines, nestled in his carpetbag.

Careful as always, he telegraphed ahead, so there was a freight wagon held for him at Fort Yellowstone, full of crates and furniture labeled *Old Faithful Inn*. He looked around, amazed at what a few days away could do. The great melt was on. The wagon had wheels again and not skids.

"Getting ready to open that hotel?" the driver said as he joined him on the wagon seat, carpetbag at his feet, Socrates inside.

"We are. Rooms are almost done. And you're hauling more furniture."

As they rode by mounds of melting slush, Ellen Found occupied his mind. He reconsidered. His heart was occupied. The obstacle was Sergeant Reeves. *We shall see*, he thought. *I've courted a woman before*.

They were almost through scary Golden Gate, that maze of curves and hoodoos where the road cantilevered out over the Gardner River far below, when the driver glanced over his shoulder. "Uh oh," he said, then something not repeated in polite company.

Uneasy, Charles looked back just as a sudden gust of blizzard wind roared down his overcoat collar, followed by icy pellets. The sky vanished in a swirl of snow.

"I can't see ahead," the driver said. Charles heard the panic in his voice. "Why'd this happen right here? I daren't move. Didja bring any food?"

Sixteen

I am afrad. It's a blitzerd. Did I spell that right? I thot the snow was gone. We all did. My father has been gon to long. Ellen wipes my tears when I cry. She cries latter, when no one noes. When Da comes hom, I will tell him I let Ellen reed his jurnal. I wunder if he will be angree.

ON THE FIRST MORNING SHE didn't wear her coat, Ellen knew it was time to plant Charles Penrose's gift of seeds on Plato's grave.

A look around suggested the coming of summer. Soon leaves would bud out, revealing that impossible green heralding spring and early summer. Already the chipmunks chattered at her.

The snow was gone from Plato's mound. Humming to herself, she made four little furrows and carefully spaced the seeds, leaving a few seeds in the envelope in case Charles wanted some after all.

"Lots of critters around soon," she told Plato as she patted his grave. "I doubt you could have caught them, but I know you would have tried."

She stood there, hands together, then turned toward the northwest as a sudden gust of what felt suspiciously like winter ruffled her skirt and showed off her ankles. The next blast brought wet and heavy snow with it. She ran inside and slammed the door behind her.

For three days snow fell without pause, the wind blowing it into monstrous drifts. The ropes between the inn and temporary housing went up again. Men shrugged and muttered about, "Mother Nature's dirty tricks," and, "That's Wyoming for you."

Temperatures dropped to negative numbers. Ellen didn't think Sergeant Reeves and his men would leave the confines of their quarters, but he came through the storm that fourth day, looking grim about the mouth. While she made breakfast biscuits and worried, he handed her a message.

"Before the telephone line went down, this came from headquarters. Mr. Penrose sent it to the YP transport barn five days ago. I don't know, Ellen."

She made herself read it. "'Arrived Bozeman. Tell freight wagon to wait for me. C. Penrose.'" She looked at Dan. "He's probably still at Fort Yellowstone, then?" she asked, trying to sound casual.

Dan shook his head. "Not according to the adjutant who read this to me. They started out three days ago. He said Mr. Penrose was eager to get back here. 'I have something for Miss Found,' he told the adjutant."

She turned away and banged the biscuit dough around. He put his hand on her shoulder, but she shook it off. "I am fine," she said through clenched teeth. He left without a word.

She was far from fine. She thought of the many places where a misstep of a horse or wrong command from the driver could send team and wagon down into disaster. *Please let them be past Golden Gate*, she prayed. *That's the worst spot.*

The men ate breakfast with their usual relish. As she refilled coffee cups, she heard conversations about summer jobs and work for the lucky ones hired to build a YP transportation barn in Gardiner, designed by Mr. Reamer as well. With an ache, she knew the transportation company was missing a wagon and driver. Better not to think about it.

How did such things happen? By the noon meal, everyone knew about the missing wagon, along with a driver and Mr. Penrose. Gwen heard it. She ran to Ellen as she sliced meat and cheese. She clung to Ellen's dress.

"I'll finish up here," Mrs. Quincy said. "Take her to your room."

Ellen picked up the child and retreated to her sanctuary, bright now with the addition of a rug like the ones in the guest rooms. Only yesterday, the carpenters applauded when Mr. Wilson proudly attached the iron numbers 1-1- 0 to a door. She heard him say, "Wait'll Mr. Penrose sees this! He was hoping we'd finish off 105 before he came back."

She held Gwen and crooned to her, telling her not to worry, that her father was a careful man and he would show up soon. When Gwen slept, it was Ellen's turn to weep.

The snow stopped a day later, but the wind blew even harder from the north and west, testing the windows, trying to get inside. "We built this inn to last," Mr. Wilson told her that night after a silent dinner. He assured her that carpenters and soldiers would turn into road crews and start out from both ends when the wind stopped.

Gwen worked quietly beside her, not leaving her side. When the dishes were done, she took Gwen's hand and walked her into the wonderful lobby. Someone had lit a fire in one of the hearths. She looked up to see the iron clock Mr. Colfitt had fashioned, ticking away the hours, untroubled by grief or fear, marking time as they waited and worried.

Mr. Reamer left the electric candlesticks on. They sent their cheery glow into the darkness as if to say, "We're here. We're your beacon." Ellen sat on a wicker chair in the step-down area before the fireplace, Gwen nestled in her lap.

"Could you do something for me?" Gwen asked Mr. Wilson when he and Mrs. Quincy joined them, hand in hand.

"Anything," the one-eyed carpenter said.

"Could you please get my da's journal from our house?" Gwen was a polite child. "And . . . and . . . could you get his flannel nightshirt? I like the way it smells."

Mrs. Quincy turned her head away. Ellen stared at the flames.

Mr. Wilson returned, snow-covered, with the journal tucked inside his overcoat, along with the nightshirt. With a sigh that made Ellen bite her lip, Gwen tucked the flannel shirt close and handed Ellen the journal. "Maybe you could read some of this to me."

Ellen nodded. "I will," she said softly, "but not right now. Let's cuddle instead."

"I understand," the child said, sounding astoundingly mature.

They cuddled all night, Gwen in tears until she wore herself out, her cheek resting on Charles's nightshirt. When Ellen was certain she slept, she took the journal and a blanket to her armchair and started to read.

Much of the journal was a laconic affair. Some entries only mentioned difficulties in getting quality lumber in Cheyenne, where they lived at the time. Of Gwen's birth he wrote, *Is it possible to love someone more? And to love someone you've only just met? I am proof of that. My girls.*

The journal grew even more spare during the time she supposed that Clare Penrose was dying. The hardest entry was the most brief: *What will I do?*

Ellen understood. *What will I do?* she wanted to ask the universe at large. There had certainly been no amazing pronouncements, no fervent declarations of anything between the two of them. She had no claim on Charles Penrose beyond that one long look he gave her when he handed her the envelope of seeds Clare had been unable to plant, and that one frank conversation neither of them mentioned again.

She ruffled through the journal to more recent days and stopped, head bowed, as Charles answered her question. It was the entry from Christmas Eve. *I want to give her something. Will she think me a fool if it is Clare's seeds? Will it say what I'm trying to say and haven't the words yet? Can I- or may I - love her too?*

It was a question for the ages. Her eyes closed in weariness and defeat. All she ever wanted to do was escape the Mercury Street Café. She hadn't planned to fall in love, not when she was simply trying to survive. But there he was, and she wanted more; she wanted him.

She glanced at the bed where Gwen slept. "In the morning I will tell you that whatever happens, you will not be alone," she whispered. "You are mine. We'll manage together."

She picked up a pencil and poised it over the page. She dated her entry April 16, 1904, and wrote in his journal, *Yes, you can love me. I won't forget Plato, but I want another cat.*

It looked supremely stupid. How could *anyone* compare an alley cat to a person? She nearly erased it, then decided to leave it there for a day or two. She could erase it later and no one would know.

She went back to her bed and tucked a portion of the nightshirt under her head. It did smell like Charles—a man's scent also fragrant with oil from wood and varnish.

Her shoulders relaxed and she slept. The wind roared on.

Seventeen

THE SILENCE WOKE HER. ELLEN sat up, startled, then relieved to see sunlight streaming through the gap in the curtains. She dressed quickly, still brushing her hair when she opened the door.

"We didn't want to wake you," Mrs. Quincy said as she handed the graniteware coffee pot to Mr. Wilson.

"I can help," Ellen said. "I need to keep busy."

And she did, all that day and the next, and the one after as the rescuers—nearly all the carpenters—hitched up teams and wagons to clear the road. The telephone lines were up by the third day as soldiers from Fort Yellowstone indicated they were doing the same. "We'll meet somewhere in the middle," Dan Reeves told her.

The sun shone bitter cold for two more days, then spring returned. Ellen woke to ice melting off the roof. Fickle, daunting Wyoming. She doubted the new state would ever have much population.

"We'll know more soon," Mr. Wilson told her as his road crew started out. He left behind the best carpenters to continue finishing the rooms. Mr. Reamer quietly directed

Charles's work. He took Ellen aside to assure her that she would always have employment with Harry Child and the YP Company. "There's a place for you here."

She understood. No one commented about yesterday's telephone call before the line went down again. Searchers from Fort Yellowstone had found one horse dead in the Gardner River, not far from Golden Gate.

Gwen didn't need to know. She still cried herself to sleep at night, but so did Ellen, who'd told her that no matter what, she was never to worry about what would become of her. "We'll stick together," she said.

Ellen should have known that the whole terrifying ordeal would end with no fanfare, no bells, no one scattering rose petals, just the sound of the big door opening.

Gwen was more attuned to her father's footsteps than anyone. She looked up from sewing hems on napkins for summer guests. "Ellen," she said uncertainly, her eyes wide.

Then came the sound of other footsteps and Sergeant Reeves's cheery, "Guess who's home!"

Gwen ran into the lobby. Ellen followed, then sagged against the doorframe as father and daughter came together with shouts of joy. She watched in utter relief, then began a checklist. He was thin. He hadn't shaved in a week and his beard was scraggly. Red eyes. The tips of his ears looked chewed up, maybe frostbitten. He was alive. She loved him.

"Got him back to you."

She took a good look at Dan Reeves, who also looked chewed up. This was the sergeant who had saved her life and hinted at marriage. "What do you mean? Don't tease."

"Just that," he said cheerfully. "We spent a night holed up with Charles and the driver. He assured me he would take good care of you. I told him I could too. He said no, that was his job."

She couldn't help a smile, her first in a week. "Thanks for getting him back alive, Dan."

"You're welcome." He looked at father and daughter. "Drat his hide! Besides, I have orders to Fort Clark, then a return to the Philippines. Orders." He kissed her cheek. "He has something else I don't have."

She gave him an inquiring look.

"He'll show you." He kissed her again and not on the cheek this time. "I told him if he didn't take good care of you, I'd know. God bless you both, Ellen."

She turned to see Charles set his daughter down and whisper to her. Gwen skipped into the kitchen, calling, "Mrs. Quincy, he's really hungry!"

Sergeant Reeves gave her a push in Charles's direction, then headed for the kitchen. In another moment she was held tight by a man who needed food, a bath, and a shave. She felt his breath against her neck. She kissed him at precisely the same moment he had the same notion, then tightened her hands across his back, pulling him close.

His week-old beard scratched her face; she didn't care. "All I could think of was you," he said finally. "I froze and starved and realized that I have a big heart with room for others. I know you want to be a front desk clerk here, but I'd rather you married me instead. I love you."

Gwen gestured to them from the dining room. "Coming in a minute, Daughter," Charles said. "I went to Butte for the machinery, not Bozeman," he said as the others left the lobby. "The Mercury Street Café burned down a month ago."

"Too bad it wasn't sooner," she said, then gasped, "*Really*?"

"Who jokes about that? I found a souvenir for you in the alley though. Put your hand in my overcoat pocket."

It was one thing to agree to marriage, but Ellen was proper. She shook her head.

"Knothead! Do it."

She pulled out a kitten who looked deep into her eyes, then cocked its head, as if wanting to know her better.

"I named him Socrates. When pickings got slim there at Golden Gate, I told him that he would eat when I did and starve with me, too."

"I told Plato that," she said softly.

"Socrates shared some of his canned milk, but I am never going to like sardines."

They sat down close together, hips touching, Ellen content to cuddle Socrates. She watched her man wolf down apple pie and nod when the cook brought in a bowl of stew. He shared his bowl with the kitten, which turned Ellen's vision misty.

Soon the dining room filled with workers, listening as Charles told of cold nights and days wrapped in blankets and rugs intended for the inn and burning some of the furniture for warmth. "I wouldn't wish that ordeal on anyone," he said simply.

"You must write about it, Da." Gwen ran into the room she shared with Ellen and returned with her father's journal. "I kept this close. Do you mind?"

"Not at all." He glanced at Ellen. "Did you read any of it?"

She nodded and spoke softly to him alone. "I understand your love for Clare. I will never intrude on your memories."

"They're wonderful memories," he told her, his lips close to her ear, "but I live in the present."

Ellen remembered. She took the journal from him and turned to the last entry, hers. "I added this. I forgot to erase it. I was presumptuous."

"Let's see. This is mine: 'Can I- or may I- love her, too?'"

He pointed to Ellen's penciled addition and nodded. "'April 16, 1904. Yes, you can love me. I won't forget Plato, but I want another cat.'"

He nodded, his tired eyes brighter. "Precisely. How about you get an ink pen and make this permanent? You know, like us."

Epilogue

IN THAT ODD WAY OF Wyoming weather, spring sidled in when everyone was hammering, installing windows, and worrying if the final load of furniture would arrive on time. Builders and staff discovered a dismaying amount of final projects even the best of planners seem to leave undone until the end, because it was the Big Stuff that mattered.

May roared in with wind and more snow, and then suddenly, silence, followed by the steady drip of ice from the Inn's enormous sloping roof. One day the landscape was gray, and the next day that impossible green of tender buds and grass. Even the geysers, paint pots, and hot springs seemed to perk up, as if aware that this inn at Old Faithful was destined for greatness.

Spring exited ahead of schedule in mid-May, as the string quartet practiced, the dining room acquired spotless white tablecloths, and rugs went down in the lobby. On his latest visit, Harry Child pronounced his project worthy of the nation's first national park.

The days lengthened and warmed like a benediction. Ellen worked long hours too, rationing her love for Charles

Penrose to quick kisses in the morning and maybe a moment in the evening by the roaring fireplace in the lobby, holding hands. What else was needed? She knew her own mind.

Then came her final visit to Plato's grave outside the kitchen door, peaceful under the over-hang of windows. "I wish you could see the inn," she told him, after looking around to make sure she was alone. She patted the grave, grateful beyond measure for the little Butte stray with the courage of a mountain lion. "I'll be back now and then," she promised. "I will."

The U.S. Army triumphed. Major Pitcher knew of a frustrated Presbyterian minister in Gardiner about to leave that town of wicked sinners, and persuaded him to come to Old Faithful for a wedding. Ellen Found and Charles Penrose were married May 30 in the lobby of Mr. Reamer's amazing inn by Old Faithful, which erupted when Ellen said, "I do." Everyone laughed.

Harry Child himself handed her new husband the key to Room 140, the final guest room at the end of the hall. "It's secluded," he confided, which made Charles blush. Gwen and Socrates stayed that night with Mrs. Wilson, the former Mrs. Quincy, who had married Mr. Wilson a week earlier. Fort Yellowstone had a federal judge who'd done the honors.

In the morning they were packed and ready to take a freight wagon to Lake Hotel, where Mr. Reamer was halfway through a remodel of that grand old dame. "I need an expert's finish work," he said, then promised Charles the lead carpenter position on the new Yellowstone Park Transportation Company barn in Gardiner. "I have more projects," he told him. "You'll be busy."

Eating leftover cake in the lobby, Mr. Child asked Ellen how she and Charles enjoyed the string quartet serenade last night outside Room 140. The violinists were still getting used to their summer job of playing for guests during dinner and dances. "I hope they impressed you," he said.

"You mean those rascals who played 'Brahms' Lullaby'?" Charles asked. His wife blushed.

And here was Sergeant Reeves, splendid in his dress uniform, but looking forlorn. Ellen leaned against Charles and his arms automatically went around her. "Dan, thanks for getting him back to me safely."

He glared at her new husband, then gave a philosophical shrug. "Drat the man, what could I do?"

"What you did."

Ellen looked around, admiring the work of a winter and knowing she would never tire of it. The first tourists were arriving tomorrow. Some projects remained undone, but it would all happen. She watched Adelaide Child instructing a pretty young thing behind the front desk. Hmm.

"Dan, go meet that front desk clerk," she said. "You look impressive right now."

He laughed at that and followed her gaze. "Yes, ma'am!"

"Will I like Lake Hotel?" she asked Charles, who watched Dan strut away.

"Yes, Mrs. Penrose, if you like cuddling with me on the front steps to watch the sun go down over the lake. It's a far cry from Mercury Street."

She relaxed in his arms. "True, but everything in my life, including Mercury Street and even Butte, brought me right here." She whispered in his ear. "Let's reserve Room 140 next year."

"Without the string quartet." He kissed the top of her head. "I've been thinking about your former name. Ellen Found. What did you find, dear heart?"

What indeed? They walked outside to look at the geyser

field, ready for summer and tourists. "You, most certainly," she said. She knew his heart.

"What else?"

"Me."

What to say about Carla Kelly? The old girl's been in the writing game for mumble-mumble years. She started out with short stories that got longer and longer until— poof!— one of them turned into a novel. (It wasn't quite that simple.) She still enjoys writing short stories, one of which is before you now. Carla writes for Harlequin Historical, Camel Press, and Cedar Fort. Her books are found in at least 14 languages.

Along the way, Carla's books and stories have earned a couple of Spur Awards from Western Writers of America for Short Fiction, a couple of Rita Awards from Romance Writers of America for Best Regency, and a couple of Whitney Awards. Carla lives in Idaho Falls, Idaho, and continues to write, because her gig is historical fiction, and that never gets old.

Follow Carla on Facebook: Carla Kelly
Carla's Website: www.CarlaKellyAuthor.com

The Widow of Daybreak

Christine Sterling

The Widow of Daybreak

A widowed young mother trying to survive. An American lawman looking to settle down. Can a mutual dislike for a gang of outlaws help them both find their way home?

Doris Whistler is learning how to survive in a town taken over by outlaws. When the leader of an infamous gang murders her husband, her choices are to tuck tail and run, or stand her ground and make Daybreak as promising as its name. It proves to be a difficult task with the good citizens in fear of the corrupt mayor and godlessness that abounds. What she doesn't expect is the support of a traveling lawman who believes in her and the tiny town she loves so much.

Buck Montgomery retired from the military to become an American lawman, and now he's looking for a town to call home. When a friend asks him to look in on the town but not fall in love with his little sister, he changes his course and heads for Daybreak, Wyoming. What he doesn't expect is to find his best friend's sister at the center of a struggle with the infamous outlaw that is holding the town hostage.

Can Doris trust the stranger who says he's there to protect her? If they combine forces, can they clean up Daybreak—and perhaps find love along the way?

Find out in this small-town, historical romance with a touch of faith.

One

DORIS WHISTLER PUSHED AT THE yards of fabric wrapped around her face as she swiped at the fresh tears. She wasn't one for fashion, but today she wanted to look her best. Her leather gloved hand ran down the side of her body and she felt the corset boning dig into her hips. Grimacing, she knew as soon as she got home the offending piece of clothing would go into the rubbish.

Normally her daily wardrobe was a long day dress with a loose top and bell-shaped skirt, covered by a linen apron, trimmed with a bit of Irish crochet. But today she donned her best dress, which was totally impractical for the small Wyoming town.

She did it for Harvey.

"I cannot believe that you left me," she sniffled, staring at the freshly covered grave of her husband. The tears rolled freely down her cheeks and disappeared into the fabric secured to her hat. She allowed the sorrow to consume her for another moment before the anger churned in her gut. Scraping the heel of her leather boot in the dirt, she swallowed the scream battering at her throat and growled at the gravestone. "Why did you decide Monday was the day to stand up to Rufus Grumblatt? It was tobacco, Harvey! Nothing worth dying over." She wiped her nose on one of Harvey's handkerchiefs she'd taken from his dresser drawer and shoved it in her reticule. "I don't know how the girls and I are going to make it without you. But we will. We will be strong for you."

Turning away, she wiped the tears from her cheeks and trudged out of the small cemetery behind the Daybreak Presbyterian Church. Doris nodded at Reverend Burns, who peered at her from his office window in the church. She appreciated that he hadn't come to console her. There were some things a wife just needed to sort out with her husband, even if he was dead. She couldn't wrap her head around the fact that it had been a mere six days, and now instead of being a happy twenty-six-year-old wife and mother, she was a widow with two small children, and a dry goods store to run in a town that God had clearly forsaken.

Daybreak, Wyoming, was a pretty little town. Doris fell in love with it when Harvey brought her here from Yellowstone. A farming community with lush valleys and prairies at the foot of the Big Horn mountains, Daybreak was a God-fearing community where folks looked out for each other. The town folks came together to lend a hand when their neighbors needed it. It didn't matter if you lived in town, or on a ranch or farm; if you needed help, someone in town would be there. That was until just over two years ago.

Two years ago was when Rufus and his gang had arrived.

Turning right on Main Street, she eyed the sheriff's office. It had sat empty for over a year now. The small houses on the side streets that she passed on her way home sat empty as well. Streets that were once flourishing were hollow. In one year, Daybreak had died.

There was an exodus after the last sheriff left. Families packed up and moved to neighboring towns. If Mayor McDougal had found another sheriff, maybe things would be different. Rufus killed Sheriff Owens the day his gang arrived in town. In the past two years, there had been over four sheriffs, none lasting longer than a few months. Eventually there just weren't any more.

As far as Doris could tell, she didn't think the mayor looked very hard for a new lawman. It was becoming increasingly apparent to her that Mayor McDougal enjoyed making money from the outlaws that rolled through town and didn't care much about the honest folk that were living and raising families here.

At the end of the street, she could see the sawmill that sat silent and empty. There was no new construction. The blacksmith's shop beside it was dark as well. The only things left in the town center of Daybreak were the saloons, the bank, the livery, the dry goods store with the millinery attached, and the undertaker's office.

The undertaker's office, however, appeared to be doing a brisk business.

She had half a mind to send a letter to her sister, Althea, pack up the girls and leave. Doris's best friend, Violet Gibbins, warned her not to decide just yet. Not when the grief was still so strong. Violet had even pointed out it wasn't fair for the girls to lose their papa and their home in such a brief span of time. Doris knew her friend meant well, but she was the daughter of Daybreak's banker.

Things were different for Violet than they were for Doris.

Violet's heart wasn't breaking, and she wasn't alone.

Doris decided she'd wire her brother, Titus, at Fort Yellowstone instead. Maybe he would have a suggestion about what to do. There had to be a solution for her and the girls, or about the outlaws. She knew there were marshals, and most towns had a sheriff. Perhaps the Army would want to do something about it?

With the way the Grumblatt Gang talked about robbing trains and taking supplies, it was only a matter of time until the Army would have to respond. If Titus told her to leave, then she would. It wouldn't make her happy, though, because that meant Rufus would win.

And Doris did not give up easily.

As if conjured by her thoughts, Rufus Grumblatt exited the Tin Star Saloon across the street, and she felt her throat tighten. Quickening her steps, she prayed she could make it the two doors down and duck into the dry goods store without him noticing her. He hadn't been to the store since the night he killed Harvey, but she was expecting his return.

Thankfully, her feet knew the way, so she could keep her eyes on him. Rufus hadn't noticed her, allowing her the opportunity to study him for the first time. If Titus asked for a description, she could give him a full one.

Rufus was not a tall man, but he wasn't short. If she had to guess, she would say maybe seventeen hands high, like the large chestnut horse in the livery. Rufus donned longish, dirty blond hair that hung in oily strands around his shoulders. An angry scar ran down one cheek and the side of his neck that he did little to hide. He had a mustache that reminded Doris of a hairy rat sleeping under his nose, but no beard, and deep bottomless eyes. Even before Harvey had died, she could tell that evil ran deep into Rufus's soul just by looking into the coal-colored orbs.

Reaching the door to the Whistler Dry Goods store, she blew out a breath as the object of her scrutiny turned and headed back into the Tin Star. It bothered her how he would stand out on the street and watch the town as if he owned the whole place. Slipping into the store, the sound of the bell proclaimed her arrival. Doris could hear Violet and the girls in the back room. A smile spread across her face at the sound of their giggles. They missed their papa, but they were still young enough that they would recover swiftly.

"I'll be right there!" Violet's voice rang out. At twenty years old, her bright blue eyes and cheery demeanor made Doris feel practically ancient in recent days. Violet was a good friend, and a wee bit spoiled. Her mother had passed away several years prior and her father was not pressing his only child to find a husband any time soon. By the time Doris was Violet's age, she was already married and had her first child. The women had become good friends when Doris had arrived in town with a baby in tow.

When the town's schoolteacher moved, Violet took over the position. The Grumblatt Gang had burned the school down, so the new one was currently in an old storage room on the side of the dry goods store. It had a pocket door that could be closed while Violet taught the day's lessons.

"It's just me," Doris called, flipping the store sign to open, and pinning back the curtains. Peeking out the window, she saw the street was mostly empty and there was no sign of Rufus or any of his miscreants. Unwrapping the yards of fabric attached to her hat, she was halfway across the room when Violet's long red curls appeared from behind the curtain that blocked the back room from sight. "Thank you for keeping the girls. I hope they weren't any trouble." Doris put her hat on the counter and walked over to the telegraph. She smiled at her friend while she checked for any new wires on the tape, before saying hello to her girls.

"It was really no trouble. Mary Ellen and Maybelle are always a joy to have. Do you feel better?"

"I don't know that I feel much of anything right now. Resentment and anger at being left behind. I said my piece for now, though. That will have to do."

Violet reached out, pulling her friend into a tight hug. "I am sorry you are going through this. I can't imagine losing a husband, but I'm here for you and the girls. I even talked to Papa about staying with you if you needed the extra help. Unfortunately, I can't take Maybelle to the school, but I can help in the afternoons while you take care of the store."

"I—I . . ." Doris gave a quick shake of her head before squeezing her friend one more time and stepping back. "Thank you, Vi. You are a good friend."

Violet giggled. "You were going to tell me you didn't need any help."

"Yes."

"It's a good thing I wasn't asking your opinion. I can't expect you to stay here if you do everything on your own. Besides, this is just until you find another husband, if you even choose to do that. I intend just to be here. That way, you don't get too lonely, and the store can keep running. I don't know what I'd do if you left."

Doris's head spun at the speed of Violet's words. "Husband? I have no desire to get remarried. And certainly not right now. I loved . . . love Harvey. No one can replace him."

The chiming of the bell over the front door cut their conversation short. Violet patted Doris's shoulder and ducked back behind the curtain. She plastered what she hoped would be a welcoming smile on her face and turned back to the counter. The smile was short-lived as she found Rufus standing on the other side, leering at her.

TWO

Buck Montgomery tipped his coffee cup back and swallowed the dredges before looking at his friend, Titus Mason. They had been friends for nearly ten years when they'd both joined the Army at eighteen, and they were as close as brothers ever since. Titus didn't talk much about his sisters, but Buck knew how much his friend valued them.

"Tell me again."

Titus ran his hand through his dark hair and leaned forward. "I got a wire today. I told you about my sister, Dory." Buck nodded. "Someone killed her husband six days ago. She's all alone up there in Daybreak with my nieces. Wire says there's no sheriff, and she mentioned the Grumblatt Gang. Seems like she thinks they had something to do with it. She asked for help. I don't know if she means help with the girls or help with the gang. I can't go right now, not with the trial coming up." Titus worked for the judge at Fort Yellowstone. His job was investigating accusations against Army personnel.

"She's asking for Army help?" Buck would want someone to go if it were his sister, if he had one, but he needed to be clear on what was being asked. He wasn't in the Army anymore, but he was a lawman. Deputized in three counties and looking for a sheriff position, if the Lord was willing.

Titus shook his head. "She just asked for help."

"Daybreak's what, two, three days from here?" He'd been planning to head out in the morning for Laramie, but that was a desire, not a need.

"I think it's four, but I haven't made the trip."

"That's better than the three weeks to Laramie." He shook his head and stared longingly at his empty cup. "I can head that way and see what's what. You want me to bring her back here?" He would follow Titus's wishes, but depending on what he found, he might not be able to leave them behind.

"Dory isn't going to let you show up and boss her around. If she needs to leave, send me a message and I'll see if I can work something out with the judge to go retrieve her and the girls. I won't make you try to reason with her, but I trust your instincts." Titus paused, standing up to retrieve the coffee pot Buck had been hoping for. "Hey, Buck, try not to fall in love with my sister. She's grieving."

Buck couldn't help it. He burst out in a belly laugh. "You're worried your sister is going to scare me and that I'm going to fall in love with her? I've put up with you for a decade. I think I can handle your sister."

Titus chuckled and shook his head. "She's not one of those girls you can smile at with your blond hair and blue eyes and expect her to do your bidding. Like I said, try not to let her break your heart." He refilled Buck's cup and returned the coffeepot to the stove before his tone turned serious. "I appreciate this, Buck. I've got to get going. Lock the door behind you."

"Aww, you think I'm handsome," Buck teased. "I'll send you a message when I get a lay of the land. And I shall do my best not to embarrass myself."

"That's all I can ask."

Titus let himself out, and Buck sat thinking about his next move. He'd already packed his rucksack for the long trip to Laramie, but he knew he'd need additional supplies if there was a change in plans. He made a hasty list of what he needed to grab from the store before heading out.

Buck knew exactly who the Grumblatts were, and it wouldn't cost him any sleep to put Rufus in the ground if he found him. He would do what his friend had asked and check on the safety of his sister, and then figure out his next steps. Giving the coffee cups a quick rinse, he let himself out of his friend's house and returned to the hotel where he was staying. He stopped at the front desk to let them know he'd be leaving in the morning and settled his bill. Working his way over to the sheriff's office, he picked up copies of the latest wanted posters on the Grumblatt Gang.

The gang was wanted all the way from Texas to Wyoming and from Nebraska to California. He let out a low whistle as he read the posters. The bounties were enough to let Buck retire early. The sheriff didn't have any additional information, but Buck knew the marshal might, so he jogged over to the office to pay Sarge a visit. Sarge was Buck's and Titus's superior until his appointment to U.S. Marshal several months prior.

Buck found the new marshal leaned back in his chair with his ankles crossed on the corner of his desk. "Hey, Buck!" Sarge called, lowering his boots. "Coffee?"

"No thanks. I just stopped by for some information."

"Sure thing." Sarge motioned to a chair. Buck hung his hat on the hook by the door and lowered his tall frame onto the wooden seat across from the older man. "What can I help you with?"

"I'm looking for an updated file on the Grumblatts."

"Grumblatts? That's Rufus and his crew, ain't it? Haven't seen much on them in over a year, but let's check the wires." He reached behind him and pulled the loose papers to the desk in front of him. "I think I have a folder on them in here somewhere. The last marshal had put one together." He opened his desk and rummaged around until he found what he was looking for. Pulling out a folder, he placed it on top of the loose papers. Buck wondered how someone with many years of Army experience allowed his office to look like a paper factory exploded inside it. As if reading his thoughts, Sarge lifted the folder and pointed it at Buck. "I inherited this mess. It is taking me forever to sort it out, so keep your opinions to yourself. Here."

"I didn't say a word," Buck replied, the corner of his lips lifting in a smirk. "Not one word." Reaching over the desk, he took the folder with the word Rufus scrawled across the front.

"Why are you looking at the Grumblatt Gang?"

Buck thumbed through the file. "Titus got a tip they're holed up close to here. I figured I'd take a mosey over and have a look for myself."

"A tip you say?" Sarge dug through the papers on his desk. "Nothing came through here." Sarge eyed him and then shook his head. "I forget sometimes that you boys don't all still answer to me. You can keep your own council or let an old man in so he can keep his mind active, you know."

Snapping the folder closed, Buck put it on his lap. "Store owner got murdered over in Daybreak. Sounds like they think Rufus might have done it and that he's still in town. I'm going to chat with the widow."

"Daybreak? Weren't you looking for a lawman position in a small town?"

"I am. I don't mind the riding, but I'd like a family before I get old."

"Daybreak hasn't been able to keep a sheriff in the last couple of years. Might be that you sort their problems out and you got yourself the local lawman position. You'd have to speak with the mayor though, and he's a right opinionated you-know-what. What was his name?" The older man got up and refilled his coffee cup, head tilted to one side as he thought about it. "McDougal; that's it. Thinks he runs the town, but between you and me, son, talk to the banker. Gibbins. If I remember correctly, he's got a sweet young daughter who's probably at a marrying age."

"You sure know a lot about Daybreak."

"I know a lot about a lot of things. Y'all just don't want to listen too often. Now that I have an office, I get to share more of those things I know. It's a better life than just shouting out orders at stubborn, thickheaded boys who want to play soldier all day."

"Hey now! I made a good soldier."

"Yes, you did, but you are still a stubborn, thickheaded boy, who turned into a pretty all right lawman."

They both laughed, and Buck started flipping through the papers in front of him, taking the time to sort them into piles by name. It would help the older man who'd never been good at sorting his paperwork.

"Buck?"

"Yes, sir?"

"He's wanted dead or alive in several territories and a handful of states. You find Rufus Grumblatt, you shoot him on sight or he's going to stick a knife in your back."

"Is that an order, sir?"

"That's a warning. The order is, don't try to bring him back alive. You want the bounty, you kill him."

"Yes, sir. Anything you hear from me, pass along to Titus."

"You two were always up to something. You have a safe trip. Go on and get out of my office."

Buck shook the marshal's hand, placed his hat back on top of his head, and went to collect his supplies.

How did it come to having two of his closest advisors bringing up marriage?

First Titus, telling him not to fall in love with his sister. Buck had no plans of doing that. Then the marshal telling him about a banker's daughter. What would a girl like that want with an anchorless lawman when she could find a better match? Clearly, there was something in the water today.

He had bags to repack before he slept. He'd head out at morning's first light. Traveling west was always easier when the sun was at your back.

Three

"MAMA, WHAT ARE WE DOING today?"

Doris looked up from her dressing table. Mary Ellen had come in without her noticing, as she was lost in her thoughts. "You have school this morning with Miss Violet. Maybelle will stay with me until you're done at lunchtime, then you'll have your afternoon rest."

"Is Papa going to come home soon?" Mary Ellen's bottom lip slid between her teeth and Doris felt her chest tighten. They were too young to understand what was happening, and she was at a loss for how to really explain it.

"Come here, poppet." She slid her chair back away from the dressing table and patted her lap in invitation. *Lord, please give me the words,* she prayed as her daughter climbed up onto her lap. "Your papa went to live in heaven, honey."

"With God?" Mary Ellen's brow crinkled as she listened.

"Yes. With God and Grandpa Whistler too."

"Oh." Mary Ellen hopped down, a frown now settled on her little round face. She had light brown hair and blue eyes like Doris, but her nose and mouth had come from Harvey. "So, he's not coming back?"

"No, honey, he's not coming back, but we'll see him again one day." Doris stood torn between reaching for her daughter again, knowing that it would be to soothe herself more so than the little girl, and letting the girl decide what she needed just then.

Suddenly, Mary Ellen turned and headed towards the door. "I better get ready for school," she said, quietly closing the door behind her. Doris wondered if she would ever understand how her daughter's mind worked. Mary Ellen would be happy one minute, sad the next, and then in deep thought another.

Sighing, she stood and looked around the bedroom that she had shared with Harvey since they moved to town. There was a bed that Harvey had made for her when they first came to Daybreak. The intricate rings carved into the headboard had always drawn her attention. The pattern mimicked the marriage quilt her mother had made them when they'd first married.

On either side of the bed were small side tables. Small gas lamps hung above the tables and Doris could see dust collecting on the globes. Harvey's Bible was still where he'd left it, on his side table. Doris had put hers in her drawer. She didn't want to think about God now. Why did He take her husband away when she needed him the most?

Above the bed, she had made a garland with blue fabric that matched the curtains she'd hung over the two long bedroom windows that overlooked Main Street. On the opposite wall was her dressing table, with her mirror, wash basin and comb set. A wardrobe made from the same wood as the bed and dressers stood next to the dressing table. Harvey even included pocket drawers that had a flap to close over them. Harvey had been successful in business and the store was a testament to that; but in his spare time, he loved to work with wood. There were many things throughout the house that would carry his memory.

Gliding to the window, she pulled at the light blue drape and looked out over the street. She could see down the entire length of Main Street from her window above the dry goods store. The remains of the charred schoolhouse still lingered at the edge of town. The two saloons and brothel were within her line of sight. Doris grimaced and wished the gang had incinerated those buildings instead. Nothing good came from a house of sin.

She could see over the livery at the horse grazing in the back pasture. It would be idyllic if she didn't know the truth. Her eyes continued to travel down the road, resting on the empty sheriff's office. Sighing, she knew she couldn't wish someone to appear, *but if she could* . . .

She gave one last glance over the street and her eyes caught Rufus leaning against a post outside the Tin Star. He reached down to strike a match on the heel of his boot. Doris watched as he lit a cigarillo and inhaled deeply before exhaling in a thin cloud of smoke. She wrinkled her nose, almost smelling the charred tobacco, but her window was closed. Her eyes followed the smoke for a moment before returning to the lawbreaker. Rufus was staring at her window with his head tilted.

She released a gasp and dropped the curtain, stepping back into the darkness of the shadows. After counting to ten, she peeked around the curtain once more, praying that he hadn't seen her. The boardwalk in front of the saloon was empty, apart from the smoldering tobacco stick discarded on the ground.

When Rufus came into the store on Saturday, she'd expected trouble. She hadn't been prepared for him to propose to her.

Propose!

Just the thought of it was enough to make her stomach roll.

Rufus assured her it was the only way to keep her family safe. She should have taken the opportunity and shot him right then. If it hadn't been for her daughters and Violet in the room behind her, she would have done it. No one in town, apart from his gang, would have blamed her if she had shot him right then. She may have ended up in a pine box, but at least she'd be reunited with Harvey.

Shaking her head to remove such morbid thoughts, she focused on her day. The store would open soon, and Maybelle still needed her breakfast. She was so thankful that Mary Ellen liked school and Doris could have a quiet morning with her youngest. Morning was typically her busiest time at the store. The women in town came in to do their shopping and chat while the outlaws slept off the previous night's activities. Most of the women refused to leave their homes after lunch time.

She straightened the drapes and turned away from the window, tripping over the chair she'd left out when she was talking to Mary Ellen. Grumbling, she tucked the chair in and hopped in place for a minute until the stinging in her toes eased a bit. Glancing in the mirror one more time, she added two more pins to her bun and straightened her blouse before she bustled out into the small living room where both girls were ready and waiting for her.

"Thank you for helping Maybelle get ready this morning," Doris told Mary Ellen as she collected their baskets from the counter where she had left them the night before. Handing one to each of the girls, she slid the largest over her arm. "What do you both say to getting this day started, before we lose the morning?"

"Yes, Mama," both girls chorused.

It didn't take them long to get down the wide steps. Maybelle wanted to walk down the steps by herself since she was a big girl now. Harvey had even put a lower railing in just last month for Maybelle to use while she practiced going up and down. Doris was glad she didn't have to carry the small child anymore. Maybelle was getting too big to balance on her hip.

Harvey had been such a wonderful papa, and the anger bubbled back up inside of her. He had stood his ground to do what he thought was right. That was something he was teaching the girls, even in death.

Always do what is right.

Doris snorted. Rufus wouldn't know what was right if it hit him in the head. If he did, he just didn't have any respect for it. A whisper of interest drifted through her mind, wondering what his childhood had been like. Did any of the Grumblatts have powerful role models?

Just that thought of having to fill both parenting roles made her tired, but what was she going to do? Find another husband? Men rarely wanted to raise their own children, let alone another man's, and here she was with two.

"Well, that's a grim look for such a lovely morning." Violet was standing at the back door, waiting for them to arrive. "Do you want to talk about it? I have a few minutes."

"Good morning, Auntie Violet." Mary Ellen raced over to hug her. Maybelle was hot on her heels, trying to keep up.

"Good morning, my loves." Violet knelt to receive the affection, but her eyes were focused on Doris.

"Perhaps this afternoon. I'm just thinking about all the moments that are coming and it made me tired." Doris let her free hand drift over the girls' heads and shook her own slightly.

"I'll be back with Mary Ellen after class. Papa said he wouldn't be home for lunch today, so we can talk about all those things when the girls go down for their afternoon rest. Right now, you need to put a smile on your face and go open the store." Violet gave Doris's shoulder a comforting squeeze before leaving with the little girl.

"Well, Maybelle, what do you think? Should we go open the store and get you something to nibble on?" She offered the little girl her hand once more and listened to her daughter babble as they made their way to the front room. Behind the counter, she set her basket down on the little table she had added for the days when Harvey couldn't come upstairs for lunch. Then she picked up Maybelle and settled her in her highchair with some bread squares to munch on.

"Mama will be right back." Doris circled the counter and noticed a man standing on the other side of the door. He didn't look familiar, and that made her nervous. She knew everyone in town, and the stage wasn't due until Thursday. Flipping the sign to open, she unlocked the door and hurried back around the half-wall to stand behind the counter.

The door opened and a tall man in dusty black pants, a light-colored dust-covered shirt and a wide-brimmed hat entered the store. He stopped as the door closed softly behind him, and the bells announced his entrance. He reached up, pulling his hat off and curly, light-brownish, blond hair appeared. When he looked up, blue eyes sparkled, and a friendly smile appeared on his face. He had a scruff of beard and needed a bath, but she still felt drawn to him. He was a stranger, but suddenly she felt safe for the first time since Harvey had died on the floor where she was standing.

BUCK ENTERED THE SMALL STORE and his eyes glanced around, acclimating to the dimly lit interior.

The woman who opened the door scurried back to the counter like a mouse and stared at him with enormous eyes. Buck stood at the door and took a moment to really look at her. She was petite, appeared to be young, with a pale complexion and light hair that he assumed was long, based on the way she coiled it above her head.

She must be Dory. Titus had given Buck a brief description of what she looked like, but his friend admitted he hadn't seen his sister in nearly a decade. Dory had done some growing up in that time. Gone were the scraped knees and freckled nose that Titus described. Instead, there was a grown woman standing in front of him.

A very attractive grown woman.

The woman cleared her throat and moved between him and the child, who was eating in a wooden highchair. "Good morning. How can I help you?"

Good, Buck thought. *She has strong protective instincts.*

He rummaged inside his vest and pulled out a folded piece of paper. "Good morning, ma'am. I need to purchase a few things, and I'm hoping you could direct me to the hotel."

Buck knew he looked a mess, but he was counting on that. His star was in his pocket, and he didn't want to look like a lawman when he arrived in town. The only sign that he was something other than an easy mark was the Colt on his hip. Her eyes drifted over him, and he wondered what she saw, but would never ask.

Finally, she raised her arm and pointed out the window. "There are several saloons in town with rooms above them. The boarding house at the end of Main, that way, offers longer term rooms for those that want something a little less rowdy. There is a bathhouse between the Tin Star and Iron Ore saloons. As for your shopping needs, there are baskets to your right to put your items in, and I'll be happy to total the items when you're ready."

A loud bang behind her caused the woman to jump.

"Excuse me for just a moment." A pink tinge high-lighted her cheeks moments before she turned away.

Buck selected a basket and started browsing. She appeared very young, but was still pretty. He added two readymade shirts, soap, and a bag of the penny candies to the basket. He moved through the store to get a better view of what was happening behind the counter.

"Sweetie, keep your spoon on your tray." He heard the woman cajoling the small child he'd spied when he walked in. "I have to go help the nice man and then I'll get you down."

"Me go!" A little girl's voice rang out loud and clear.

"Maybelle, I need you to stay here."

"No, Mama. Me go!"

Buck leaned his head against the post in front of him. Well, it appeared the woman was the widow and Titus's little sister. He still hadn't decided if he would tell her who he was. Hopefully, she wouldn't hold it against him. He wanted to introduce himself, but he didn't want to alarm her. The part about knowing her brother was only going to be mentioned if he had no other choice. He didn't know if Titus had sent a wire out heralding Buck's arrival, but he didn't want to introduce himself to the widow until he'd had time to bathe.

"Sorry about that." She reappeared from behind the counter with a little dark-haired girl with green eyes, just like Titus, on her hip.

"No trouble at all, ma'am. Who is this little darling?" He reached a finger out to chuck the little girl on the chin, but her mama turned her away from his reach. "I apologize." He tucked his hand in his pocket and placed the basket on the counter.

The woman took items out of the basket and wrote the prices on a piece of paper. "What brings you to Daybreak, Mr . . . ?"

He tried to hide his grin at her not-so-subtle question. "Montgomery. My name is Buck Montgomery."

He watched her glance to the ceiling as if remembering something, then she shook her head, causing the little one to giggle, before returning to her tallying.

"What brings you to Daybreak, Mr. Montgomery?"

"I'm just passing through on my way to Laramie, and thought I'd let my horse have a rest. This looked like my best option to rest and restock my supplies."

"You're going all the way to Laramie on your horse?" Surprise colored her voice as she slid the tab across the counter to him. "That will be fifteen dollars."

"Yes. Sprocket doesn't mind a long trip if we take our time." He counted out the bills and laid them on the counter. "Thank you so much for your help, Miss . . . ?"

"Oh! I'm so sorry. I'm Mrs. Doris Whistler. I own this store."

She sure is pretty with pink cheeks and that one strand of hair that was escaping her well done hairdo, he thought.

"I'm surprised your husband isn't working the counter."

"My husband is dead. Enjoy your time in Daybreak, Mr. Montgomery." With that, she turned and walked purposefully away from him. He prayed he hadn't made her cry.

Letting himself back out onto the boardwalk, he carefully closed the door behind him before looking around. He'd noted the abandoned sheriff's office and the church on his way in. Buck's next stop was the bank, but a greasy-haired man standing under the Tin Star Saloon sign watching him caught his attention. Placing his hat back on his head, Buck felt every nerve in his body come alive.

The rumors of Rufus Grumblatt being in Daybreak were true. As he lived and breathed, that man was standing directly across the street, giving him what Buck was sure was a threatening look. Ignoring the man, Buck turned and headed down the street towards the bank. Sarge had told him to talk to Gibbins, which was exactly what he intended to do.

Buck noted a small classroom next to the store. A red-haired teacher gave him a smile when their eyes met, and he groaned to himself. However old that girl was, she was even younger than Titus's sister. Suddenly, he felt like he was eighty, not a mere twenty-eight. Pulling the door of Daybreak Savings and Trust open, he was greeted with another empty building. This town didn't appear to do much of anything before noon.

"Can I help you?" An older man in a crisp white shirt and clean black slacks came out of the back office. Buck recognized the way he held his body. No wonder Sarge had sent him here. Gibbins had spent some time in the military, too.

Four

"HE'S SO HANDSOME."

The back door clanged shut as Violet let herself into the back of the dry goods store. Doris didn't have to ask whom Violet was referring to. She understood it was the mysterious stranger. If she hadn't been made wary by his untimely appearance, she would have agreed with Violet too.

"We don't know anything about him."

"That is not true." Violet grinned at her as Doris put together the afternoon tea tray with snacks. "At least not anymore." Violet came every afternoon to have a cup of tea and a chat before the girls woke up. Then she would take them out to play or entertain them upstairs until Doris closed the store.

It had been three weeks since she had buried Harvey, two weeks since Rufus proposed, and a week since the stranger rode into town. Had it really been that long since she buried her husband?

"What did you do, Vi?"

Anticipation slid through her veins. Doris would be a liar if she didn't find the handsome stranger slipping into her thoughts since he appeared that day in the store. *It made her*

141

feel disloyal. She was supposed to be in mourning, not wondering about strangers in town with curly blond hair and happy eyes.

"I didn't do anything, goose." Flouncing down on the nearby chair, Violet was the image of innocence. The tone of her voice said otherwise. "Mr. Montgomery joined Papa and I for dinner last night. He's friendly and much older than I thought. He's going to Laramie, but is staying here for a bit."

"What made him change his mind?"

Violet shrugged, and it reminded Doris that her friend was younger; and never being married made all men appear to be eligible. *Why did the idea of him taking an interest in her friend ruffle her feathers?*

"That I don't know. The question is whether I can get him to marry me before he leaves." Violet bit her lower lip and Doris shook her head.

"If he marries you, you won't be the schoolteacher anymore." Doris picked up the teapot and swirled it before pouring two cups. Handing one to Violet, she continued. "If he's really going to Laramie, I would miss you very much. I'm sure there is someone in this world who thinks that Rufus is charming and handsome, too. Don't pin your hopes on a man you don't know well enough to measure yet."

"Oh, Dory. I'm just daydreaming for now. He's probably too old for me anyhow."

The chiming of the bell above the front door robbed her of the chance to make a quip about age. Popping up out of her chair, Doris hurried to the counter. There had been a steady flow of customers this week, as well as friends coming to say hello. Some even dropped off food. While she was thankful for that blessing too, each time someone brought a meal, it brought another wave of sadness with it.

"Can I help you find something?" She couldn't see

anyone when she entered the store, but she was sure that someone was here. "Hello?" She called again, opening the divider. "Violet, go upstairs," she hissed. The hairs on the back of her neck rose as her friend slipped past her to the back stairs. Doris watched for a moment and then stepped onto the floor, determined to see if someone had come in.

Suddenly, a hand gripped her arm and pulled her between the bolts of fabric that lined the wall. She braced herself, thinking she would hit the floor. The smell of alcohol, stale tobacco, and unwashed clothes assaulted her senses. Fear coiled in her belly as she recognized Rufus seconds before his lips crashed down on hers. Her hands slapped at his chest and face, fighting to get away from him. He held her tighter, one hand holding the back of her head, the other gripping her hip tightly.

She kicked at his legs, twisting to free herself, and the sound of fabric tearing echoed loudly as she fell backwards toward the floor. The weight of his body against hers meant he was falling with her, and Doris tried to bring her knees up to put some distance between them when her back hit the floor.

As quickly as Rufus appeared, he was gone.

She closed her eyes and lowered herself to the ground, curling into a ball to protect herself from whatever might come next. She hoped whatever stopped him would encourage him to leave, but her hope was dwindling.

"Get your hands off me, stranger!" he growled.

Doris opened her eyes to find Buck Montgomery holding Rufus by the back of his neck.

"I don't think so, *stranger*," Buck replied, tightening his grip.

"That's my wife and you have no business interrupting us." Rufus jerked himself away from Buck, causing Doris to shrink back.

"I'm not your wife!" Tears were streaming down her cheeks, fear and embarrassment battling for superiority inside of her.

"You'll be my wife soon enough. Since I got rid of your husband, no one is going to challenge me by taking what's rightfully mine. The first thing I'm going to do is remind you that a wife's supposed to submit to her husband's wants and desires." He reached for her, but Buck stepped between them.

"What do you mean, you got rid of her husband?" His tone was menacing, but Doris felt safe in his shadow.

"He left her." Rufus twitched a shoulder.

"You killed him!" The words exploded from her, and she couldn't stop what came next. "You stood right there, and you shot him when he wouldn't give you the tobacco for free. That's what you did!"

She noticed Buck didn't say anything. He seemed to grow several inches taller as he listened to the two of them. The next thing she knew, he stepped forward, lifting Rufus clear off his feet, and hauled him to the front door, throwing him out onto the sidewalk. Doris rolled back on her heels and pulled herself to a standing position, using the wall as leverage. She rushed to the window to peek out into the street. She didn't know this man, and yet here he was doing something that no one else in town had done for her.

"Best you leave her alone from here on out. She's not alone anymore." Those words sent chills down her spine. *He didn't know her. Why was he willing to risk himself for her?*

"You're a dead man, stranger. You hear me? Deadman walking!"

Buck shut the door and turned his back to Rufus, as if he wasn't the slightest bit concerned. Doris's breath hitched in her throat.

"Can you come away from the windows, please? He won't hesitate to shoot you in the back."

She didn't think she could take another dead body in her store, but she didn't want to be left alone to deal with Rufus, either. Buck glanced over his shoulder, and it freed her from his gaze for a few seconds. Rufus had disappeared, probably into the alley to sleep off the liquor. All she could do was pray that he was drunk enough that he wouldn't remember what happened today.

"Are you all right?" Buck's words washed over her, and warmth filled her belly.

Brushing the hair from her eyes, she realized that her hair had fallen from its pins. She worked with shaky fingers to put it back in order. "I have had better days. I don't know how to thank you."

Buck watched her, his brows furrowing as his eyes searched her face with eyes as blue as the summer sky. "Are you really going to be his wife?"

Doris shook her head. "Do you think for one moment that I would consent to marry a man like him?" Her hair fell once more. Sighing, she pulled the pins out, allowing her light brown locks to fall around her shoulders. "You wouldn't know, would you? He proposed to me a few days before you came to town. I don't want to marry him, but I don't know of anyone who's going to stop him, either." She walked to the counter and dropped the hairpins. "Everyone in this town does what he or the mayor says." Snorting, she picked up a pack of hairpins from a display of women's accessories. "You'd think that Rufus was the mayor, not McDougal."

Resting her elbows on the counter, she dropped her head into her palms. She wanted to have a good cry and wake up to it being just a bad dream.

145

"Surely the minister wouldn't marry a nonconsenting female." Buck was now leaning against the counter opposite her. He was close enough that his breath caressed her cheek, and she could count his individual eyelashes. It should be criminal for a man to have such long eyelashes and beautiful blue eyes.

"I don't know, but the mayor does what Rufus wants, and there's not a sheriff in town." She hiccupped and buried her face in her hands once more. *Please, Lord, don't let me cry in front of this man.*

"Don't cry, Mrs. Whistler. Everything will be all right."

His long fingers brushed against her cheek, and the scent of soap and warm leather teased her senses. Doris wanted to linger, but she pulled away. She didn't know him, but he reminded her of someone. She just couldn't figure out who. Her husband was barely cold in the ground and this man was causing chaos in her system. *That needed to stop now.*

BUCK PULLED HIS HAND AWAY from Doris's cheek, anger still gripping him. He wavered between scooping her up into his arms and promising to keep her safe for the rest of her life, and stalking out of the dry goods store to cut off Rufus Grumblatt's hands for daring to touch her.

"Did you need something?" Her voice cut through the debate in his head, and he blinked twice, focusing on her.

"Is there a way to send a wire in this town?" Buck knew that there was. He'd seen the message she had sent to Titus.

"Yes, of course. I send the wires. If you'll write your message down for me. I can take care of that right now, though I wouldn't expect a response until tomorrow." She pressed a pencil and paper towards him. "It'll be twenty-five cents."

"Thank you." He needed to figure out how was he going to get a message to Titus without her figuring out the connection. *Why did it matter if she did?*

Facts are facts. Might need a friend. Laramie will have to wait. B.M.

He'd have her send it to the marshal's office. Sarge would understand and pass along the info to Titus. It wouldn't surprise him if some of the other men he'd served with suddenly had a genuine interest in visiting Daybreak in the coming days. Brothers in arms always came when called.

He passed the note to Doris and slid some change onto the counter. "I'll come back around lunchtime tomorrow to see if you've gotten a response. Here's the money for the wire, and a bag of those mint sticks you've got." He didn't need more candy, but he hadn't quite figured out how her business was doing, and he wanted her to be able to afford to eat.

"Thank you for saving me." The quietness in her voice made his chest ache. Maybe Titus hadn't been teasing him when he warned Buck not to fall in love with his little sister.

Love? That couldn't be right.

"Ma'am, I would want someone to help my widow or sister if they were in a similar situation. I'm glad I was here to help."

"But how did you know I needed help?"

She wasn't going to let this go, and he wanted to kick himself. He would not tell her he had seen the scoundrel come into the store and made it a point to follow, or that the banker had given him access to the apartment above the jail while he was in town. Some things were better left unsaid.

"I didn't. I had a message to send and when I came through the door, I heard you shout."

"Maybe Harvey was looking down on me then. It's embarrassing." Doris was sending the message at the station in the corner behind the counter. Buck was sure he was not supposed to hear those words.

"What brought you to Daybreak?" He wanted her to keep talking, and not thinking about the things that could have happened.

"My husband wanted to build a better life for us. There was a terrible wildfire where we lived and so we got in a wagon and headed west. Daybreak was the first town we'd come to in several days. It was small and friendly, and they didn't have a store. We stayed."

"And now that he's gone? Why stay?" He wasn't trying to be harsh, but if he was going to help her at all, he needed to understand how her mind worked.

"This is my home. We raised our girls here. I have a brother in the military close to here, and a sister in Virginia. Right now, we stay."

He admired the stubborn tilt of her chin; she was not a wilting flower. "What about Rufus?"

"I . . . I don't know. I wasn't planning on having to fight off his advances. He killed my husband over the price of tobacco. Now suddenly, he's decided he wants to marry me. The whole town is afraid of him or in his pocket, and I'm not really either of those, I suppose."

The curtain to the back room opened, and red curls popped out. "Is everything all right out here?" Violet Gibbins appeared, and Buck wanted to bang his head on something. He'd noted her advances at dinner the night before, but he didn't want to have to tell her how he was more interested in the widow next door. "Oh! Hello, Mr. Montgomery. Are you joining us for dinner tonight?"

She looked up at him with hopeful eyes. Buck needed a way to gently discourage her affections.

"Miss Gibbins. Thank you for the invitation, but not tonight. I have a meeting with your papa right now, then will be otherwise engaged this evening."

Buck noticed both women's faces turn red, and he took a moment to replay his words in his head. Now they would expect him to be with a girl at the saloon. Giving a mental shrug, he decided it would be best to let them make their own assumptions until it was time for the truth to come out.

"I understand." Miss Gibbins nodded, stepping back away from him.

"I sent your message." Doris smiled, stepping back up to the counter. "I think I'm going to close early today. Did you need anything else?"

Buck wanted to cheer but contained himself. If the store was closed, she was upstairs, which gave him freer movement around town. "That's it for me today. I would suggest staying indoors tonight. If he gives you any more trouble, please let me know."

"You don't need to be a part of my troubles." She sucked her bottom lip between her teeth, and something twisted in his gut. He wanted to take his thumb and free that round, bottom lip, and wasn't that just the daisy's uncle. He shook his head to clear it, tipped his hat to them both, and pivoted, taking long strides to the door.

Buck turned the sign to closed and glanced back at Doris. "Come and lock up. I won't leave until you've done so."

Moments later, he heard the latch settle into place on the door and gave a sigh of relief. At least she listened to the words he said. Rufus was leaning against the wall outside of the Tin Star, glaring at him. Acting as if he hadn't seen him, Buck turned away and headed to speak with Mr. Gibbins.

It was time for a new lawman in Daybreak.

Five

DORIS GROANED AND TRIED TO roll over. She didn't want to get out of bed; her whole body ached, not to mention her brain. The events of the day before had played out repeatedly in her nightmares. The reality of what would have happened, if Mr. Montgomery hadn't come into the store, crashed down upon her when she opened her eyes.

She would rather pull the covers back over her head and wish everything away, but the girls needed breakfast, and she had to open the store. Doris decided she had no choice but to speak with Mayor McDougal. *Not that he was going to do anything about Rufus,* but she had to try. That man just couldn't go around battering people.

"Dory! Dory! Wake up!"

Violet's voice rang through the tiny apartment and Doris bolted up in bed. Violet had a key in case of emergencies. She never used it, so Doris wondered what was wrong. Had she really slept that late? Glancing at the windows, she noted the sun was barely rising. That wasn't the cause for shouting. Her bedroom door flew open, and her friend came running to her side.

Leaning on her elbows, Doris looked at Violet. Her red

hair was still in her nightcap, curls tumbling down her back. She wore a wrapper tied tightly around her nightgown. Dainty toes peeked out from underneath the lace edge.

"Vi, what's wrong? Why are you here in your night-clothes, and where are your shoes?"

"Get up! Look out the window. Something is happening!"

Doris groaned and flopped back on the bed, lifting the side of the blanket as she closed her eyes. "You could just lay down with me. It's too early to get up." She had no intention of rising this early, and whatever was happening in the streets was certainly none of her business. Violet bounced onto the edge of the bed, pulling at Doris's arm. Opening one eye, she looked at Violet and groaned. "Why don't you tell me what's happening?"

"Because I don't know, silly! Papa told me to come over here and lock all the doors. He said there would be no school today, too." Violet wrinkled her nose. "I didn't cancel school."

That was enough for Dory. Sitting up, she moved her legs over the side of the bed and toed around for her slippers. Slipping them on her feet, she pulled the coverlet around her shoulders and stood, offering Violet an edge before walking to the window and peering through the curtains.

Below, she could see a group of men gathered in the middle of Main Street. Rufus and his men were on one side with Mayor McDougal. Violet's papa and several other men she recognized from town were staring them down on the other side of an invisible line that seemed to run from the door of her store across the street to the Tin Star.

What was happening?

"Mama?" Mary Ellen called from the doorway of the bedroom.

151

"Go back to bed, baby. Violet had a bad dream."

"I'm scared, Mama."

Doris moved from the window to the door. "How about I tuck you in?" Mary Ellen nodded and rubbed her eyes. "Come on, sweetheart." She glanced back at Violet, who was riveted to the scene below, and then led her daughter back to bed, tucking her in and kissing her forehead. "I love you."

"Wuv you, Mama," Mary Ellen murmured, but she was already asleep as Doris stood up and straightened the blanket around the small child. She checked on Maybelle, who hadn't stirred, and then quietly tiptoed back to her bedroom.

Violet hadn't moved from the window. She pressed her nose against the glass and turned her head to the left and right before moving to make room for Doris to peer out the glass once again.

"Do you think it's going to be a gunfight like at the O.K. Corral?" Violet whispered, leaning into Doris's shoulder.

"Oh goodness, I hope not. Wait. Look, they're lining up. Who is that down there beside your papa?"

There was something familiar about the figure, but she didn't recognize him. *Look up,* she silently commanded. As if the figure heard her, his head tipped back slightly, and Doris recognized Buck Montgomery seconds before she saw the silver star on his vest.

Her fingers lifted to her mouth and suddenly things made a lot more sense. He wasn't in town just because he was passing through. He'd come looking for Rufus, and that's what his note yesterday meant.

"What is the meaning of this?" Mayor McDougal called out. Rufus took a step forward, his legs splayed, arms crossed, and his eyes locked on Buck.

"Clyde, I thought you might like to meet the new sheriff." Mr. Gibbins nodded toward Buck, and someone let out a growl. Doris's eyes snapped back to Rufus. She was sure the growl came from him.

"Isn't that Mr. Montgomery?" Violet leaned closer, and Doris could only wonder how her friend hadn't recognized him right away, considering how smitten she seemed to be with the man.

"Mm hmm." Doris pushed Violet a bit to the side. "Shh, I can barely hear anything." She gently cracked the window open, and a soft breeze carried the conversation into the room.

"Daybreak doesn't have a sheriff." Rufus stepped forward again, but Buck and the men surrounding him didn't move. Dory felt herself step back on his behalf.

This is silly, she thought. He doesn't even know I'm here!

Mr. Gibbins continued. "The people of the town of Daybreak need a sheriff. The Lord saw to it and brought Marshal Montgomery to our town. He has graciously accepted the position."

"Temporarily." Buck's deep voice was clear, and she knew he hadn't even raised it.

"There cannot be a lawman in Daybreak unless I appoint one," McDougal blustered. His face was turning red, and she could see sweat glistening in the early morning light.

"I am a lawman. I was passing through a town where a murder, and an attack on a woman, have taken place within days of my arrival. The community is asking for something to be done, and it is my responsibility to do what I can to help with the safety of the people of Daybreak."

Doris felt as if God had riveted her feet to the floor. *Maybe He had heard her prayer after all?*

Violet pressed against Doris once more. "When do you think he decided he was going to be the sheriff? Was that why he was talking to Papa?"

"Violet, for heaven's sake, be quiet so we can hear them." Dory wrapped an arm around her friend, but her eyes locked on the two men that seemed to want to decide her future. Why hadn't he said he was a sheriff? Was he even really a lawman? Her mind was racing through what she knew about the man and where he'd come from. Did he mention where he had been before he came to Daybreak?

"You can't do this, Gibbins." McDougal shook his fist.

The banker pulled on the edges of his jacket. "Actually, I can. You're the mayor of this town. As such, you're to keep the people of Daybreak safe, and their needs heard. If you can't come to see things our way, we'll hold a special election and find someone who will."

She watched as Buck stepped forward and the men to the right of Rufus shot nervous glances at their boss. They clearly weren't prepared to fight this morning. She doubted the Grumblatt Gang was sober, or if they had even gone to bed yet.

"Well, now we know why your papa canceled school for the day." Dory smiled at her friend, silently worrying about the violence that would come from this.

"But what does that mean? A sheriff? We haven't had a sheriff since they caught the last one in a compromising position over a year ago."

Moments like this were when the six years between them felt like a lifetime. Doris pushed away from the window and grabbed Violet's hand, dragging her to the bed. They sat on the side of the bed, and Doris kicked her slippers off, tucking her feet underneath her.

"It means times are changing here in Daybreak. The Grumblatts need to find a way to run Montgomery out of town. Montgomery needs to get rid of that horrid man."

"Or kill him."

Doris shrugged her shoulder. "Or kill him."

Something deep inside her warned that the only way McDougal and Rufus were getting rid of Buck Montgomery was if he was in a box at the undertaker's. She prayed that wouldn't be the outcome. Buck kind of reminded her of Wyatt Earp, and the stories that Titus used to tell her, before he went off to fight his own battles.

"What about that special vote Papa mentioned? Do you think anyone in town would run against the mayor?"

"Maybe your papa, but he's a businessman and must protect you. I can't think of anyone in town who would want to take up that mantle. At least no one in this town has shown that kind of initiative while we've been here."

"Harvey would have."

"Yes, Harvey would have."

"What about you? You could run for mayor."

Doris snickered. "That's absolute nonsense. Women don't run for office. We may be able to vote, but I don't think Wyoming is ready for a mayor that's a woman."

"I think it must be you. I'll talk to Papa about it." Violet bounced lightly on the bed before jumping to her feet and straightening her nightgown. "I'm going to start breakfast while you get ready for the day."

Violet disappeared into the hallway, leaving Dory alone with her thoughts.

Run for mayor?

What an idea, indeed.

She didn't want to run a town.

The person who took the job and secured the election would need to be someone who wanted to make Daybreak profitable again. They would need to bring business back to town. The person would have to make a future for the children in Violet's classroom, and keep people safe from heathens like Rufus and his gang.

Placing her blanket back on the bed, she gathered her clothes for the day. Her dress was on a peg by the window, so she couldn't help but look once more out into the street. The crowd of men was gone, and an odd twinge of disappointment settled in her belly.

Buck made it clear he was only here temporarily.

Maybe if she could get Buck to marry Violet, he would stay in town, and then someone else could be the mayor!

Yes, that was the solution.

Then Doris could grieve and figure out what her next steps were for her little family.

Undoing the braid in her hair, her thoughts wandered over everything that had happened in the last month.

Maybe she should find a husband. Was it too late in life for her to find someone else to be a papa to her girls?

Was there such a thing as a mail-order groom?

With these thoughts running through her mind, she quickly dressed and went to find Violet and start her day.

BUCK WAS SATISFIED WITH HOW his morning had gone.

There had been no bloodshed, and the look of pure hatred on Rufus's face would fuel Buck's joy for several days. It felt good to come out of hiding, so to speak. When he had spoken to Mr. Gibbins the day before about the events that had happened with Doris, they agreed to speed up their timetable. Things in Daybreak could not continue as they had been.

He stood in the doorway of the abandoned sheriff's office. The whole place needed to be cleaned. He saw that dust and cobwebs covered every inch. The upstairs apartment and jail were just as filthy, but it felt like he belonged.

Now he just had to make sure that he didn't end up dead. Maybe Sarge was right. He should have shot Rufus the first time he laid eyes on him. He'd spent the last three weeks quietly meeting the men of the community. They all had the same concerns. The ranchers, the business owners who weren't on the take, and Gibbins. There hadn't been a sheriff in nearly two years who had lasted for more than a couple of weeks. The mayor started changing when a new group of outlaws came into town and he spent more time in their company. McDougal abandoned the friends that he'd had for years in favor of collecting a piece of the winnings from the saloons and brothels. The more saloons and gambling houses, the more money McDougal made.

Glancing around at the dust-laden interior, Buck planned his next steps. First, he would clean up his new office and the holding cells so he could assess the facilities before making his second plans. To do that, he would need to get cleaning supplies at the dry goods store, and that would give him a chance to check on Doris.

He needed to make sure she was, in fact, fine. Buck didn't want to send a note to Titus informing him that Doris was hurt.

How long did a woman typically spend in mourning? he wondered.

The thought lingered in his mind all the way to the store. He preferred that question to whether Titus would still be his friend, if he pursued his growing affection for the man's little sister.

The bell rang overhead, and Doris's head popped up from behind the counter. She looked a little disheveled today. She'd piled her curly hair loosely on top of her head, and dark circles rimmed the bottom of her eyes, telling him she had slept no better than he had. When her eyes landed on him, a small smile appeared, and she seemed to take a deep breath.

"Hello, Mr. Montgomery. How can I help you today?"

Marry me.

He stilled, wondering where those words came from.

Biting his tongue so the words didn't slip out, he rested his hand on the door handle and asked, "Have you been busy this morning?"

"No, it appears the ladies in town will not be shopping today. Something about a bunch of men in the middle of the street at dawn."

She was teasing him! Reaching behind him, he flipped the lock on the door, and took long strides across the room until the only thing separating them was the counter. Resting his palms on the counter, he leaned over until they could almost touch each other. He wondered what her lips tasted like and whether she would protest the kiss. "What do you know about men in the streets at dawn?"

"It looks like Daybreak is getting a new sheriff." She raised her head to look up at him. The tip of her nose brushed against his chin, sending shivers down his spine.

"It appears that is the case." If he tilted his head, their lips would meet, but did he dare?

Doris stepped back and huffed. "You are on your way to Laramie."

"I was." He wasn't sure where this was going, but the distance let him clear his head.

"And you came from Fort Yellowstone."

That wasn't really a question. He didn't answer her. She was clearly working something out. She blinked at him before shaking her head and turning away. He wished he could read her thoughts.

"I need to get some cleaning supplies, unless you know

of someone in town who would like to earn some money cleaning up the sheriff's office and living quarters."

"When the unmarried women hear that the building is occupied, they will come in droves to help you settle in. They will clean it up in no time, feed you, and you won't have anything to worry about. You won't need much of anything from the store at that point."

Was that regret he heard in her voice?

"Would it make you sad if I didn't stop in?"

The rattle of the door disrupted the moment, and Buck turned to find Rufus standing outside of the store, with a scowl that was likely permanent after the events of this day.

"Probably. We have to let him in," Doris sighed. He could only imagine that it was the last thing she wanted to do in this moment.

"Do you want me to unlock the door?" When she nodded, he moved back across the room.

"Buck?" The tremor in her voice stalled his hand from unlocking the door, his head turning to look at her. "Please don't leave."

"I'm not going anywhere, honey; we have a whole silent conversation to finish before this day is done." When she nodded her head, he turned back to the door, flipping the lock and opening it to the outlaw on the other side.

Rufus pushed past him with a growl and headed straight to the counter. Doris was still there, but she had stepped back further to put proper distance between them. Buck shifted to stand to the side. Nothing bad was going to happen in this building unless it was Rufus Grumblatt's death.

"I spoke with Reverend Burns. You and I are getting married tomorrow afternoon."

Rage pumped through Buck's veins, his hands clamping into fists, but he kept silent.

"I told you yesterday, I'm not marrying you."

Good girl, Buck thought.

"Here's the thing, Dory. That's what he called you, right? Dory? Well, now you're going to be my wife. You can say yes, and we can make this painless for everyone, or I can find creative ways of encouraging you." Rufus glanced at Buck, and leaned in over the counter, assuming that would block out his next words, "Or people are going to die. Should it be the new sheriff . . . or maybe the pretty teacher?"

"You can't do that," she answered, but Buck could hear the fear in her voice.

"Oh, I can. The only thing that's going to stop me is my ring on your finger and your body in my bed. Think about it, sweetheart. How many people must die before you say yes?"

Rufus didn't wait for an answer. Pivoting, he stalked past Buck with a smug smile on his face and winked. Taking a deep breath, he ignored the outlaw and returned to his place at the counter to check on Doris.

"What am I going to do?" she whispered as her knees buckled.

Buck swung himself over the counter in time to catch her before her head hit the edge of the table behind her.

Six

DORIS WOKE UP WITH A throbbing in her head. She opened her eyes and closed them promptly, counting to ten before opening them slowly, allowing the light to filter into her brain. Someone had tucked her into her own bed, with a solid weight pinning her down on one side.

Had she imagined it?

That explained the war drums beating a steady rhythm behind her eyes.

Buck was now the sheriff.

What about that conversation with Rufus?

Maybe it was a nightmare.

She'd heard that widows could sometimes turn to lunacy, and Doris prayed that wasn't the case. The last thing she wanted was to be sent to the asylum. She closed her eyes once more, and the weight disappeared, followed by heavy footsteps sounding across the wooden floors.

"She's awake," Violet called, and Dory grabbed her head, moaning at the noise.

"Please, Violet. There is no need to shout. I'm going to need a powder for this headache."

"Dearest, I wasn't shouting." The weight returned, and

Doris opened her eyes to see Violet sitting beside her on the bed. She leaned over and gently brushed the hair from Doris's forehead with cool fingers. "I'm sorry that your head hurts, but it sounds like you had quite an ordeal before you fainted."

"I did not faint." Doris tried to lift her head, but it wouldn't budge.

"You shouldn't scare a fella like that," Buck's voice teased from the doorway. Despite the pain, she turned her head to the side and smiled. Seeing his face was worth the agony. Concern was thick on his face and there was something else there behind his eyes.

"It wasn't just a bad dream?"

Both Buck and Violet shook their heads. Doris tried to move, and the weight at her side shifted, pulling her focus away from his deep blue eyes. Maybelle was fast asleep against her hip, and Mary Ellen sat watching from the far corner of the bed.

"Are you going to die, Mama?"

Doris could see the tears welling up in the little girl's eyes. Carefully, she freed one arm from the blankets and embraced her daughter, taking care not to wake the younger girl.

"No, baby. I'm not. I just—" Pausing, she cut her eyes to Buck, and he nodded at her. "Mama had a fright this morning and my brain says it needs to rest."

"I don't want you to go live with Papa and Grandpapa. Me and Maybelle need you here."

Pulling Mary Ellen closer, Doris closed her eyes, showing her love and a confidence she didn't feel to her daughter. She had no plans on dying, but even if she married Rufus, there was no guarantee that he wouldn't just kill her when he got bored, or if she burnt dinner. There had to be another way. She just needed time to think.

Leave it to him to decide the wedding was tomorrow, probably hoping to distract Buck from whatever schemes they currently had running.

"I'm glad you're awake, Mrs. Whistler. There are some things I need to attend to, but if it's all right with you, I'd like to come back around dinnertime to see how you're feeling."

She wasn't sure when he'd knelt beside the bed, but he was closer than was probably proper. "I'd like that. Maybe Violet can make something light for all of us for dinner?" She glanced up at her friend, who nodded. Doris knew Violet would go invite her father over as well. Since Violet's mama had died and since Harvey had passed, Mr. Gibbins had developed a habit of coming for dinner once a week. Doris was extremely grateful to them both for keeping her company.

"Then I'll see you for dinner." He tenderly raised his hand and swept her hair away from her face. "Don't hurry to get up. You're allowed to take the rest of the day."

Why did this moment seem so intimate?

Despite the crowd, it felt like it was only the two of them in the room.

"Please don't die today." Her words were lighthearted, but her voice was serious. "I don't want to tell Titus that I cost him his friend."

Buck's face stretched into a broad smile, unsurprised she'd figured it out, and he chuckled quietly. Pushing up off the floor, she could see his shoulders still shaking from silent laughter.

"I'm flattered you don't want me to die, honey, but your brother is the least likely to blame you for my death. He'd probably tell you I courted it. When I come back for dinner, you'll have to tell me what gave me away." He gave her forehead a light kiss and gave her shoulder a tender hug before he left to attend to his sheriff duties.

163

"So, he will not be my husband." Violet perched on the edge of the bed beside her. There wasn't any criticism in her voice, only a tinge of sorrow. "What's this about your brother?"

Inhaling deeply, Dory slowly lifted herself up and shifted closer to the head of the bed, pondering what to share with her friend.

"He only half confirmed my suspicions. I sent Titus a message seeking advice after Harvey died. I think Buck was Titus's solution. Probably not to take an interest in me, but to assess the situation. The fact that my brother hasn't arrived here yet must mean that he is busy, but he wouldn't send someone he didn't trust."

"Are you ready to talk about what happened this morning after you left me?"

The weight on her left shoulder shifted, and Dory glanced at Mary Ellen. Both girls were now fast asleep atop the comforter. Violet got up and put a blanket over Mary Ellen before returning to Dory's side.

"Rufus came to the store. Mr. Montgomery and I were talking in private. He had locked the front door when he arrived, which angered Rufus. He says I'm going to marry him tomorrow or people are going to die. How can I make sure that you, the girls, and all the others remain safe without marrying him, Vi?"

"Me? You're not responsible for protecting me. My papa would be upset to think you thought that responsibility fell on your shoulders. We also have a sheriff now. If you ask me, he seems rather smitten with you. Don't let that scourge, Rufus, scare you into making decisions that don't have to be made. We'll think of something at dinner tonight." Violet stretched out her arm, rearranging the pillows behind Doris's head, and then draped the quilt over her.

"I'm so tired, Violet." She couldn't keep her eyes open.

"I know, sweetie. Close your eyes, and I'll come back to check on you in a little while. Do you want chicken and dumplings for dinner, or ham and vegetables?"

"Dumplings would be lovely." Dory's eyes closed, her mind considering how lucky she'd been to find a friend like Violet to walk this path with her.

BUCK WAS A GOD-FEARING man. He embraced the concept of an eye for an eye, and he only condoned violence if it was necessary. Two such occasions would be if he was protecting himself, his family or his property; or if it were in a time of war.

His ability to stay collected was something he took pride in.

His urge to take Rufus Grumblatt out was fighting to overpower his common sense. Rather than going to the Tin Star first, where he was sure the man would be, he opted to go to the church to chat with Reverend Burns. He needed to find out where the Reverend stood on the matters in town. It was a short walk to the Daybreak Presbyterian Church and the large wooden doors. Buck removed his hat and entered the sanctuary. Once his eyes adjusted to the darkness, he spied the reverend standing at the altar.

He walked down the aisle, his boots thudding against the wooden floors. The reverend looked up and smiled, placing the papers he was reviewing to the side. He approached Buck, his hand held out in greeting.

"Hello, Buck, how can I help you?"

Buck shook the man's hand and took a moment to choose his words carefully. "Reverend Burns, I was

165

wondering if you have time to hear me out? I have a few queries and I appreciate your thoughtful nature."

"Of course. Let's go into my office and we can have some coffee while you gather your thoughts." Buck accompanied the man through the chapel to an office that was small and full of books, papers, a desk crafted from wood, and two overstuffed chairs. "How do you like your coffee?"

"Black is fine, thank you." The reverend disappeared to fetch the coffee while Buck wedged himself into one of the chairs. He tried to cross his leg, but the arms were so thick with padding that he just gave up and let his boots rest on the floor.

"Here you go," the reverend said, handing Buck a cup of coffee and sitting down in the chair behind the desk. "Now, what's on your mind?"

Buck took a sip of the hot brew. He wanted to time his words carefully so he could watch the reverend's reaction. Resting the cup on his knee, he cleared his throat.

"I've heard that you intend to hold a wedding here tomorrow afternoon. I know you heavily oppose the issues going on in this town. So, I'm surprised you are supporting the people I'm supposed to remove." Buck saw the man's face become pale and his Adam's apple bob wildly. The reverend closed his eyes briefly and Buck watched the man's lips move in a silent prayer. "Help me understand how you ended up in the predicament to pressure Mrs. Whistler to marry this man who murdered her husband, and attacked her in her own shop."

"Mrs. Whistler?"

"Yes." Buck put his cup on the ground. "What leverage do they have against you to force you to perform this farce of a wedding?"

The other man's eyes snapped open, and anger swiftly

replaced fear. "I'm not performing a wedding for Mrs. Whistler. We just buried her husband!"

Buck exhaled in relief. He had been on edge since Rufus announced his "engagement" to Doris. The thought of the gentle widow marrying such a ruffian hurt his heart. "Then who do you think you're marrying?"

The reverend held his cup close as he spoke. "I'm uniting Kenneth Wardell and a girl from the Tin Star in marriage. Why do you think I'm performing a marriage for Mrs. Whistler? Who is she supposed to be marrying?"

"Rufus Grumblatt enlightened Mrs. Whistler a few hours ago that you would marry them tomorrow. If she resisted, he was going to start killing people in town. Mrs. Whistler had quite a fall from the news and is now recuperating in her bed." His cheek was twitching wildly, and the desire to wreak havoc was growing rapidly inside him.

"Sheriff Montgomery, I will force no one into marriage, and I never have in all my congregations. I would trust that my character will represent me, even though we haven't known each other for too long." The man stood from behind his desk, downing his coffee and coming around to where Buck still sat. "What are you going to do about this?"

"That's the problem, Reverend. I am well within my rights to gun the man down based on the warrants he has. However, it's going to cause a conflict with the mayor, and as you do not have a judge in town, McDougal can make the whole situation difficult. I also cannot allow Rufus to murder people in Daybreak because he didn't get his own way. So how would you like me to handle this?" Buck knew exactly how he was going to handle it. He just wanted to make sure that he still had friends on the town council once things were done.

"If we knew what to do about Rufus Grumblatt and his friends, frankly, we wouldn't need you, Sheriff. I'll speak to the other council members, but we will back whatever move you make."

Those were the words that he needed to hear. Rising from his chair, he took his leave, thankful that the reverend would inform the rest of the council. Buck, however, needed to visit Mayor McDougal.

It was time to make a proper introduction and make his intentions abundantly clear. A plan formed in his mind, and he felt a sense of determination by the time he arrived at his destination. The mayor's house was larger than most in town, with a wrought-iron gate separating the property from Main Street.

A short whistle pierced the air just as his hand touched the latch of the gate. Looking over his shoulder, a movement toward the edge of town caught his attention. Clearly, his chat with the mayor would have to wait. He gave a quick look toward Main Street. All was quiet, and while part of him worried about that, the other part knew in two hours it wouldn't be. For now, he had to seek the source of the whistle.

Reaching the tree-lined path, a smile bloomed on Buck's face. Sarge and Titus were standing in the thicket to the side of the road. "Well, aren't you both a sight for sore eyes?"

Titus clapped him on the shoulder in a brotherly hug. "So, did you fall in love with my little sister yet?"

"I've not been here long enough for that to happen," Buck teased. It was the closest to *yes* he was going to get before he told her himself.

"Pay up! I told you she'd win." Titus stretched out his hand to Sarge, laughing loudly when Sarge placed the five honey cubes in his hand.

"You could have waited another month, Buck," Sarge groused. "And you should have shot Rufus on sight like I told you to."

"It took you long enough to get here," Buck said, slapping Sarge on the shoulder. "Don't worry, you'll get your honey cubes back, I'm sure."

"I know you have a plan, Buck. What is it?" Titus asked.

"Let's get back to the sheriff's office and I can fill you in."

As the trio made their way back to the town, Buck felt calmer than he had since he first arrived.

The fight in Daybreak was just made a little fairer.

Seven

DORIS WOKE TO A DARKENED room.

She knew she had dozed with the girls most of the afternoon, but now they were gone, their little voices carrying from the kitchen down the hallway. She dragged herself up out of bed and gave herself a minute for the throbbing to cease before turning the gas lamp's dimmer switch and allowing light to permeate the room. Slowly walking to the wardrobe, she needed to find something to wear for dinner. Every step was a struggle, as it was too hard to even lift her feet.

What was she going to do when Buck left?

It was strange how fast she had become so attached to him. The announcement that he was a lawman made sense. She hadn't once seen him go into the saloons. He was spending most of his time with Mr. Gibbins, and he had made it a point to come into the store every day since he'd arrived. It was impossible for a single man to eat that many peppermints each day. His belly would ache something fierce.

She picked a purple long-sleeved day dress that she'd made in the fall. Though it was a bit too big since she'd lost weight following Harvey's death, the fabric was comfortable. He'd always said she looked pretty in it, and today she wondered for a moment what Buck would think. Sitting down at the dressing table, she observed her reflection. Despite her exhaustion, her eyes were brighter than they had been in a while and color was returning to her face. Taking the pins from her hair and laying them on the table, Doris picked up her brush and started counting the strokes as she ran the bristles through her long hair.

"I can braid that for you," Violet spoke from the doorway, causing Doris to jump slightly in her seat.

"Thank you, Vi. I don't know what I would do without you."

"Good thing you're never going to find out," Violet teased, taking the brush from her hand and smoothing her light brown hair one more time before parting it into sections. "Mama taught me to do a Dutch braid when I was no older than Mary Ellen. I think it would be good for tonight. It's just family, after all."

"I learned coifs, not the braids that you do. They're lovely really." Dory found it so relaxing to have someone playing with her hair. It was a far cry from the way her mother used to do her hair with a firm hand. "Would you want to teach the girls?"

"I could teach Mary Ellen. She's a quick learner. Maybelle is still too young." Violet hummed to herself while she went about the over-under pattern. "The ladies are going to come to the store tomorrow for tea and a chat about your campaign."

"Vi, I told you I don't think I should run. Look at what happened today."

"Of course, you feel that way. However, what happened today is exactly why you should run. How many times have you said that the mayor should just do his job and make them leave? It's time for things to change here in Wyoming, and there's no one better to make them change than you. Plus, if we want to get the mill and smithy back in business, they're going to respond more quickly to a woman asking someone to fill the position."

"You have it all figured out, don't you? Why don't you run for mayor?" Gazing at her friend's features in the mirror, Doris noticed the doubt flitting across her face before she put it aside.

"I can't run. Papa owns the bank, and everyone knows him. Any naysayers would say that if I won, I only won because of Papa, and that isn't something I want." Violet paused, tying a ribbon around the end of Doris's hair, finger combing the long strands that hung down her back. "This way you can do it. I can teach. Mr. Montgomery can handle the law things, and we can all live happily ever after." She patted Doris's shoulders. "You look beautiful."

A knock on the downstairs door ended the conversation, and Violet went to let the men in for dinner. Clearly, Violet seemed to have it all figured out, but happily ever after seemed like a childish ideal these days. Doris slid her feet into her house shoes before entering the main part of the apartment.

What she found stole her breath away.

"Titus!"

Her feet were running at the realization that her brother stood at the door. She slammed into him, hugging him tight, while laughter erupted around the room.

"Told you she wouldn't mind having you join us for dinner." Buck's voice cut through the air, and she turned on him.

"You DO know my brother. I was right!" She advanced

on him like a wolf on a rabbit. If he had said that was why he seemed familiar and who he was, then she could have spent an extra two weeks trusting him instead of worrying that he was the new Rufus, threatening everything she had left. "Why didn't you just tell me so?"

"Dory," Titus called from behind her, but she didn't listen.

She was almost close enough to swat Buck, if he would just quit backing up, but he was getting closer and closer to the far wall.

"Sweetheart, I didn't want to tell you that Titus sent me. I was just going to check on you and move on. I didn't expect to stay and be your hero," he chuckled.

Buck's words stopped her in her tracks, and her breath caught.

She blew out a frustrated breath as the memories of the last month flitted through her mind. His actions weren't a result of Titus sending him. Nobody with any sense would go against her brother. Yes, Buck stayed because of Rufus and his gang, but it appeared to be more than that. She couldn't be sure, but she had the feeling that he was showing interest in her.

Could things be any more confusing?

"Dory." Violet's words cut through the single-minded focus in her head. "There are more people here than your brother and the sheriff." Doris turned, embarrassment coloring her face as she noticed another man she didn't recognize standing next to Mr. Gibbins.

Leaning over to her friend, she whispered in Violet's ear, "This is why I am not qualified to be mayor, Vi." Smiling at her guests, she stepped back and waved them inside. "I apologize, gentlemen. Please come in."

There were chuckles all around, and Dory glanced over

her shoulder to send Buck a look that she hoped clearly said their discussion was far from over.

B̲UCK LOOKED AROUND THE TABLE.

Somehow, he'd ended up at the head of the table with Maybelle on one side of him and Mary Ellen on the other. He could get used to Saturday evenings like this with friends and family gathered, safe and sound.

Whoa there, boy, don't get ahead of yourself.

It hadn't escaped his notice that Titus was clearly infatuated with Violet. His best friend was hanging on to her every word, and each time Titus would say something, Violet would respond with a series of giggles.

It would be wonderful if Titus would move to Daybreak. Then he'd have his best friend close. They could settle down, raise their children together . . . *whoa, again.*

Buck shook his head. He was getting ahead of himself.

"Sheriff?" Mr. Gibbins's voice cut through Buck's thoughts. Clearly, the banker had been trying to get his attention for a while.

"I apologize. What was that?"

"How was your first day as sheriff?" Gibbins winked at him.

Buck wiped his mouth and placed his napkin on the table. "Let's see. I rescued a damsel in distress, spoke with the minister about his ethics, and was on my way to the mayor's house when these two showed up." He thumbed his hand at Sarge and Titus, who both grinned.

"Hey now. He said he needed friends," Titus explained, leaning close to Violet. "So, his friends came to visit."

"What is the problem with Burns?" Gibbins paid attention to the facts. Buck admired that quality in him.

"Nothing's wrong with Burns, but I needed to verify that for myself. I wanted to discover where his loyalty rested. I'm eager to have a conversation with the mayor of Daybreak, to discover what in his role is so appealing."

"He won't be the mayor for long. Dory is going to be the new mayor," Violet interrupted with a grin on her face. "It's a perfect plan, Papa!"

"Is that right, princess?" Gibbins smiled at his daughter. "Why don't you let us lesser mortals in on your plan? When it's just us men, we can chat about the issues of the town." Gibbins smiled at his daughter, and Buck glanced at Maybelle and Mary Ellen. He thought it might be terrifying to see what the two of them would be up to, in a couple of years. If they were his, he'd probably indulge them like Gibbins indulged Violet.

Mary Ellen noticed him looking and leaned toward him. "Are you going to be our new papa?" Her words were barely loud enough to hear.

"Why do you ask?" He leaned down so that they could give the appearance of a private conversation, though he was sure everyone could hear them. *How did she know what he was thinking?*

"Uncle Titus likes you, but I've never met him. Mama loves him though, and she always tells me about what a good big brother he was. That's why I must be a good big sister. Maybelle looks a little like you, so kids won't pick on her, and my mama needs someone to love her, so she doesn't just leave us like Papa did." There were no tears in her eyes, just a straight explanation about her thought process without judgement.

"What do you need, Miss Mary Ellen?"

"Arthur McBee would quit pulling my hair if my papa was the sheriff."

Buck threw his head back and laughed. Noticing Mary Ellen's face coloring in embarrassment, he cut himself off and leaned back in. "I could make him stop pulling your hair even if I'm not your papa."

"Yes, but . . ."

"What are the two of you talking about over there?" Doris's voice cut through the air, and both Buck and Mary Ellen straightened. The little girl appeared the picture of innocence. She shot Buck a sideways look, and he gave her a small nod. Her wishes were safe with him.

"Mary Ellen was just telling me about what a good big brother her Uncle Titus is to you. I'm hoping that he's just as good of a friend and I will not upset him too much with my next action." Buck pushed back from the table and noticed Mary Ellen looking at him with wide eyes, her little heart-shaped mouth rounded into an O. He patted her on the head and rounded the table to stand between Titus and Doris. "Titus, we've been brothers for a long time. What was the last thing you told me before I left Yellowstone?" The tension in the room was making him itchy. He hadn't even kissed Doris yet, but he knew that if he didn't marry her, he was going to regret it for the rest of his life.

"I told you not to fall in love with my sister." Titus leaned back, crossing his arms over his chest. "You looked me in the eye and told me you weren't concerned about that."

Buck nodded. "I said that. But I didn't expect to be watching your sister from a distance. I had plans for my life that were thrown out the window when you came and asked if I could come to Daybreak. I'd told Sarge over there that all I wanted was a town to protect and a place to build a family. I've found both here in Daybreak." Moving to where Doris was seated, he took her hand. It was so small compared to his. Her fingers were stiff as he wrapped his hand around them, trying to impart some warmth into the cold digits. He didn't let go as he knelt beside her. "I know you're still grieving, and I'll wait if you ask me to, but I love you and the girls. I ask for the honor of your hand in marriage and letting me be their new papa."

Doris put her fingers up to her lips and stifled a sob. Tears streamed down her face as she shook her head no, then yes, and no once more. With a choking gasp, she pulled her hand from his and pushed back from the table, knocking the chair over.

"Forgive me," she said as she hurried down the hallway, Violet in pursuit.

"I think she'll say yes," Mary Ellen announced, getting up from her chair and going to the sideboard. "While we wait on Mama, let's have dessert!"

The little girl came back to the table with a plate of brownies and handed them to Titus.

Buck took his seat and looked at his friend, who shrugged before accepting the plate.

As Buck waited for the plate to make its way around the table, he stared at the hallway, wishing for Doris to reappear. For the first time in his life, Buck was at a loss. He simply didn't know what to do.

Eight

"GO AWAY, VIOLET. I DON'T want company."

Doris sat on the edge of her bed and gripped Harvey's handkerchief in her hands. She ran her thumb along the embroidered H as she looked at all the things she'd collected over the years. A thick layer of dust coated her beloved items because she had been too busy to take care of the housework since . . . She released the handkerchief, dropping it into her lap and sighing.

Why was everything divided into before Harvey's death and after he died?

Why did he have to leave? Why did she miss him so much, but then feel guilty if she even considered taking action to secure her and the children's well-being?

It was common knowledge that widows should be in mourning for at least a year after their husbands died. She didn't feel like that was necessary. She would always love Harvey, but she also knew that he wouldn't want her sitting around wearing black or moping. He would want her to move on with her life. Make sure the children had a papa. *Maybe even find love?*

Harvey was generous that way. She didn't know if she had it in her to feel the same way.

If she was the one who perished, would she want Harvey to find love again?

She sat with the thought for a moment. It wouldn't bother her if he did.

But what if she was married to Buck?

The prospect of him finding love again if she passed away crushed her.

Why would she feel so different about the two men?

Would Harvey like Buck?

He probably would. Harvey liked Titus, and Buck and her brother were a lot alike.

She realized that over the past weeks, when she needed someone, Buck was there. When she went to sleep at night, Buck was the last person she thought about. He was the first person she thought about in the morning.

Harvey was like a comfortable shoe. They had grown up together and everyone expected them to get married. So, they did.

A loud knock echoed through the room.

"Violet, I said I didn't want company."

The door cracked open. "Not even me?" Titus poked his head in, his broad shoulders filling the door frame.

"I guess you can come in." She was glad to see him. It had been at least six years since they were last together. They exchanged letters, but it wasn't the same as having her brother right in front of her.

He looked good, tired and a little bulkier, but there was a peace about him she couldn't recall ever seeing in him before. She watched him approach her dressing table chair, flip it around and sit on it, his tall body straddling the back of the chair.

Rubbing his thumb on his jaw, he looked at her with steely eyes. "Well, you sure made a mess of things this time, Dory."

"Which part?" She didn't know if she should laugh or cry. Tears welled up in her eyes and she clenched the handkerchief even more.

"Oh, Squirt, don't cry." He leaned over the back of the chair and grabbed her hand. "Let's see. You found one of the most wanted men in the entire country. You lost a husband and took over his business. Then you made one of the most stubborn men I've ever met fall head over heels in love with you. I'd say you've been rather busy these past few weeks. Whatever you do, Dory, you do it with force."

Doris gave a half-laugh, half-sob. "He's not in love with me."

"Oh, he loves you, Squirt." Titus squeezed her hand. "I gave him a direct order not to fall in love with you. Sarge suggested he court your red-haired friend. He didn't do either of those things, did he? He then proposed in front of the few people he has respect for in this town. And what did my sister do? Run off and lock herself in her bedroom."

She dabbed at her eye with a handkerchief, still clinging to Titus's hand. "I did do that, didn't I?"

"Yep, you did that."

She couldn't help it. Giggles rose within her, her tears flowing freely. She was a complete mess, and there was still a man out there in the next room who wanted to marry her. If that wasn't a God thing, she wasn't sure what else could explain it. Looking at Titus, she hoped he could guide her now, as he had always done.

"What am I going to do?"

"Do you love him?"

"I don't know," she whispered. "I like him."

"What are you worried about?" Doris shrugged her shoulders. Titus tapped her knee. "Look at me, Dory."

"What if Rufus kills him, too?" There. She said it. She was afraid that Rufus would kill Buck, so she didn't want to risk falling in love.

"Rufus Grumblatt is a dead man walking, and he will not kill Buck. That man is one of the most evasive and well-trained soldiers I've ever met. I need to decide if I should tell the man I trust with all our lives to step back. Or should I just punch him in the nose for taking liberties with you?" His eyes were light, but his words rang true, and it startled her out of her thoughts.

"I. You. Don't lay a finger on him!" Doris stood and lightly punched her brother in the shoulder. "He has been a perfect gentleman. I just need some time. Do you think he'll be mad if I tell him that?"

Titus stood and pulled Dory into his arms, wrapping her in a brotherly hug. "I think that is a good idea. He'll be overjoyed that it's not a no. Do you want me to send him in here and rescue him from all the brownies Mary Ellen is feeding him, or do you want to come back out and join the rest of us?"

This was one thing she adored about Titus. He'd always been a powerful advocate for giving her options.

"I don't want to embarrass myself any more tonight."

Placing a kiss on the top of her head, he released her and pushed her towards the chair. "All right then, I'll send him back here to talk with you, but the door stays open."

"Yes, sir," she laughed. Watching her brother walking away, their conversation ran through her mind. What would Buck think about her running for mayor? And how could they take down McDougal?

BUCK WATCHED VIOLET USE A napkin to scrape off as much of the chocolate brownies from the little girls' hands as she could. She was very good with the children, and he knew she would make an excellent mother one day.

"Let's get you poppets washed up and to bed."

Buck watched Mary Ellen's forehead crinkle at Violet's words.

"I don't wanna. I wanna wait for Mama."

"Mary Ellen," Buck said from his chair. "You heard Miss Violet. Help Maybelle get washed, and I'll make sure you get to see your mama before bed."

The little girl narrowed her eyes. He could tell she was tired and overloaded with sugar. He narrowed his eyes back, daring her to say something.

"Mama didn't say yes, yet."

"Your mama might take a bit of time to decide. It wouldn't be good for her to return and find you not ready for bed, or the kitchen in a mess, right?"

Kicking her shoes on the carpet, Mary Ellen mumbled under her breath. "Can we really come back?"

"Are you going to help Maybelle?"

"Yes." Moving around to where Violet had lifted Maybelle out of her chair and set her tiny feet on the floor, Mary Ellen grabbed her sister by the hand. "Come on, Maymay, let's go wash up and get our night shirts on."

His eyes tracked the girls down the hall as far as he could see, only to hear chuckles coming from the surrounding seats.

"What?" He eyed the men at the other end of the table.

"That little girl has you wrapped around her finger." Gibbins burst out laughing.

Sarge looked rather pleased with himself. "Looks like all your wishes might come true sooner than you think."

"I'll take my chances with that. We just need to do something about Rufus first." Glancing around to make sure there were no little ears within hearing distance, Buck continued, "He told Dory that she was going to marry him one way or another tomorrow. When she resisted, he listed off the people in town he intended to kill. We must make sure the women stay inside until this is resolved, and they should have someone with them."

"Agreed." The other two men nodded.

"I don't work for the next few days, so I volunteer to have the first watch. I think they can all provide me with entertainment for a few days." Gibbins grinned, leaning back in his chair. "Those girls might as well be my grandbabies. Violet won't be providing me with any grandchildren soon."

A dark shadow crested the entrance to the dining area. Buck glanced up to see Titus walking back towards the table.

"Well, I'm glad you three are agreeing on things, but Buck here needs to go chat with my sister." Titus settled himself back at the table, then gave Buck a look with raised eyebrows. "I got her to quit crying. I know you are serious. You wouldn't have risked our brotherhood. But now you need to go listen to her. Try not to make her cry some more. You hear?"

Buck blew out a deep breath. "I hear you."

He felt like he was walking to a court martial as he headed for the bedroom to find out his fate. His only goal now was to keep her from crying, but he was more worried about his own tears. He tapped lightly on the door and waited for her to admit him.

"Come in," Dory called out.

He wasn't prepared for her to be nestled in at the head of the bed. He saw her cheeks were blotchy, and her nose was a glossy red, suggesting she had been crying.

"Hey, there."

"You can come all the way in." He realized he was still standing in the doorway. He stepped in and started to shut the door. "Don't do that. Titus was very clear that the door must stay open."

"Of course, he was." He chuckled, coming to perch on the end of the bed. "He said you wanted to talk to me?"

His throat was dry, but his palms were wet. He didn't like being unprepared, and he was unprepared for this conversation.

She took a deep breath and looked at him. "Why do you want to marry me?"

"Well, then I could have my peppermint sticks for free." He saw a faint smile break out over her lips. "I want to know that I can kiss you whenever I want. Mary Ellen asked if I'd be her papa, and I loved the feeling that came with that. I love you, or I think I'm in love with you. I don't have any experience with this feeling that's eating at me from the inside out. I know my belly feels worse when I'm not with you."

"That does sure sound like love. What do you mean, though, that Mary Ellen asked if you'd be her papa?"

"That's what we were talking about at the table when you interrupted us." He slid up the bed slightly. "You know what love is supposed to be. Do you think you could love me?"

He wasn't at all comfortable with this vulnerable display, but if he had to beg her, he would drop on his knees before her, God, and everyone in town, if needed. He reached out, brushing his fingers over her cheek lightly. As her eyes fluttered shut for a second, it captivated him. She leaned into his fingers, then slowly opened her eyes.

"I am of two minds. I loved my husband very much. I'll love him until I die. But he's gone and won't be coming back. When I think about you, I can't imagine not having you in my life, and the thought of anything happening to you fills me with despair." She reached up and tangled her fingers in his, pulling his hand down to the bed between them. "Just because I love Harvey, doesn't mean I don't have enough room to love another man. This isn't a no, but I need some time. Can I have some time, Buck?"

It took everything inside of him not to jump and shout. It wasn't a yes, *but it was not a no*. "Sweetheart, you can have all the time you need. I'm not going anywhere unless you ask me to go."

"Truly?"

"I promise." He leaned forward and gave her the softest kiss possible, barely a brush of their lips together, but it was better than anything he could have ever expected.

"She said yes!" Mary Ellen shrieked, running down the hall, and Dory dropped her head to his shoulder, laughing.

"Do we correct her?" he asked with mock concern.

"Not tonight. Let's just let her have her joy. Perhaps it will make it easier to get her in bed."

Nine

DORY THOUGHT SHE WAS GOING to retch.

She was stuck in the back room of the dry goods store moving bolts of fabric, while the women of Daybreak gathered at a table drinking coffee and nibbling cookies. Mr. Gibbins was overseeing the store, as Buck insisted no one go out front, not even Dory, until he determined it was safe.

It was her store!

How dare he tell her what to do.

Yet here she was, listening to Violet chatter about whatnots.

"Dory. Dory! You need to come and join us," she insisted.

"Thank you, but I should get these new fabrics out front. They won't sell back here." She lifted several bolts of calico and turned towards the curtain that divided the back room from the front.

"There's no need for that," Sandra Taylor said. She was an older widow who lived in town and had her nose in most of the goings-on. Waving her arm around the room, she eventually motioned to the bolts of fabric in Doris's arms. "The people who will buy the fabric are right in this room. I think we should look at it after we finish. So you see, Doris, you don't need to take it out there."

"That's an excellent idea. Thank you, Mrs. Taylor." Violet was practically jumping in her seat. If she clapped her hands, she would remind Doris of Mary Ellen.

"All right, I suppose it can wait." Returning the bolts to the stack on the counter, she noticed Violet was patting the chair next to her.

"You can sit here, Dory." Turning to the rest of the seated women, Violet grinned. "I thought this would be a good time to discuss the future of our beloved town. As you know, things have been changing in Daybreak over the past week. We have a new sheriff. My father and your husbands have been working tirelessly on plans to bring our community back together."

Doris saw some women nodding their heads, and it made her aware of how many details she had overlooked while trying to finish her daily obligations. Guilt ate at her, and she wondered if she had let people down along the way. No one had said anything to her, so she just continued to listen to Violet.

"Mayor McDougal has done a poor job of representing the best interests of this town. He strongly opposes the prospect of having a lawman control the wrongdoings and acts of aggression. This includes the recent murder of Dory's husband!" She looked at Dory then with a sad smile on her face, as the women murmured their apologies. "My father mentioned the other night that the town could have a special election and have the current mayor replaced." Violet could not contain herself any longer as she finally gave in and clapped her hands.

"What does that mean for us?" Mrs. Burns asked, shifting forward in her chair, eager to hear what Violet had to say.

"We can vote! There are more women in this town right now. Wyoming gave us the right to vote in 1869. I say we vote Mayor McDougal out."

Mrs. Taylor snorted. "If you can find someone to run against him."

"We've already found someone," Violet squeaked. An eruption of voices broke out in the room. Doris took a deep breath. Violet reminded her of a child in so many ways, even if she was her best friend.

Pounding her cane on the floor, Mrs. Taylor demanded order in the room. "To whom do you refer, Miss Gibbins?"

Doris cleared her throat. She had never voted, even though the opportunity had been available for nearly forty years. Her mama said it would cause chaos and division. She'd allowed Harvey to speak for the household and many other families behaved similarly. The head of the home would cast a vote to represent the entire home. Women were encouraged not to vote, even though they had the opportunity to do so.

Pushing back from the table, Doris stood and looked at the other women.

"She meant me. I'll do it." The women blinked slowly and then, with a clap from Violet, the women broke into applause. "I'll do it." She stood, looking at the other women. "We have power that we don't use. The men in this town want to keep us down. I'm specifically talking about McDougal and his team of cronies. Rufus thinks of all women like chattel. It is time we take our power back. I'm not talking about being disobedient to our husbands or the law. I'm talking about using the law to our advantage."

"What do you suggest?" one woman asked.

"The mayor doesn't care what we think. So, we tell him. We use our voices. We use our vote. I'm tired of being afraid to walk down the street. I can't open my store without worrying that someone will come in and rob me . . . or worse." Her voice cracked but she had to keep going. "Rufus demanded that I wed him today, regardless of my opinion. If I said no, he was going to kill people." She paused, taking a breath. "I'm tired of being afraid. I don't want to raise my girls to be afraid. I want the future that Daybreak promised each of us when we arrived. This town could be profitable, comfortable, and safe if the Grumblatts weren't here. So why does the mayor allow them to stay? If elected as your mayor, I will ensure we have an honest sheriff, a Godly council, and we will take back our town by cleaning up the streets and removing the outlaws."

Applause broke out around the room. The women of the town were hugging each other, and then they were hugging her and Violet.

"I hope the mayor is ready, because it's going to be a long week for him," Marlee Sanderson said, looking over the group. Her husband was one of the older councilmen in town, and Dory wondered what she was planning. "Do you want to be mayor tomorrow, Doris, or would Tuesday suit you? I have heard the men talking about a special vote, and most of the people will be in town tomorrow for church. Right, Eileen?"

"The church makes the most sense," Mrs. Burns agreed. "I'll talk to Peter so that he is prepared. We can have a luncheon afterwards."

They spent the rest of the morning planning things out—who would bring what to the potluck, who would request their husbands to go out and let others know—and all agreed that the first establishment that was going to close would be the Tin Star.

"Excuse me, ladies," Buck's voice rumbled through the

room, right around lunchtime. Everyone stopped to give him their attention.

"What can we do for you, Sheriff?" Violet smiled at him, and Dory tried not to laugh. She knew he'd support her, but the innocent act of her best friend made her want to giggle.

"I'd like to request that either you all stay gathered here for a time until I come back, or let me know if you need to return home. But I humbly request that everyone stay away from Main Street this afternoon."

Dory knew immediately that something was happening, and the urge to ask him not to do whatever it was rose strongly in her. She shifted towards him with little thought, while glancing around the room.

"There are children here," she murmured, and he nodded at her. Of course, he knew that already.

"Sheriff," Violet called from the front of the room. "We will stay here. Everyone plans to be here for the day and the children are upstairs."

"I appreciate everyone's help." He looked out over the group, and Doris tried to absorb some of the confidence he was radiating. It helped relieve some of her anxiety. "Can I speak with you for a moment?" He extended a hand to Dory.

Without a word, she put her palm in his and let him lead her into the hallway at the bottom of the stairs. "What are you going to do?"

"Sweetheart, I will not tell you that. I just want you to stay inside and out of sight until Titus or I come back in here."

"Please be careful."

"I promise I'm going to be just fine. Sarge and Ned Sanderson are going to stay in the store down here. Is there enough room upstairs for the group?" He placed his hand on the back of her neck, his thumb stroking the pulse point in her throat.

"Of course." Doris swallowed hard.

His lips came down and brushed hers, once, twice, then settled in hard for a moment before pulling back. "I love you. I'm not rushing you, but I want you to know. I love you. It's time to go."

He gave her a quick hug and then ducked back through the curtain to the store.

"Ladies, let's go upstairs, where we can all be more comfortable," Doris called from the doorway.

"Nosy, too." Violet giggled. "Dory has windows facing the street."

BUCK WASN'T LOOKING FORWARD TO the upcoming confrontation. The town needed to be rid of the wickedness that filled the streets. He would have rather solved the problem without using force, however, the Grumblatts and McDougal wouldn't back down. Knowing the women and children were safe put his mind at ease. It allowed him to zero in on the task and handle it as effectively as possible.

Titus was standing to his left, his friend's hand flexing over the handle of his revolver.

"I don't understand why the banker is here," Titus repeated himself for the third time, and Buck finally took the bait.

"Are you so oblivious that you cannot recognize his behavior? You haven't chatted enough with him or Sarge to find out who he is?" If he hadn't done either, that would have been more shocking. When Titus failed to respond, Buck looked at his friend, who was now a deep shade of red. "Any other objections?"

"No."

"I'd like to point out that once you're done discussing who I am, the men are in place and we're running out of daylight." Gibbins gave them a look of displeasure, and Titus grew more embarrassed.

"Then it's time to dance." Buck stepped out into the middle of Main Street and fired a shot directly into the air. "Rufus Grumblatt, come out!"

He could hear doors slamming, but his eyes didn't stray from the entrance of the Tin Star. Buck had seen Rufus at the bar before the crowd gathered outside, so he knew he was still inside the building. When no one appeared, Buck pointed his gun in the air once more.

The swinging door of the saloon slammed against the outer wall of the building, and Rufus strolled out. "Whaddaya want?" he slurred, weaving from side to side.

"What do I want *today*?" Buck asked, grinning at the outlaw. "Today, I'd like to arrest you on the charges of robbery, murder, assault, and other immoral acts. Tomorrow, I'm going to marry Doris Whistler. It seems a fitting wedding gift."

As if on cue, Rufus reached for the pistol on his hip, but Buck was faster, and seconds later Rufus was dead on the boardwalk in front of the Tin Star, one bullet straight through his head. Without their leader, the rest of the Grumblatt Gang attempted to flee down the alleyways and through the bushes. Gibbins, Titus, and Sarge shot those that stayed and fought, mostly in the leg or arms. Buck was glad none of Daybreak's citizens were hurt in the melee.

He wasn't interested in any of the men but Rufus; he was the one with a bounty on his head. The rest of the men—Titus and Sarge could handle. He watched as they gathered up the fallen gang to place them in jail to await trial. Most of them would meet their fate at the end of the gallows, and that would take a few days to construct.

Suddenly, an ear-piercing shriek filled the air. Buck felt his blood curdling as he spun on his heel towards the dry goods store. A flash of blue appeared in front of the large window, the same color as the dress Doris wore that morning. She was being dragged towards the empty sawmill.

Buck lifted his pistol, but he was out of bullets. He could see that McDougal had a wild look in his eyes and a pistol poking Doris between the ribs.

"McDougal, you don't want to do this," Ned Sanderson called out from the doorway of the store. Buck could see that Ned's face was bruised and bleeding. He held a shotgun with shaky hands. "Let her go."

McDougal threw his head back, and his maniacal laughter filled the street. "I don't think so, Ned." He lifted his pistol in the air and waved it around. "That new sheriff just killed my baby brother. This is a family matter and doesn't involve you."

Buck had a sudden epiphany. A familial tie explained why McDougal did nothing about Rufus and his gang. The mayor had welcomed his brother and his friends into town with open arms. McDougal pulled Doris closer to him and pointed his pistol towards Buck. Everything happened so quickly, but it appeared like time was standing still. Sarge had moved around the bushes and appeared behind McDougal, ripping Doris from the mayor's arm and pistol-whipping him as a shot rang out into the street.

Buck saw Doris's mouth open, but no sound came out. He felt his shoulder jerk backwards and his feet buckle underneath him. He yelled as the pain of a white-hot poker ravaged his flesh. Hitting the ground, Buck rolled to his side and grabbed his arm, the blood washing between his fingers.

He looked up, noticing a few wisps of clouds scattered about in the brilliant blue sky.

Then the cacophony began. He heard yelling and boots thudding on the dry ground. The blue sky disappeared as shadows appeared over him. He felt the brush of fabric against his face as Doris pushed everyone away and kneeled next to him. He saw her mouth moving, but he couldn't make out the words.

Don't cry, sweetheart. He tried to reach up his hand to wipe her tears away, but it wouldn't move. *Don't worry, Dory. I'm not dying,* he thought as the darkness enveloped him and he passed out.

Ten

DORIS SAT IN THE CHAIR, holding Buck's hand.

"Madame Mayor?"

She turned to see Sarge standing in the doorway.

"Stop that. I'm still Doris."

"I just stopped by to see how you were faring."

"I'm all right." She turned back to look at Buck. He was so pale lying on the pillows. When she'd seen him fall . . . *she didn't want to think about it.*

"I brought you a cup of coffee."

"Thank you." She didn't move when he placed it on the small side table.

"He'll be all right. He is one of the toughest men I've ever seen."

"Then why hasn't he woken up? It's been four days."

"The body's gotta heal. Just takes a bit of time. He was lucky it didn't hit bone."

"I don't think I can do this."

Sarge pulled up a chair. "Look at me." She couldn't keep her eyes off Buck. She didn't want to move lest he take his final breath and she missed it. "Look. At. Me. Now. Doris."

Blinking slowly, she turned her attention to the older military man.

"He is not dying. I know he's not going to leave you anytime soon. So why don't you go across the street and take a bath, get a hot meal, and spend some time with your babies? You've not left his side since we brought him up here." He removed the grip she had on Buck's hand. "I'll stay here with him. The doc should be back soon. Go on now."

"When are you and Titus leaving?"

"I'll leave in the morning. The wagons arrived that will take the prisoners to Fort Yellowstone. Titus is going to stay here, since the only lawman is out of commission."

"Where is my brother?"

"He's probably across the street, making eyes at that pretty redhead and being fed treats by your daughters." Sarge cupped her elbow and assisted Doris to a standing position. "Do you need me to get someone to escort you home?"

Doris shook her head. "It's just across the street. I'll be fine." She rubbed her hands on her skirt. It was one of her favorite day dresses. Bright blue with black lace. Now it had dark brown stains on it where the blood had dried. There would be no salvaging it.

"Thank you, Sarge. I'll be back."

She leaned over the bed and brushed Buck's dirty hair from his face. After pressing a kiss against his clammy forehead, she nodded to Sarge and headed down the steps from the sheriff's office and living quarters to the main road.

Closing her eyes, she lifted her head to the blue sky and let the sun warm her face.

She prayed as she had been praying for the past four days.

For God's mercy and blessings.

That He protect the town she loved so much.

For His favor to shine on her children.

For a gathering of His angels to protect Buck as he heals.

For him to open his eyes . . . so she could tell him how much she loved him.

Yes, she loved him.

Doris finished her prayer and then walked to the store. Mrs. Burns was behind the counter and greeted her as she came in.

"How's Buck doing?" the reverend's wife asked.

"He hasn't woken up yet. Were you busy today?"

"Mrs. Taylor was looking for the dark chiffon that she saw last week. The green one with the white dots. I wasn't sure where to look, so I told her I'd ask you and then have it cut when she comes back later in the week."

"I'll find it. If it isn't in the back room, then it is probably in the boxes underneath."

"I think Violet was tidying up."

Doris gave a tired chuckle. "Well then, who knows where it might be? But I'll find it. Where are Vi and the children?"

"She took them up for their afternoon naps. They are just precious, Doris."

"I could use an afternoon nap. Are you all right staying for longer?"

Mrs. Burns shooed Doris with her apron. "You go. My husband is making the rounds. He'll be stopping by to see Buck soon and then he'll be over to pick me up. I don't think anyone is coming to relieve me, so I'll just close the store."

"Thank you, Mrs. Burns. I can't believe the town has come together again to help me."

"I can't believe you are now the mayor."

"In a street election, no doubt."

After Sarge had rendered McDougal incapacitated, her position as mayor was all but secured. But there still needed to be an official vote. Voting took place the following day during Sunday worship. Since she needed someone to run against, Ned Sanderson put his name on the ballot, knowing he wouldn't win. Of the thirty-five votes, three went to Ned. The rest went to Doris. The three people that voted for Ned were old farmers who couldn't envision a woman leading the town.

"My husband said the council would get together soon."

"Yes. This week."

"Are you moving into the mayor's home?"

Doris rubbed her forehead. "I honestly don't know. I like my home."

"What about the store? You won't be able to do both."

"I don't know about that either."

Now she had a new set of questions to answer.

"I better get upstairs and get cleaned up."

"You do that, dear. Have a good rest."

Doris heard the bell and saw a few customers enter the store. Not feeling up to company, she slipped behind the curtain covering the hallway and raced up the stairs.

"What are you doing here?" Violet asked as Dory entered the living space at the top of the steps. "Is everything all right?"

"I live here," Doris replied. "I'm tired. I'm dirty. I stink and I'm hungry."

"Well then. Let's feed you, wash you, and put you to bed." Violet gave a little laugh. "You go take a bath first and I'll make you something to eat."

Doris could barely keep her eyes open as she went to the bathroom and filled the large clawfoot tub. Indoor plumbing was a luxury that she was very grateful for. Dropping her clothes on the floor, she crawled into the hot water and quickly scrubbed herself from head to toe until all traces of the unfortunate day were gone.

When she was done, she dried herself and slipped into her bedroom to find a clean day dress. She didn't even bother with the layers of undergarments. She just wanted to lie down and take a nap for an hour, and then she'd head back to see Buck.

"Can I come in? I brought you some tea and a snack," Violet asked, tapping on her door.

"I'm dressed. Come on in." Doris opened the door since she knew Violet had her hands full.

Violet placed a tray on the bed with a pot of tea and a plate filled with soft scrambled eggs, toast, and a broiled tomato. "I wasn't sure what you would like, but I thought this would be easy on your stomach."

"Thank you, dearest. I am hungry."

"Do you want me to brush your hair while you eat?"

"I don't think I have the strength to lift my arms right now."

"Take your plate to your dressing table and eat, and I'll fix your hair."

She simply nodded. Responding was too much of an effort.

As she ate, she looked at Violet in the mirror. Her friend hummed as she gently pulled the brush through Doris's hair. "Were the girls good?"

"They were. They missed you."

"Thank you for watching them."

"It was my pleasure. Titus was . . ." Violet paused and turned away, but not before Doris caught a blush breaking out on her cheeks.

"Titus? Titus was?"

"The girls like their Uncle Titus."

Doris nibbled daintily on a piece of toast. "And their Aunt Violet? Does she like Titus?"

Violet pressed her hands to her cheek. "Oh goodness. Would it bother you if I did?"

Before Doris could respond, there was a ruckus at the bottom of the stairs.

"Doris! Doris, come quickly."

Doris dropped her toast and rushed to the top of the stairs. Looking down, Reverend Burns stood at the bottom, his wife holding onto his arms. Doris felt her heart beating in her chest.

Oh no. She should never have left.

"Is it Buck?"

The Reverend nodded. "Come quickly."

"What's wrong?" Violet called over Doris's shoulder.

"He's waking up."

BUCK'S EYES FLUTTERED OPEN, AND he saw the prettiest sight he could imagine.

Dory was leaning over him. Her hair was a mass of damp curls cascading around her face. Her face was scrubbed clean, and he could see a smattering of freckles across her nose. His ma called them angel kisses.

"Dory," he croaked. His throat was so dry.

"Get him some water," she demanded. She stroked his forehead with cool fingers. "I'm here, darling."

Moving his hand, he found hers pressed against the sheet. Wrapping his fingers around it was an effort, but he'd spend whatever energy he needed just to touch her. "How long have I been sleeping?" He estimated it had been two or three days based on the way his body ached. He knew from previous experiences that bullet wounds took several weeks to heal.

"Four days."

"She never left your side," Titus said from the end of the bed.

"Except for an hour ago, when I ran across the street." Doris gave his hand a squeeze.

"Here's your water, son." Sarge passed Doris a glass, then helped Buck sit up in bed.

Doris guided the glass to his lips as he drank small amounts of water. "Don't go too fast." She gave a half-chuckle. "If I knew all that I had to do was leave to get you to wake up, I would have done it sooner."

Buck leaned back on the pillows. "I'm done." Taking Doris's hand once more, he looked into her eyes. "I don't want you leaving me again."

"I won't," she murmured.

Buck wanted to marry her. "Are you going to marry me now?" He told her he'd wait, but he wasn't expecting to be shot. "I'm not waiting until we are alone again to ask you."

Doris laughed. "If we are going to be married, I cannot have you getting shot again. My nerves won't survive it."

"Yes, ma'am." He'd agree to just about anything if she would let him put his ring on her finger.

"You need to listen to her. She's the mayor of the town now," Titus said.

"Mayor? So, the vote went through?"

"It did," Doris said. "Violet was correct. I'm learning every day. I don't know much about the job, but I'm learning. Daybreak needs someone who loves this town to lead it."

"That it does." He looked around the room at his friends. "Get out of here. I need to talk to my lady."

Titus pulled a watch from his pocket. "Five minutes. That's all. And the door stays open."

"We should go downstairs anyway and check on everyone."

"You'll fill me in later, Titus?" Buck asked as the men headed towards the door.

"Maybe. Right now, you need to rest and if you are lucky, you can kiss my sister."

Doris blushed and turned her head towards Buck's shoulder as he laughed out loud.

Once they were alone in the room, he used two fingers to turn her chin towards him. "What's going on in that pretty head of yours?"

She pretended to pick a piece of lint from the pillow. "Doc says you need to rest for two weeks. No gun slinging, no fights." Her eyes were serious as she looked at him. "I can plan a wedding by then."

"So, you're the mayor now?" She bit her bottom lip. "That changes things a bit."

"In what way?" Her brow furrowed with worry.

"What's going to happen with the mercantile?"

Her shoulders slumped. "I don't know. I may have to sell it. I can't do everything. There's a lot of work to do."

"You just said I cannot do anything for at least two weeks."

"I said you have to rest for two weeks."

"They shot me in my gun arm."

"What does that mean?"

"It means I may not shoot again."

"What?"

"I think you should start looking for a new sheriff, and I'll manage the store."

"Do you have someone in mind?" Her eyes twinkled as she tilted her head.

"Titus," they said together, laughing.

"I love you, Dory." His left hand came up and grasped the back of her head. Pulling her down towards him, he took his time coaxing her bottom lip out with brief kisses that made her laugh. He took advantage of that new opportunity to settle his mouth fully over hers, silently promising her all the good things in life she could ever want, and claiming the widow of Daybreak for his own.

Epilogue

June 1909, Daybreak, Wyoming

DORIS LOOKED DOWN AT HARVEY'S tombstone and dropped a daisy on the grave.

She wasn't angry anymore, and she thanked God every day for releasing her anger and bitterness that Harvey was gone. She praised Him even more for bringing Buck into her life.

Running her finger along the engraved sandstone, she traced the letters that spelled out Harvey's name and the date of his death. The wind brushed against her cheek, as if Harvey were caressing her skin. She closed her eyes, and she could almost hear his laugh. He'd told her she could do anything she wanted to do if God was in her corner. She found difficulty in accepting this. She had never heard of a woman mayor before . . . and now she was one! The first woman mayor in the state of Wyoming!

"I came to say goodbye, Harvey," she whispered. "I'll still come to visit, but it will be different." Doris wasn't sure how long she was staying to chat with Harvey, but she'd committed to settling things within herself before she married Buck. "I know that you're not here anymore. That you are in Heaven with my parents. But I feel a little less crazy standing here and talking to you, than standing in the middle of a room talking to the ceiling. I wonder what it's like where you are, but I don't want to join you anymore. There are too many things to do, and I hope you understand that."

The breeze washed over her once more, and she smiled into it.

"If I'd have known you were going to be this agreeable, I would have come sooner." She brushed a bit of dirt off the headstone. "I'm getting married tomorrow, and I pray you'll understand. Our vows were until death do us part. I realize I'm not dead, Harvey. I'm pretty sure you'd understand that I want to marry the man who will die for me and our girls. I think you'd like him. No. I know you would."

A meadowlark landed on top of the grave marker and tilted its small head to look up at her. Doris giggled, as Harvey loved the meadowlarks. The male meadowlark sang from the fence post to find a mate, its yellow belly showing outward to draw attention until a female finally answered the call. Harvey would tease Doris that she was his female meadowlark.

"I won't ever forget you, my dearest. You were my first love; the father of my children and you were my friend. I just thought I should tell you. Violet says you already know, but I needed to tell you."

Arms wrapped around her waist, and the little bird hopped from the gravestone to the arm that pulled her close. Buck placed a kiss against Doris's hair. "Are you almost done?"

"I am. I was just saying goodbye."

Buck gave her waist a squeeze. "Hi, Harvey," he said

over her shoulder. "I want to say thank you for such a wonderful family. I'll take care of our girls, don't worry about a thing."

The wind rustled once more, and the meadowlark sang again from its perch on the nearby fence. Harvey wasn't a man of many words, but it almost felt like the bird was offering a blessing to them. Linking her hand in Buck's, they made their way back through the small cemetery and out onto the boardwalk in front of the church.

"I love you." She rose on her toes to offer him a brief kiss.

"And I love you."

"I didn't know that you were coming to the cemetery," she said, as he led her back towards the dry goods store.

"I came to tell you that the reward money came in. Titus identified the body of Rufus Grumblatt and let the judge know to wire the money here."

Sarge and Titus had taken Clyde McDougal and several of Rufus's men to Fort Yellowstone to be tried before the federal judge for their crimes against the nation. She didn't know how many of those crimes McDougal was involved in, but Buck thought that the reason Daybreak didn't have a lawman was Clyde's way of protecting his family.

"That's wonderful, Buck. What are you going to do with it?"

"It's enough for me to retire on." He led her across the street.

"Oh. I thought you were going to work at the store once you were feeling better." Doris was crestfallen. Now that he had access to the reward, maybe working at the store would be too mundane. Then she noticed the twinkle in his eye. "What are you thinking?"

"I thought my wife had her eye on a pretty little Victorian house in town."

"The one with the flower garden on the side?"

"Yes, the very one."

"It's rather large. Wouldn't we be better living above the store and saving the money?"

Buck shrugged. "We could. But I thought the house would be the perfect size to raise our children."

"Mary Ellen and Maybelle?"

"Yes. But I would like to have more children. And I thought there wouldn't be enough room for six above the dry goods store."

"Six?" Doris laughed. "You want six children?"

"Well, we need to keep Violet's mind off your brother."

"True."

"A teacher needs students. So, I thought six would be a good number."

"We'll need to rebuild the school."

"We can do that. I think we're rebuilding the town, Madame Mayor."

"We're rebuilding more than that, Buck. We're rebuilding our lives."

THE NEXT DAY, DORY WATCHED as Violet finished adding sprigs of wildflowers to Mary Ellen and Maybelle's braided crowns. There was a tap on the bedroom door, and Mr. Gibbins poked his head in.

"Ladies, if you're ready, it's time." He'd offered to walk her down the aisle since he was the closest thing Doris had to a living father.

"I think we are. Aren't we, sweethearts?"

"Yes, Mama!" they cried in unison.

They were nearly as excited as she was about the

wedding. Buck had been spending time in the evenings playing with them and listening to Mary Ellen's six-year-old woes. He'd even had a chat with Arthur McBee about ways other than hair pulling to get a girl's attention. It had solved one problem, but did nothing to prepare them for the day he brought Mary Ellen a box with a live frog inside.

Kissing her girls on top of their heads, she gave them each a quick squeeze. "Go with Aunt Violet and I'll see you soon." She watched as the girls practically ran out the door. Violet gave her a wink and blew a kiss as she scampered after the young girls.

Gibbins took her arm and walked her from the reverend's house to the small church across the yard. Doris paused for a moment and looked at the headstones on the other side of the churchyard.

"Something on your mind, Dory?" Gibbins asked.

"Do you think Harvey would be upset with me?" she couldn't help but ask, glancing at him.

"Doris, good men love their wives to the best of their ability for their whole lives. They don't ever think about the cost of dying because they fully intend to be here. I think Harvey would be proud of how well you've handled things since he left, and thankful that Buck will step up and love you and those girls for the rest of his life now, too."

"Thank you," she mumbled, blinking rapidly as they continued walking and approached the front steps of the sanctuary. She wiped her tears. There was no need to weep when she ventured through the entrance and into her future.

The front doors opened, and Doris couldn't believe her eyes. The whole town of Daybreak had taken their seats inside the small chapel for the wedding.

Violet and the children walked down to the front of the church where she directed them to sit in the first pew before taking her place at the front.

Then Doris saw him.

Buck stood tall in his dark suit, with Titus standing next to him. Her brother leaned over and whispered something in his ear, and Buck grinned.

Warmth flowed over her as she took careful steps to meet him at the altar.

"You look beautiful," he whispered.

Doris's face hurt from smiling. "You do too," she said, then laughed.

"Dearly Beloved," Reverend Burns began. "We are gathered here today to join Buck Montgomery and Doris Whistler in holy matrimony." Doris knew in that instant everything was going to be as God had intended, from the moment that Rufus had taken Harvey from her. "Who gives this woman away?"

"The community of Daybreak and I do." Mr. Gibbins handed Doris's hand to Buck before returning to his seat at the front of the church with the girls.

It felt like a lifetime had passed since the day of Buck's shooting. Her patience was rewarded when she heard the phrase she had been longing for. "You may now kiss your bride."

With shaky fingers, Buck lifted the thin veil from her face and cupped her cheek. His lips came down to caress hers until her mouth opened under his, and the whoops in the room echoed from the ceiling.

"It is my honor to present to you, Mr. and Mrs. Buck Montgomery," Reverend Burns announced as they pulled apart. The congregation laughed, and soon she was running down the aisle and out the front door to greet the new day with her husband.

Join Christine's newsletter and get a free book:
https://dl.bookfunnel.com/gsk52ipap6

Thank you to Holly Dahle, Vickie Waters, Lou Klassan, MaryEllen Cox, Kerry Rubel, Jeannette Harbottle and Miriam McLean for suggesting the character names in this story. I'm so happy you are part of the Chatters family. -xo Christine

Thank you so much to my Street Team and Beta Readers, Sandy Solara, Sue Krznaric, and Theresa Baer, for helping me chapter by chapter to complete this book in time!

I am so grateful to Heather Moore and Carla Kelly for allowing me to be a part of this anthology and for Laura Ashwood, who recommended me.

Check out more books by Christine

If you enjoyed this story, please check out The Flat River Matchmaker Series, which starts with *The Farmer's Bride.*

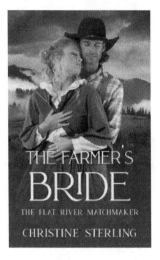

A woman needing a home; a man needing a helpmate and a marriage of convenience that meets both of their needs.

Forced from her home, Elizabet Garrett needs to find a husband, and fast. What she doesn't anticipate is meeting a man who is nothing like she expects, but just might be the answer to her prayers.

Disabled after a farming accident, Peter Arkin lives on his small homestead nursing his demons and a broken dream. Forced to face another harsh winter alone, he sobers up and agrees to allow a local matchmaker to find a suitable mail-order bride. But hurtful rejections for his handicap leaves him reluctant to keep trying.

Does he have enough faith to take one more chance? Will Elizabet be able to see beyond his injury and be the helpmate he needs? Is there a chance that they can find the love and healing they both desperately seek? Find out in this small-town historical romance with a touch of faith.

USA Today bestselling author **Christine Sterling** writes sweet wholesome romance with a touch of faith and humor. She has written over seventy-five historical western and contemporary small-town romances. Most of her stories take place in the plains of Nebraska or Colorado, but she will write wherever there are cowboys needing to find love. Her favorite stories involve tight-knit families, and you will often find character cross-over in many of her books.

She lives on a farm in Pennsylvania with her husband and four dogs and can be found in her garden with a notebook and a cup of tea.

Follow Christine on Amazon.
Follow Christine on Goodreads.
Follow Christine on BookBub.
Join Christine's Chatters Reader Group:
https://www.facebook.com/groups/148223709303134
Get a free book when you sign up for Christine's newsletter.

May I Kiss the Bride

Heather B. Moore

One

VIOLA CONSTANCE DELANY GRIPPED THE handle of her hatbox as the train jerked into motion. The shrill whistle of the engine was almost deafening, but Viola's proper upbringing stopped her from covering her sensitive ears like a four-year-old child.

Steam roared past the window where Viola sat as she watched her beloved San Francisco fade away. Not that she loved the train station or the industrial buildings close to it, but the green hills and weeping willows and scarlet flowers would all be missed. Especially once she arrived at her destination: the desolate, arid, windy, hot, bleak, colorless—did she mention *desolate*?—Wyoming.

"For the summer," Father had told her.

Viola had known better than to argue. Her parents had wrung their hands of her. She was frustrated. They were frustrated. And the only solution to this frustration seemed to be sending Viola to work in a small bakery owned by her mother's sister, Beth Cannon, who, until this past week, had been deemed one of their "unfit relatives."

Oh, Viola had argued. Begged. Even cried real tears.

Nothing had swayed her father. He was a banker, after

all, and oversaw the fortunes of the very wealthy. That took a certain stoicism and a hardy constitution.

So when Viola's engagement of the year had turned out to be the flop of the year, Father refused to let the high society on Nob Hill have the last word about his daughter. As a result, she was heading on a noble mission of mercy to aid her poor dear aunt who ailed with rheumatism.

All right, so the details were accurate, but the sentiment behind them . . . None of this would have even been considered if Percy Johnson III hadn't been discovered visiting a brothel in Chinatown. The papers had been full of the incident. Cartoons had even been drawn.

Mother had written the letter to Percy, signed by Viola, formally breaking off the engagement.

Viola hadn't cried as much as she thought she might over her broken engagement. Oh, she did cry. But after the first day, she decided she felt relieved. She'd started courting Percy because his father was her father's boss. They'd been a natural match. Sure, Percy was handsome and charming, dressed at the height of fashion, had impeccable manners . . . but Viola couldn't say she was head over heels with him.

"Sir! You cannot go into first class!"

The door at the end of the train car thumped open, and Viola snapped her gaze up to see a man stride into the first-class car. A cowboy.

Viola blinked, then blinked again. Was she seeing a mirage? The man looked like he'd stepped off the Cowboy Wear page of a Sears catalog.

"Sir!"

The cowboy kept walking, his gaze shifting from one bench to another. His eyes skimmed over Viola. She tried to make herself small—invisible if possible. The only problem was, she was the single occupant on her bench, and the bench across from her was empty. Every bench throughout the rest of the car had at least two occupants on them.

The cowboy's gaze landed on her again.

Despite the shadow of his brim, his hazel eyes seemed to penetrate right through her.

Viola tried not to stare at the cowboy, who was clearly out of place in a refined first-class compartment. Meals would be served on real chinaware, for heaven's sake.

She turned her chin sharply toward the window, but she saw his reflection there anyway. Tall man wearing a cowboy hat, woven shirt fraying at the collar beneath a rawhide jacket that had seen better days—or years—black trousers, and black boots that needed a good polishing.

Viola wrinkled her nose as he plopped down on the bench across from her. She waited for the unpleasant scent of dirt, hay, or cattle, or all three, to reach her. But she only caught the faint whiff of green grass and fresh air. Not so bad. His long legs would have bumped hers if he'd sat directly across, but he'd at least sat at the far end of the bench, closest to the aisle.

"Sir!" The shouting attendant finally came into view, and Viola took a peek at the blustering man with his twitching mustache and strawberry-red face. "You . . . cannot . . . sit . . . here." His breath heaved. "First-class passengers only, sir."

The entire car had gone silent; even the sounds of the train's wheels chugging upon the tracks seemed to dim.

"You'll thank me later." The cowboy tugged something silver and metal out of his breast pocket. "Sheriff of Mayfair."

Viola stopped breathing for two reasons. First, Mayfair was where her aunt's bakery was, and second, the cowboy took off his hat and looked directly at her.

The man had been imposing with his hat on, striding through first class like he owned the place, but with it off . . .

The eyes she thought were hazel were, in fact, green. A deep green that reminded her of pine trees on a rainy day. And his dark brown hair fell over his forehead like it had just been waiting to escape. But what caught her attention the most was a scar that traveled from the edge of his eyebrow all the way to his ear.

Instead of a disturbing disfigurement of his face, it only made him look stronger, more dangerous, and if possible, more confident.

"Now," the cowboy said in his deep, slow tone, "if this fine lady is all right with me sharing her space until we reach Cheyenne, then I'll stay right here."

The cowboy's eyes remained on her, apparently waiting for her answer. Viola wondered if her throat could open enough to speak at all.

"I, u-uh, y-yes, you may sit there." Her voice stuttered, but at least she got the words out.

The attendant opened his mouth, then closed it again. His gaze locked on the cowboy's impressive scar. "I need to speak with the conductor."

The cowboy set his hat upon his head. "You do that, sir."

The attendant nodded, then took a step back, his throat bobbing up and down. Another step back, then the attendant turned, hands fisted, as he strode off.

People went back to their conversations after the attendant left. Weren't they bothered that this huge cowboy had sat himself down among them without paying for first-class passage?

A moment passed, then two, and Viola kept her gaze on the passing scenery outside the widow. They were moving through a valley, and the green hills were bright and green in the sunlight beneath the wispy, clouded sky. Oh, how she would miss California. She could only hope that the summer in Wyoming would speed by, and when she returned home, all the gossip pages would have moved on.

"Ma'am?"

She turned her head at the cowboy's low rumble.

"Might I store that hatbox for you? It's a long ways to Wyoming."

Viola drew it closer. "No, thank you. I don't want it jostled or stepped on."

The cowboy's expression didn't change, but something shifted in his eyes. Almost imperceptible. Amusement? If he was laughing at her, or thought she was too protective of her hat, then he was an impertinent man.

She rerouted her gaze. She didn't need to worry. From the reflection in the window, he'd tugged down the brim of his hat, stretched his long legs forward, folded his arms, and promptly fell asleep.

Viola waited a good five minutes before she looked over at him again. How could he fall asleep like a fly knocked out of the air and instantly dropped? His breathing deepened and he might have even been snoring softly. It was hard to make out above the noise of the train.

She released a sigh and returned to her window-watching. As each mile passed, she wondered if it was possible to die of boredom working at a bakery in middle of nowhere-Mayfair. Starting to bake cakes and pies, and mixing bread dough from before sunup sounded like a slow death. Didn't her mother, or Aunt Beth, for that matter, know that Viola couldn't cook, or bake, a lick?

She could, she supposed, do things with a lot of instruction. Hopefully, she and Aunt Beth wouldn't butt heads too much, although one small spark of interest flickered in her mind. What had taken Aunt Beth to Wyoming in the first place? And why was it such a family secret?

TWO

REYNOLD CHRISTENSEN WENT BY REY. Sheriff Rey. Or just Rey. Didn't matter to him. But never by Mr. Christensen, which now interrupted a rather sweet dream he was having about a certain blonde woman who'd just baked him a pie and presented it to him at the town social. He'd been hungry when he boarded the train to Cheyenne, but now he was ravenous. He was just about to slice himself a piece of the still-warm dream pie when someone blurted in his ear "Mr. Christensen!"

This was no dream.

He shoved his hat back and opened his eyes to see not one, but two men in uniform glaring at him. One of them was probably the conductor. The other was the red-faced attendant he hadn't the pleasure of formally meeting yet.

Rey gave up on his dream of pie and pulled his legs in, straightening to face his visitors.

"If you've paid first-class passage, then you can stay here," the conductor said, his steely gaze quite impressive. "If not, the attendant will escort you to a different car."

Rey should have known it would come to this; he was just hoping to get a nap in first. He reached into his shirt pocket and drew out a folded and partially crumpled telegram from the governor of Wyoming, then handed it over. Rey had only had to read it once to know that he must answer the call, even though it meant cutting his visit short with his mother. He didn't love leaving his eight-year-old daughter behind in San Francisco, but she'd never forgive him if he ended their vacation so soon.

So, here he was, hopping on this train at the request of the governor.

The conductor's face had gone chalk white at reading the telegram. "Is this true? And how does the governor know?"

Rey lifted a shoulder. "Received threats, I guess. Might not be this exact train though. Other lawmen are jumping on all trains headed to Cheyenne this week. Your luck is getting me." He took the paper back, folded it, and tucked it into his pocket. "Now, if you don't mind, I have sleep to catch up on."

He thought that tugging down the brim of his hat and closing his eyes would be hint enough, but apparently, the conductor had more questions.

"There's only one of you?" the conductor said in a near whisper. "If what's in that telegram is true, we need more than just one lawman to defend—"

Rey snapped his eyes open. "Hush. You want panic from your passengers? Believe me, I can get the job done. Now, you do *your* job, and if—*if* the time comes, I'll do mine."

Still, the conductor and the attendant didn't move.

"Off with you," Rey muttered. "There's nothing to worry about until we cross into Wyoming territory. I'll be wide awake and keeping watch by then." He motioned toward the windows. "First class has the best view. We might not even have to stop the train."

Rey kept his voice low so the other passengers wouldn't overhear—but he knew the woman on the bench across from him clutching that infernal hatbox could hear every word. To her credit, she kept her gaze averted, focused on the passing landscape.

The conductor's eyes were wide, but the attendant's eyes were even wider.

Rey again tugged his brim down and closed his eyes. After a hushed debate, the men left. The sound of their retreating footsteps was a welcome sound—almost like a lullaby melody.

Now, back to his pie dream. But his mind wouldn't settle. He could truly smell food somewhere—likely in the adjacent dining car—so mealtime must be close. He wasn't exactly interested in mingling with any other passengers and engaging in small talk over a meal, so he'd wait until the last possible moment before entering the dining car. Sure enough, a bell jangled and the passengers in the first-class car began to file into the dining car.

If Rey's stomach would just be quiet, he could get a decent nap in, but it wasn't to be.

Because it seemed that everyone in the first-class car, except for the woman with the hatbox, had left. Rey's eyes might have been closed, but it wasn't hard to sense these things. First of all, she'd have to move past his legs and possibly step over them. She did neither.

In fact, she cleared her throat and spoke.

"Mr. Christensen?"

He opened his eyes. He might try to ignore a conductor and an attendant, but he'd never ignore a woman. "Rey."

"Rey?"

"Short for Reynold. I don't stand on ceremony, ma'am, and I don't expect others to."

She blinked. Slow. Her gray eyes reminded him of the stormy Pacific. Bits of her blonde hair had escaped the confines of the hat she wore atop her head, and he wondered what she'd look like with those locks unpinned.

"My name is Viola Delany." She extended her gloved hand across the space between them.

Rey could have been knocked over by a gust of wind. This was no wilting flower of a woman. He shook her hand. Her fingers were delicate, but her grip was firm—something the hatbox was a witness to.

When they released hands, Viola continued, "I didn't mean to eavesdrop, but it was quite impossible not to overhear your conversation with the conductor." She drew in a breath that fluttered the ruffles of her blouse about her neck. "I couldn't help overhearing you mention that something is going to happen when our train crosses into Wyoming territory?"

Her accent was prim. Her voice soft yet forceful as if she were a woman who was used to giving orders and having them carried out. She had to be in her mid-twenties, he guessed, yet she had the directness of a matron much older.

"You heard right, ma'am."

Viola folded her gloved hands atop her hatbox, her gray eyes not leaving his. "What is going to happen?"

Well, her question was direct, he'd give her that. But the question *he* had was whether he'd answer it as directly. He didn't take this woman for someone who'd get hysterical— but no one really knew until one was put into a dire situation. Was her backbone as strong as she acted it was?

"I can't predict the future, ma'am, I'm only here at the request of someone, just in case there is an incident."

Viola's dark brow raised. It was a bit of juxtaposition with her face—to have such light-colored hair along with dark eyebrows. He found it quite pleasing, he decided. She was pretty, yes, but not in the conventional sense.

"I'm not asking you to predict the future," she said in her prim voice. "If that someone is the governor of Wyoming, like you indicated to the conductor, then I'd like to know the contents of your telegram."

Something stuck in Rey's throat, and he coughed. "It's confidential."

Viola's eyes widened slightly, but she said in a completely calm voice, "It wasn't confidential when you handed it to the conductor."

"He's . . ." Rey paused.

"A man?"

"A man in authority," Rey corrected quickly.

Viola's brow raised a titch higher. Then, with precise movements, she set her beloved hatbox onto the bench at her side and gathered her skirts about her. She rose and walked two steps, turned, and sat right next to him.

So close that he caught her scent of something fancy. Perfume, likely. It wasn't displeasing.

Her hand appeared in front of him, palm upturned, fingers extended. "May I read the telegram, Rey?"

Perhaps it was the way his name sounded in her prim tone, but he found himself drawing out the telegram once again and unfolding it.

She took the paper and read through the few short lines. When she raised her gaze to meet his, he saw the expected wariness mixed with surprise in her eyes.

"We're going to be robbed?" she whispered.

"We don't know for sure," Rey said. "The governor received threats and has ordered lawmen on all trains heading into Wyoming this week. We might be lucky. Seems that the governor refused to let one of their friends out of jail, so this group of thieves have threatened revenge."

Viola drew in a slow breath, neatly folded the telegram, and handed it over. She didn't move, didn't speak for a long moment. It was a strange thing for this woman to be sitting so close to him. They somehow breathed in tandem, or maybe Rey was just aware of her every inhale, exhale, and the way her fingers interlocked as they sat upon her lap.

"What's your prediction, Rey?"

"Truth?"

"Truth."

"This train has a first-class car, which means more wealth packed into suitcases." He paused and glanced down at her. Viola kept her gaze straightforward. "There's a high chance this train will be robbed tomorrow morning by dawn."

Her intake of breath was sharp, but still, she didn't move. "And you're going to stop it how?"

"By shooting first."

She turned to look at him then, her chin lifting, her gray eyes flickering to his. "You think you can hold off a posse of train robbers by yourself?"

"I don't have a choice. Unless you want to take over one of my pistols. Would you shoot a man, Viola?"

Three

VIOLA HADN'T PLANNED ON SLEEPING; in fact, she'd highly doubted she'd be able to manage it, but somehow she opened her eyes in the middle of the night. The sleeping cabin was pitch-black—save for the swath of stars through the window. She'd purposely kept the curtains open since she wanted to see the train robbers if they happened to be riding horses alongside the train.

She had to know when to duck.

Which is what the sheriff had told her to do. When she'd confirmed that, no, she didn't know how to shoot a pistol, and, no, she wasn't willing to kill a man, he'd told her that she should plan on hiding beneath her sleeping bunk if the train was forced to stop. At the very least, stay below all windows if shooting started.

Well. It was quite a wonder that she fell asleep at all.

The train hadn't slowed, and the steady chugging of the wheels upon steel rails hadn't changed. So what had awakened her?

Pulling her robe about her dress, she climbed off the sleeping bunk and stepped up to the window. She had decided not to change into her night clothes. If she were going to be robbed, it wouldn't be in her nightgown.

The stars raced by and the moon seemed to bobble a bit.

Were they in Wyoming territory yet?

She looked toward her closed door and wondered about the sheriff. Was he awake, watching and waiting like he said he'd be? What if he'd fallen asleep and didn't see the train robbers until it was too late? What was his plan? To stick his arm out a window and start shooting? Again her mind returned to the possibility of him falling asleep and then all havoc breaking loose.

There was only one thing to do.

Find him and make sure he was ready for his job.

Viola tied her sash about her robe, securing it closed, then she opened the compartment door. All of the other doors in the sleeping car were closed, and everything seemed quiet and peaceful.

She moved along the corridor, the floor rumbling beneath her. Once she reached the dining car, she scanned the place, only to find it empty. She headed toward the lounge with the benches where she'd first met Rey. The gaslights had been turned off, so it took her a minute to adjust to the darkened interior.

Rey sat in the same location she'd left him. He wasn't stretched out though, with his hat pulled low. No, he was leaning forward, elbows on knees, as he studied the window. Through the window, the sky had lightened from a deep black to a murky gray. She guessed it would be some time before the sun rose, but the landscape was taking shape and form.

"You're safer in your sleeping cabin, Miss Delany," Rey's voice rumbled in the near darkness.

She shouldn't be surprised he'd heard her come in, but

she flinched all the same at the sound of his voice. She walked to the bench and sat across from him. "See anything?"

He shifted his gaze to her, but she couldn't see much of his expression on his shadowed face.

"Nothing yet, but that doesn't mean nothing's out there."

His words sent a cool chill through her. He'd shed his rawhide jacket, and it sat on the bench next to him. This allowed her to see the two pistols in a holster strapped to his hips.

She turned to look out the same window he was watching. She couldn't make out anything unusual, apart from fields of grass and groups of trees. She couldn't even see roads or houses. Eventually, the gray gloom softened and pinked. The sun moved closer to pushing over the western horizon, and Viola began to make out more details. The pale green of sagebrush. The deeper green of summer leaves on trees. The stretches of yellow-green grass blowing in the wind.

Suddenly Rey stood and swept off his hat.

Viola popped to her feet. "What is it? Did you see them?"

His eyes landed on her for an instant. "Saw something. Hold my hat."

She grasped his hat with both hands and stared as he slid not one, but two pistols from his holster belt. He didn't check to see if they were loaded, which meant he'd already loaded them.

"Rey," she said as he stepped away from the bench. "Can I . . . help?"

A small grimace appeared on his face. "Keep my hat safe."

Was that all? Not that she could manage a pistol, but surely . . . maybe she could alert the passengers? "What if—"

"Get back in your cabin," he cut in. "Stay hidden. And if you're a praying woman, I wouldn't mind a good word put in for me."

Viola opened her mouth to respond, but Rey strode toward the door that connected to the next car. He tugged it open, stepped through, then closed it firmly behind him.

Something in her belly tugged and she had the sudden urge to hurry after him. Surely she could do more than pray. Instead, she rushed to the window. What had he seen? And was the train slowing?

Her heart hammered its way up her throat as her gaze moved across the landscape speeding past. Grass, sagebrush, trees, a river . . . Then she saw it. Or more accurately, *them.*

Five riders atop horses. The beasts were charging ahead of the train as if in a race to the next train depot. But there was no train depot coming up, and the horses were sprinting, their eyes wide, their mouths open as if in a scream. The riders had whips and they were using them generously on the horses' flanks.

Viola hated all five men on the spot. First, they dared to rob this train and steal from hardworking folks, and second, they were terrorizing their horses. Viola didn't know what she'd do if they boarded the train and demanded valuables, but she wouldn't be hiding underneath any bunk. She'd give them a piece of her mind.

Gripping Rey's hat in one hand, she scooped up his jacket with her other hand. Then she marched to the connecting door. Opening it, she found another corridor leading to another car. Rey must have gone through there. So she did too.

The next car was a storage car. Filled with crates and trunks. The windows were high and let in very little light, but she continued through and opened the next door. The engine was louder now, and she must be getting closer to the front of the train. She entered the next car to find it was another storage car. Still, no Rey. How far had he gone?

She was about to open the next door when the train lurched, accompanied by a high-pitched screech. Viola lost her balance and fell next to one of the crates. Were they completely stopping? And did that mean Rey hadn't been able to stop the train robbery?

Were the robbers climbing aboard even now? Had they shot Rey?

Viola's stomach soured as panic raced through her. She gripped the nearby crate to haul herself up, but before she could stand, the door burst open in front of her. The tall figure coming through the door could have been anyone. The morning sunlight behind the man obscured his features, but when he spoke, there was no doubt it was the cowboy. Alive.

"Ms. Delany?" he barked. "What are you doing here? I thought I told you to stay in your cabin."

Relief shot through her so swiftly, she had to keep ahold of the crate. "I wanted to check on you."

He didn't seem amused. In fact, his face was pale, and perspiration stood out on his forehead. That's when she noticed. Blood soaked his shirt. It seemed to be everywhere. One of his hands gripped his stomach while the other hand still held a pistol.

Viola's knees gave out and she again slid to the ground. This time, everything went black.

Four

"I'M FINE," REY INSISTED AS the town doctor poked at the skin surrounding the stitches on the side of his torso. "But that cattle prod is cold."

Doc Smithson chuckled. "If this was a cattle prod, you'd be on the other side of the room by now." He held up the small, blunt metal instrument.

All right, so it was only about five inches long, but Rey was bruised and the skin was tender.

"If this really hurts," the doc mused, "it might be infected."

"It does hurt, but not a lot," Rey said with a sigh. "I'm just complaining."

Another grin from Doc Smithson. His red mustache was trimmed as thin as a pencil and his eyebrows as bushy as a runaway caterpillar. The man was a skilled physician, but he had a bit of an unsympathetic way about him.

Case in point, he slathered on some red medicine, slapped a bandage over Rey's stitches, then used a large amount of tape to close every seam possible. Which would hurt like stepping on hot coals when Rey had to peel it off.

"That bandage isn't going anywhere," Rey said in a dry

tone. "Even if I was a bull rider, I think it would stay in place."

Doc's hand came down on Rey's shoulder, and he hid a wince. Things were bruised on his body that had never been bruised before. The shoot-out with the train robbers had thankfully been short and effective. Rey had yet to hear if any of the five robbers had been fatally wounded. He knew he'd gotten a good shot at three of them.

The riders had sped away before Rey could get a good look. Besides, there was only so much time he wanted to spend on the roof of a speeding train. He knew he'd been shot, but the pain didn't kick in until he was trying to climb down the car and land on the platform in one piece. He'd ordered the open-mouthed engineer to speed up the train again.

Then Rey had been intent on heading back to the lounge car and seeking out a doctor when he'd opened the first compartment door to find Viola. On the ground.

Panic had nearly gutted him. Had she been shot by a stray bullet? It seemed impossible, yet . . . why had she been on the ground? But before he could demand more answers, she'd gone whiter than a sheet blowing in the summer wind and fainted.

After that, he couldn't exactly account for events. Someone—likely the conductor because of the name "Mr. Christensen" repeated over and over—came into the train car. And that's when Rey had passed out. From lack of blood, it seemed.

When Rey had next opened his eyes, he was splayed out on a surgeon's table in Cheyenne, and Ms. Delany was nowhere to be seen.

He wondered what had happened to her. No one seemed to know. Not the train station master he'd gone and questioned after he could walk more than a couple of feet. Not the ladies at the women's auxiliary who knew everything that went on in Cheyenne. And not Mr. Baxter, who owned the most reputable hotel in town.

So, today, with hope gone of finding out if Ms. Delany had recovered from her own malaise, he was headed back to Mayfair. They were missing a sheriff, after all.

Because the doc had ordered him not to ride a horse for another week, Rey hired a driver to take him back home in a carriage. As he settled onto the bench, he was finally able to clear his mind and think about things that didn't have to do with shoot-outs, stitches, or the mysterious Ms. Delany. She could be in another state for all he knew. She'd never said what her final destination was.

From all accounts, she'd been traveling alone. What did that mean?

Rey shoved those questions away—questions he'd never get answered. He redirected his thoughts to his small ranch and horses and whether Barb and Jeb were doing all right acting as caretakers in his absence. He could at least report back to his daughter about how her favorite horse, Sky, was doing when Rey returned to San Francisco in a couple of weeks.

He relaxed into the seat and enjoyed the small reprieve. He was sure to get an earful from Deputy Thatcher when he showed up at the office. Thatcher was never quiet on any matters, big or small.

"Whoa," the driver of the carriage said, tugging on the horse's reins to slow down the animal.

Rey stuck his head out of the carriage window to see that up ahead, there was a crowd on the boardwalk that ran along Mayfair's Main Street. Other carts and riders had slowed down, and now there seemed to be traffic. In the tiny town of Mayfair.

"What's going on up there?" Rey asked the driver.

"Don't rightly know." The driver pushed his hat back a few inches and mopped his brow with a seen-better-days handkerchief. "The line of people is going to the bakery."

"Must be a two-for-one special?" Rey said, mostly to himself. He'd get out and walk if the carriage was going to be this slow. But his place was a half mile out on the other side of town, and the morning was only getting hotter.

As it was, the carriage practically crawled past the bakery, and Rey peered at the crowd. Interesting that those in line were all men. In this town, the women did the shopping while their fellas worked the ranches. But then again, most women did their own baking. So maybe that's why the men were filling up the line.

"Hello, Sheriff!" a voice called out.

Rey tipped his hat to Mr. Brunson.

"You're back already?" another voice called.

"How are you, Gerald?" Rey said to a hooked-nose man.

Other men in line turned and greeted Rey. He knew them all by name, as a matter-of-fact.

"Looks like y'all have a sweet tooth today?" Rey said to a young man named Wallace.

Wallace laughed, displaying his impressive buckteeth. "Sure do, Sheriff."

The carriage continued on, and Rey had a feeling in his gut that he was missing a vital bit of information. He ran through the men in the line—they were all single—so that made more sense. None of them had wives to bake for them. Must be one whoppin' pastry sale.

The line extended to the next corner, and Rey's eyes about popped out when he saw Thatcher wielding his pistol, confronting a man in a dingy white cowboy hat.

"Hold up," Rey called to the driver. "I'll be getting out

here. Can you drop off my things at my house? I'll spot you a few more dollars."

The driver tugged on the reins, and soon the carriage pulled to a stop. The men in line watched with interest as Rey climbed out, adjusted his hat, and rested his hand on his holster.

"Sheriff." More than one man tipped his hat and nodded in greeting.

Rey kept his gaze on Thatcher. Was it possible that his deputy had gone rogue in his short absence? Was Rey about to witness a gunfight or—heaven forbid—be in the middle of one?

"Thatcher, what's happening?" He strode to his friend and acting sheriff, an older man with a bit of a pot belly, graying handlebar mustache, and with arms as strong as an ox.

Thatcher swung on Rey, gun still pointed.

"Easy," Rey said. "What's going on?"

"Boy, am I glad to see you," Thatcher huffed. His eyes were bloodshot, and Rey hoped the man wasn't hitting the bottle during working hours again. It was tricky to keep law and order in a town where the lawmen themselves were being disorderly.

"This here line isn't supposed to be added to after two p.m.," Thatcher blustered. "I promised Beth I'd make sure there was a cutoff."

Beth Cannon was the baker who ran Main Street Bakery. Been doing it before Rey moved into town. A sweet yet outspoken woman. Had been struggling with arthritis the past year, so she'd hired a couple of girls to help her with the baking in the mornings.

Rey wasn't sure what exact time it was, but he assumed it was now after two, thus the struggle.

"Come on, Thatcher, I got here late on account of my horse going lame," Billy Warner said. "Can't blame me for that. Tell 'im, Sheriff Rey."

"Did everyone run out of food the same day or something?" Rey asked to no one in particular.

"Oh, this man isn't buying anything," Thatcher said, pointing at Billy. "The likes of him are just taking a look." He turned his full attention upon the man. "So, get out of line. No money, no line. After two, no lining up to peek."

Billy scowled, but he shuffled away, hands in his grimy pockets.

"Thatcher," Rey said, "put your gun away and tell me what all this fuss is. Looks like a parade, but I don't see any silver marching band or dancing ponies."

Thatcher grumbled something incoherent, but he holstered his pistol. "It's Beth's niece. Venice, or Vanna, or something. She's a looker, and all the men want to get a look."

Rey frowned. "I didn't know Beth had a niece."

"None of us did," Thatcher said. "But she's the talk of the town. Hair the color of summer wheat—"

"Eyes like a thundercloud," Gerald said from somewhere down the line. "The kind of storm you want to get caught in."

"Smile that lights up the whole darn sky," Wallace added.

The men in the line all nodded, and that's when Rey saw it. Each one of these unmarried men had that *look* in their eyes. Like they'd been dumbstruck. Some might call it lovestruck.

"Well, I'll be. Sounds like an angel," Rey said through gritted teeth.

"Oh, she's an angel, all right," Mr. Brunson chimed in. "Sang in the church choir yesterday, and I could have sworn the birds stopped singing outside to listen."

"My heart may never recover," Jeffrey said, clutching said heart. Jeffrey was a reed-thin man who could normally be found at the saloon this time of day. He looked the most sober Rey had ever seen him, wearing a clean button-down shirt.

Rey couldn't deny that his curiosity was piqued, but he also knew any single, unmarried, half-pretty woman in Mayfair would get plenty of attention. He wasn't a regular churchgoing man, so he'd just have to skip out on hearing angels sing. He just hoped that Beth Cannon was getting the rest she needed, because from Rey's viewpoint, standing on the crowded boardwalk, the bakery was busier than ever.

He turned to Thatcher. "How long has this been going on?"

Thatcher paused a moment and counted on his stumpy fingers. "This is day five. The niece arrived one day, and by the second day, the lines were forming. Beth had to take me aside, and we set up some ground rules."

Rey nodded at this. Made sense. But as he scanned the men in line, bouncing in their cowboy boots, mopping their foreheads and necks in the heat, cracking a few nervous jokes, Rey decided that the line was indecent. The bakery wasn't a circus peep show. Beth Cannon was one of the most respectable women in town—not respectable in the churchgoing sense—but respectable because she was one of the original homesteaders and was, as far as he knew, the oldest citizen of Mayfair.

"I'm the end of the line," he announced. "Thatcher, you go ahead and get yourself a cold drink."

"Thank you, sir," Thatcher said with an eager nod and hurried off, giving out a couple of glares at loitering men for good measure.

Might as well see what all the fuss was about, Rey

decided, and whether he needed to put more measures into place to keep Beth Cannon's niece away from so many prying eyes and gossiping men.

Five

VIOLA DIDN'T MIND THE GAWKING, not exactly. She'd found it charming the first couple of days. The bakery had also sold clean out by lunchtime. And even though the morning gals whom Aunt Beth had hired were making almost double the breads and pastries, they were still selling out.

"Viola! Come here!"

Viola sighed and wiped her floured hands on her apron. She'd been assigned pie duty, which she decided she liked over the kneading of bread dough or dipping donuts into hot fry oil. She headed around the back counter where she worked with a view of the storefront and joined Aunt Beth at the register.

"This key is stuck."

Again.

Aunt Beth wasn't exactly a complainer, Viola had been quick to realize, but when she was having a bad day, she had zero patience. Like today. Her white peppered hair resembled a bird's nest upon her head, and the rolls of her fleshy neck shone with perspiration. Summer afternoon in Wyoming in the middle of a bakery was not for the infirm.

"Here." Viola took ahold of the offending key and wriggled it to the left. The key popped back up. "Now try."

Beth continued fanning her face with an apple-filling-splotched fan. With her free hand, she poked at the key. A number 8 typed out. "That'll be eight cents, LeRoy."

LeRoy, a man with more freckles than a spotted dog, grinned. "Thank 'ee, ma'am. Here's a dime. Keep the change." He winked directly at Viola.

"Move on over," a man behind him demanded. The man clutched a crumpled hat in his hand, his clear blue eyes focused on Viola.

She smiled politely at him, then returned to the pie counter.

"Hey, why can't the keys stick when I'm being helped?" the man complained when Beth rang up his order of one apple tart without any trouble.

Viola hid both a smile and a sigh. As amusing as all these male patrons were, who happened to be single, available men, at some point everyone needed to do something other than purchase baked goods. Didn't they have cows to feed and horses to ride? This was the middle-of-nowhere Wyoming, after all.

"You'll be the belle of the barn dance if you go." Sidney sidled next to Viola.

The girl, a couple of years younger than Viola, had a gap-toothed smile and eyelashes that went on forever.

"Oh, I don't think I'm going," Viola said, picking up from their earlier conversation that felt like hours ago. A *barn* dance? In the hay, with everyone stomping around in cowboy boots? Sounded dreadful. Yes, Viola was helping out her aunt at her bakery, and she did enjoy singing in the church choir—mostly to please Mother though, who'd told Viola to get her aunt to church, "To save her soul."

Besides, Viola hadn't taken waltz lessons in order to dance with any of the men staring at her now with their moon eyes and tobacco-stained teeth. Not every cowboy chewed and spit, that she knew, since the sheriff from the train hadn't. At least not on the train . . . but his teeth had been a nice, clean white too.

Yes, she'd noticed.

Not that she'd thought about him much. Only to wish him well and a full recovery in her private thoughts. She'd heard the rumors of him recovering in Cheyenne after a surgery to remove the bullet. Which must have been why he'd been bleeding so much and why she'd fainted . . . Who knew she fainted at the sight of blood? It wasn't like she'd ever been witness to a train robbery before.

If she did see him again, and that was *if* . . . she'd ask politely after his well-being and hope that he'd forgotten how she was utterly useless in a dire situation. Instead of running for help, she'd slid to the ground like a discarded rag doll. Her heart still thundered when she thought about that morning.

Since arriving in Mayfair, she'd learned that not only was Rey the sheriff of this small place, but he was *the* man. The two shopgirls were half in love with him. She'd learned more about Sheriff Rey in five days than she knew about her ex-fiancé after over five months of courting.

Another reason she was anxious about their first encounter. Rey was a widower. Had been married to the love of his life—according to the shopgirls Sidney and Della—and he had a daughter from the union. "Looks just like her mama. Poor Sheriff. Every time he looks at his child, he grieves over his dead wife."

That logic sounded a bit extreme, but what did Viola know about widowers, or cowboys, for that matter?

"I'll have one of those peach pies," a male voice droned from the front counter. "And I'll pay an extra dollar if the miss can bring it to me herself."

Viola snapped her gaze up.

The man in question was named Gerald—he'd introduced himself to her each day. And each day, his words became more brazen. Obnoxious, even. Did he know that the end of his rather large nose twitched when he spoke?

Usually, Aunt Beth chased off such comments, but she looked over at Viola *expectantly.*

"What?" she mouthed, but Beth's painted-on brows only raised.

In fact, the entire shop of men in line waiting their turn were looking at her. If she did this for an extra dollar, what might tomorrow bring? What choice did she have though? A dollar was a dollar.

She pasted on a smile, then picked up the peach pie nearest to her. Holding it aloft, she walked around the counter and set it down in front of Gerald. "Have a nice day, sir."

Without waiting for a reply, she turned and walked back to the pie counter.

"Thank you, miss," Gerald said, his voice having an added squeak to it.

"I want that too," the next man in line said.

His name started with a W, Viola remembered. She quickly averted her gaze. Making eye contact with him might only encourage him to be more brazen.

"I want the cherry pie, and I'll pay *two* extra dollars if the miss brings me the pie *and* kisses me on the cheek."

Laughter roared through the bakery, and Viola's cheeks flamed. She kept her gaze on the crust she'd been rolling out. Anger churned in her stomach, spinning hot. Aunt Beth had better kick the man out, or she would.

Aunt Beth did no such thing because another voice boomed over the laughter. "That's enough. No special favors. Wallace, you're out of here, and don't come back."

Viola *knew* that voice. *No. No. No.* Not here—not like this. When her hair probably matched the bird's nest of Aunt Beth's. Not to mention being covered in flour and bits of dried pie crust. She dragged her gaze upward to see Wallace sputter. Red-faced, he spun toward the man who'd dared issued the orders.

Viola already knew who'd walked into the bakery.

All laughter died, and only one set of boots walking forward could be heard.

She couldn't keep her gaze off the tall cowboy. His size made the bakery shrink like a dollhouse. His eyes were the same—green beneath the cowboy hat he'd asked her to hold. He wasn't wearing his leather jacket, but his shoulders filled out the denim shirt he wore just as nicely. Viola's gaze skated to his torso, seeing a bulk probably from bandaging, and she wondered how his injury was healing. He could obviously walk and order people out of the bakery . . . if that was any indication.

When she'd first seen him, he'd been shaved, and now dark whiskers outlined his jaw. Coupled with his scar, he looked more like an outlaw than an honorable sheriff. In this moment, Viola saw him as Sidney and Della must—the handsome, strong, tragic widower. A man of authority and stoicism. Honorable to the bone. Respected by all.

"Sheriff?" Wallace blubbered. "I-I'm sorry. I didn't mean—"

Rey's hand clamped on to the smaller man's shoulder. "*Out.*"

Wallace nodded, his face even redder. He pushed through the other men, nearly stumbling in the process.

When he made it out the door, Rey set a hand on his holstered gun.

"Any other knuckleheads want to be banned from Beth Cannon's bakery?"

Heads shook, and *no's* were mumbled.

Rey's gaze swept those standing in the bakery line, lingering on a couple of the men. Then he turned to face Aunt Beth. "I hear you have a niece in town helping out."

Beth's smile curved wide. "That's right. She's all the way from San Francisco. Welcome back yourself, Sheriff. Heard *you* got shot saving a train full of people. Looks like you're up and in fine form now."

"Missed my heart by a mile," Rey's deep voice rumbled.

Something flipped in Viola's stomach. Oh, who was she fooling? Everything inside her was flipping and flopping like a fish on the San Francisco wharf.

Because right then, Sheriff Reynold Christensen finally looked at her.

Six

IF SOMEONE HAD TOLD REY last week that looking at a woman could take a man's breath away, he would have laughed and said those were words of a fanciful poet. Not that Rey was an expert in poetry, but he heard the way men talked about women. He also knew the way men fought over women. And he remembered what it felt like to love a woman with your whole being so that you'd do anything for her. Even if it took mortgaging the ranch to send away for some fancy city doctor, only to have the miracle cure fail.

He also knew that his heart, which had been doing just fine—healing slowly and being content with his life as sheriff, dad to one little girl, and keeping law and order in Mayfair—had suddenly been jolted. Yet there was no lightning coming through the bakery roof that he knew of.

But that's what felt like had happened when he turned his gaze upon Beth Cannon's niece. Who happened to be the woman from the train. *Miss Viola Delany* herself. Risen from the train-car floor and restored to her senses. Changed from her prim white blouse of ruffles. Now she wore a sky-blue dress and light pink apron, dusted with flour. Gone was her smart hat angled over her gray eyes. The stormy Pacific was clear in her gaze now, her face framed by wisps of blonde hair that had escaped the bun tied at the nape of her neck.

Her dark brows and dark lashes were just as he remembered them though. Nothing had changed there. But her cheeks were flushed pink, likely with the heat of the ovens and certainly had nothing to do with seeing him—a jaded cowboy who'd been through a thing or two in life.

It was probably a good thing that Viola Delany spoke first, because for the first time in his life, Rey had no words. Maybe the proverbial cat had really stolen his tongue and buried it beneath a mound of hay in the farthest reaches of a barn somewhere.

"Sheriff Rey." Viola's cool gray eyes skated over his person as if she could see the outline of his tighter-than-a-lasso bandaging. "You have recovered. The whole town has been praying for you."

Rey's throat bobbed. Now, why didn't this woman seem surprised to see him? And how did she know what the whole town was doing? This was *his* town. Wait . . . He'd told her where he was from, and she hadn't returned the favor, which meant she'd known all along they'd run into each other.

He took off his hat. First, because he felt like he was standing in front of a blacksmith's kiln, and second, because it gave him another moment to collect his thoughts. But he reached up too fast for his hat—clean forgetting about his healing wound—and hissed out a wince.

"Sheriff, you should sit down," Beth said at the same time Viola's softer voice added, "You don't look so good, sir."

Oh no. Don't faint now. You're the sheriff here. To protect and defend. Not to wilt and be coddled. These thoughts ran through his mind faster than the imaginary lightning that had struck him earlier, but thankfully, someone had the foresight to scoot a chair behind him and sit his rear down.

Rey didn't faint after all.

"You all right, Sheriff?" Had Thatcher's voice always been that loud?

Where'd he come from anyway? Sure enough, the man was leaning over him, his breath stinking of whisky. They were going to have a serious talk later.

"I'm fine," Rey mustered, but his thoughts were spinning faster than a dust devil, and his throat felt like he'd swallowed his grandpa's pipe smoke.

"Take him back to the nook under the stairs. There's a bed there."

Beth Cannon had spoken. Her voice was an octave too high, but that wasn't as irritating as the several pair of hands forcing him to his feet, supporting him, and propelling him through the bakery, past the hotter-than-Hades ovens, and into a closet.

Well, it wasn't a closet, but close enough.

He heard other voices. Women. Men. All fussing over him.

"I'm fine," he repeated, but no one paid him attention.

Voices rose and fell, blended together, until blessedly, mercifully, there was only one.

Viola.

"Try this, Sheriff Rey." Her voice was soft, still prim, yes, but he really didn't mind that.

He dragged his eyes open. The light was dimmer in the nook under the stairs. And he was on a small bed that would better fit his daughter than his own six-foot-something frame. But he wasn't in a position, or of the mind, to point that out right now.

Viola sat next to him, perched on a small slice of

247

mattress, which meant that her hip was nestled against his hip. *Well.* He'd process that later.

Right now, she held out what looked like a cool glass of something, and his throat was practically screaming for it.

He reached for the glass and their fingers brushed. Her hand was warm and soft—just as a woman's should be—so there was no surprise there. If he could command his pulse to calm down, he would have, but his pulse wasn't listening.

He drained the cool glass of lemonade, then handed the empty glass back to Viola. "Thank you, ma'am."

"You don't need to be so formal with me, Sheriff. Ma'am is for someone who is older than you or a stranger." She tilted her head. "You almost fainted."

"No . . . I was just hot. The bakery is an inferno."

The edges of her mouth lifted, and the gray of her eyes lightened. He didn't think he fully appreciated her smile on the train. Now he was making amends.

"Bakeries are generally warm, and it's summer in Wyoming."

"Both of those facts are true." His heart did a double thump when her smile grew. "You seem to work fine in the heat. Rolling out pie dough and putting up with gawking men."

Her dark lashes lowered, and her hands curled around the empty glass. "I don't mind the heat. It doesn't make me faint. Not like seeing a man covered in blood."

Her cheeks were definitely pink, as was that mouth of hers.

"I'm sorry if I startled you."

Viola's gaze lifted again, her gray eyes steady. "When? In the bakery just now, or on the train?"

He had to think about that for a moment. "Both?"

Another smile stole across her pretty features, and he

knew that a moment or two longer of this smiling back and forth might lead to something that he'd definitely regret later.

"Apology accepted, sir."

"Rey."

She blinked. "Rey."

"That's better." He winked, and he had no idea how in high heaven he thought he could wink at her. Too late to take it back now. "Now, if you don't mind, I need to make sure all those men out there are on their way outside with their purchases. Don't need the womenfolk harassed. This here is a business establishment."

Viola Delany's hand pressed against his chest. If he wasn't well and stuck before, now he truly was. "You're not moving an inch until the doctor comes and looks you over."

This was a voice he hadn't heard before. A commanding voice with plenty of authority. A voice that maybe a mother would use on a child, or a woman would use on a husband.

"I didn't know you had a bossy side, Viola."

Her brows lifted a fraction. "There's a lot you don't know about me, Rey."

Was it possible to stare at a woman too long? What would the poets have to say about that?

"Now, let me see that bandage of yours," Viola continued in her bossy voice. "Unless you have a hunchback on the side of your torso, it seems you have enough bandaging to outfit the Red Cross for a month. You only got shot once, right?"

Rey grinned. "Right."

"And the scar on the side of your face? Is that from another fight with train robbers?"

He touched the scar on his face. "Nothing so impressive. Fell off a horse."

"Ah." When Viola took it upon herself to unbutton his shirt, he wasn't sure if perhaps he had fainted and was now dreaming a dream he probably shouldn't be dreaming.

Yet this was no dream, although it might be a slice of heaven. Her warm, delicate fingers worked deftly, only brushing against his skin once or twice.

"Ah." Viola's gray eyes gave nothing away, unless he counted the purse of her lips. "Just as I thought. No wonder you almost fainted. Who bandaged you up?"

"Doc Smithson."

"Whoever Smithson is, there's no need to be a zealot about medical care and bring a man close to fainting." She began to pick at the edge of the bandaging tape. "I think he's rearranged your ribs in the process."

Rey sucked in a breath as Viola peeled off one edge of the bandaging. It was both painful and relieving. The tightness loosened but left behind the burn of sore skin atop of deep bruising.

"Sorry, I'll be quick," Viola murmured.

He sucked in another breath and focused on her face, her hair, her eyelashes. Anything but the pain of the bandage tape being ripped off his skin. "Tell me," he rasped. "Where'd you learn to administer medical care? You don't seem to care for blood."

Her gaze flicked to his, then back to her task. "Volunteered at the Red Cross a few times. Never treated a real patient though. Mostly cut bandage strips and rolled them up."

She tugged a particularly tight section, and he winced, then locked down his jaw to keep from groaning.

"There." She wadded up the discarded bandaging and set it aside. "Now, let's take a look."

He didn't know what he expected, but it wasn't her

prodding the area around his stitches. Her touch was light, though, and although there was a bit of an ache, he didn't mind her soft fingers on his skin.

"The swelling is down," Viola pronounced. "And the bruising is changing color. All good signs." Her eyes lifted to his face. "You'll live, Sheriff Rey."

He shouldn't laugh because truthfully, it hurt, but he laughed anyway. "You did a lot more than cut bandage strips and roll them up. Are you a secret nurse-in-training? You fainted when I walked into the train car, yet you have no qualms now?"

When her cheeks bloomed pink, he knew he'd struck a chord somewhere, but he wasn't sure what it was.

"I guess I'm not in shock over your potential death anymore." She moved her hands to her lap as if something on his torso had burned her. "Besides, my father would never let me become a nurse. I've just read a few books about medicine and medical care, that's all."

Her words might be nonchalant, modest, even, but Rey sensed that behind this woman's prim demeanor was a dream of something beyond what her life was in San Francisco.

"What would your father think if you were professionally trained?"

Viola lifted a hand and tucked a stray lock of hair behind her ear. "That's not possible for a woman like me. My parents will find me a husband, one who's properly rich. I'll have two children, a boy and a girl. The boy will go into law or banking. The girl will be beautiful and marry another rich man. And when I'm in my rocking chair, tapping away my final days, wanting to be a nurse will seem like a faded dream of a girl I once knew."

Rey gazed at her for a long moment, and she gazed right back.

"Well, if you want my opinion, Viola Delany, you can have the husband and two children, plus follow your dream. It's 1905, ma'am."

Seven

Viola had no idea why she'd gone and told Sheriff Rey things that she hadn't even told her own mother. When she once brought up nursing school to her father, he'd blustered and ranted, firmly putting her back into the place where she was expected to exist. And the months and years had passed. Now she was twenty-seven and working in a tiny bakery for an aunt.

"You look like him, you know," Aunt Beth said as she perched on the wooden stool in front of the shop register.

Viola paused in peeling the bushel of peaches she'd been working on for the past hour. Sidney was peeling apples, and Della was sweeping the floor.

"Who?" Viola's mind had been on Sheriff Rey an inordinate amount of the time since his near fainting in the shop six days ago. He was much recovered now, or at least he seemed to be when he stopped in each day at 2:00 to shoo men out of the shop and make sure there were no troublemakers.

He merely tipped his hat at Viola, greeted her aunt and asked if there was anything she needed, then strode out.

Oh, she'd seen him about town. And if they made eye contact, he'd nod and tip his hat.

Viola was about ready to knock that hat off of his head, if only to get him to say more than a two-word greeting.

"Your father," Aunt Beth continued. "You remind me of him."

Viola couldn't have been more surprised. People always told her she looked like her mother—same blonde hair, similar height, and curvy build.

"You have his eyes." Aunt Beth looked toward the windows, her painted brows pinched.

Viola wouldn't say her aunt looked exactly like her mother—but there were plenty of similarities between the two sisters.

Now Viola blinked. She supposed her eyes were the same color as her father's, but no one else had really commented on that.

"You have his forthrightness and stubbornness," Aunt Beth continued as if she were performing a monologue with an audience of three.

Della had stopped sweeping, and Sidney had stopped peeling apples.

"I'm not sure that's a compliment," Viola teased, because Aunt Beth sounded bleak, subdued, and something prickled at the back of Viola's neck. What had brought all of this on?

Aunt Beth pushed herself up from the stool, then rubbed her hands as if they ached, which they probably did.

"Do you want me to put on that cream for you?" Viola offered.

"That would be nice, dear," Aunt Beth said in a tone that sounded like she was thinking of something else entirely. "Do you think you girls can run the shop today? I'm quite tired."

Viola's mouth nearly dropped open, but she nodded anyway. "Of course."

"Can I run the register?" Sidney asked in a hopeful tone.

"I don't care who does it, but there must be a double count upon closing."

"Yes, Miss Cannon." Sidney gave Della a triumphant glance.

Della's scowl lasted only a second, then she returned to sweeping.

"Come, Viola," Aunt Beth said.

Viola followed her aunt up the stairs to the second floor, where she lived in a suite of rooms that included a tiny kitchenette, a sofa by the window, and two narrow beds in the bedroom.

When Aunt Beth settled on the sofa, she drew an afghan about her legs even though it was plenty warm.

Should Viola be worried even more now? She fetched the cream that the town doctor had said would ease the swelling and aching in her aunt's hands. Sitting next to her, Viola began to rub the cream in.

"You have a nice touch," Aunt Beth said in that faraway voice again. "You know, I wanted to go into nursing too."

Viola's mouth did drop open then. "You—you heard what I said to Sheriff Rey last week?"

Aunt Beth's mouth curved into a smile. "Yes, of course. I couldn't leave my niece alone with a virile and unmarried man. Doesn't matter how ill he might be. Wouldn't be proper."

"The sheriff would never—" Viola cleared her throat. "He's an honorable man, but I'm sure I don't need to tell you that." She was still trying to remember their conversation exactly and what Aunt Beth might have overheard.

"He's been keeping an eye on you, you know," Aunt Beth said.

"On *me*?" Viola rubbed her aunt's wrist a little harder than she'd intended to. When she realized it, she softened her touch. "He's looking out for all of us in the shop. It's his job."

Aunt Beth chuckled at this, then she drew her hands back. "Viola, you're a grown woman, but sometimes I think you only see what you want to see—and ignore what's right in front of you."

Heat climbed up Viola's neck. "I see what's in front of me—"

But Aunt Beth held up her hand. "Now, sometimes it's better to listen, especially to a woman who has years more experience than you in matters between men and women."

Viola could only stare at her aunt. Beth had never been married or engaged, never had children . . . Had she a string of lovers in the past no one in the family knew about? It was hard to imagine her wild-haired aunt, in her plain cotton dresses and perpetual flour underneath her fingernails, with extensive experience with men.

"I'm listening," Viola said, because what else could she say? She was more curious and eager than a mouse searching for crumbs in winter.

"When your mother and I were young women, she was always considered the pretty one. The bright, sparkly, outgoing Cannon sister. I was the studious one. Always reading. Always dreaming of far-off places. I read everything. Medical books in which I imagined myself as a nurse. Legal books in which I wondered if I could follow in Clara Foltz's shoes and become a female lawyer in California. Science books in which I dreamed of joining a safari trip to the African continent."

Viola had read books about all those subjects, but she'd always known she was meant to follow in her mother's footsteps and become a society miss. "So nursing was one of the things you considered?"

"Yes," Aunt Beth said. "I wasn't like you—invested in it—because I loved to dream so much. I used to go on long walks with a book tucked under my arm. I'd slip into one of the San Francisco hotels and sit in the lobby. Not to read, but to listen to the conversations of those around me. Travelers intrigued me. And that's when I met your father."

Viola moved to the edge of the sofa and turned more fully toward her aunt. "I thought you and my mother met Father at the governor's ball."

"Oh, that's when your *mother* met him." Beth released a sigh accompanied by a smile. "I fell in love with him first, you know. I still remember the moment your father walked into that hotel lobby. He was dressed like a gentleman, and his eastern accent only added to his intrigue. He spoke rapidly to the hotel concierge, then swept his gaze about the lobby, stopping on me."

Aunt Beth touched a hand to her throat as she continued. "He asked me for restaurant recommendations, and we fell into a conversation after that. For over an hour we talked of everything, and he told me he was interviewing for a job at the bank. That he'd be in town for a week or two, sightseeing. I had planned to show up in the lobby the next day, and maybe the next, if only to speak with him more. But that night, he arrived at the governor's ball."

Viola had heard stories about the governor's ball—from her parents, never from Aunt Beth.

"That night at the ball, your father only had eyes for your mother. It was like someone had snuffed out the candle burning inside of me, forever plunging me into the dark." She gave a sad laugh. "At least that's what it felt like at the time. Nineteen-year-olds can be dramatic."

But Viola didn't smile or laugh. How had she not known Aunt Beth had loved her father? She felt both repelled and fascinated. "Did Mother know? Did my father . . . ?"

"No one knew," Aunt Beth continued. "At least not directly. I think they both suspected. I left the morning after they'd announced their engagement at Christmas dinner. Packed my things, jumped on a train heading east, and got off at Cheyenne."

Viola had no words. She hadn't known any of this.

"I refused to go to the wedding," Aunt Beth said. "I made up an excuse of being ill." She shrugged. "Never had the desire to see the two of them together. Thought that maybe I'd find another man, or I'd follow one of my dreams after all. But none of that happened."

Viola released a breath. "I'm sorry. I had no idea."

Another shrug from Aunt Beth. "How could you?" She reached out and patted Viola's hand. "Now, run along. The shop will be opening soon, and you have a lot of admirers coming to see you."

"None I could ever take seriously," Viola said. "My parents would have a fit."

Aunt Beth chuckled. "That's what makes it so entertaining. I know you've been smarting over your broken engagement, but it's quite comical that your parents would make you hide out here. The one place they'd never stoop to visit. And the one place where you are at the most threat of having your heart stolen."

"What do you mean?" Although Viola knew what her aunt meant. Her racing heart was proof enough.

"You're not one of those stuffy city folks," Beth said. "You might look like your parents, and you might have finer manners than most people in Wyoming, but you're a dreamer. You want to look beyond the trappings of wealth and privilege. You want to make a difference in the world, and how will you do that living under the weight of someone else's expectations? If there's one thing I could tell you to do—based on all my experience and all my regrets—it's to take a chance on your dream. If you don't, you'll never know if it would have worked out."

Viola's thoughts spun with all that Aunt Beth had told her. She rose to her feet and moved to the door leading to the stairs. "Thank you for telling me your story. I didn't know, and I'm sorry that you went through such heartache."

"Oh." Aunt Beth waved a hand. "It was all for the best. I see that now. Your father was on the fast track of elite society, and your mother happily went along with him. I'm content in my small-town bakery. It might not have been an original dream, but it suits me just fine. The quiet life, the nonjudgmental life, a life of feeding people delicious food— what could be better?"

Viola smiled as she paused at the door. "Wyoming isn't so bad?"

Aunt Beth grinned. "Not so bad at all."

Viola's thoughts felt weighed down as she descended the steps. Aunt Beth's secret was out, it seemed. All these years—she'd been living her second choice in life. Alone, but not alone at all. Every person in the town admired Aunt Beth, greeted her, visited with her—she was surrounded by a different kind of family.

Viola had never had that in San Francisco. No, her days were filled with social visits or joining her mother on committees for one thing or another. Her close friends she'd grown up with were all married, and some had children of their own. Her only independent time was when she volunteered for the Red Cross.

She walked into the kitchen and settled into making the

first round of pies. The routine had become a comfort in a way. She could let her mind wander yet keep her hands busy. The morning passed quickly as Viola got pies into the oven, then rolled out more crust. Sidney chatted merrily with the men who had lined up to make their purchases.

Even without Sheriff Rey directly in the shop, the men were much better behaved. They didn't add on extra dollars and make demands. They paid for their orders, tipped their hats at Viola and the other girls, then shuffled out.

Viola hadn't realized how much she was watching the door when Deputy Thatcher walked in—instead of Sheriff Rey.

"How y'all doing?" he asked, nodding to Sidney. "Any trouble today?"

Sidney flashed the older man a smile. "Everyone's been well-mannered."

"We have," Phil said, a stout man with intelligent eyes. "In fact, I was just about to ask if these pretty ladies will be at the barn dance tomorrow night."

Sidney blushed quite fiercely, which Viola found intriguing. Did she have an interest in the cowboy named Phil?

"I'll be there," Sidney declared. "How about you, sir?"

Phil's gaze cut to Viola, then returned to Sidney's, where it should be. "I'll certainly be there. Maybe you can save a dance for me? I'd be right pleased."

Sidney's coloring deepened. "I'll consider it."

Viola wanted to laugh. Sidney was way past considering.

"What about you, Miss Delany? Will you be at the barn dance?" another man called out.

Viola looked over to see a man named Billy, who was a regular at the bakery. Someone had mentioned he was a cattleman, which probably explained why his clothing looked like he'd just climbed off a horse. He was usually quiet, as far as his words went, but his gaze was always on her as if he were trying to read her very thoughts.

"I haven't decided yet," Viola said, which was true, but even if she went to the barn dance, it wouldn't be to dance with any of these men. She'd already told Aunt Beth that she'd help at the pie table. Stay behind the scenes. The way things were looking, Aunt Beth might not be going to the barn dance.

Billy shuffled forward in line, not responding, but not looking away either.

The stares and comments were still a bit of a novelty. They didn't bother her too much, although Billy was a bit brazen with his staring. There were other single women in town—Viola had met them, along with Sidney and Della. They might be a few years younger than Viola, but they were definitely interested in courting and getting married.

"She'll go," Sidney said brightly. "It can't be a barn dance without our newest friend there."

Viola wanted to know why not when Deputy Thatcher slapped a hand on his thigh. "Oh, geez Louise, I forgot about that. Sheriff better be back by then. I can't throw out all the drunks on my own."

Back? Where was Sheriff Rey? Out of town? Should he be traveling after being so recently recovered from his surgery? Curiosity burned inside of her, but she didn't dare ask any questions with so many listening ears about. And were drunkards a main part of the barn dance? Maybe she'd stay clear after all.

"Oh, that's right." Sidney rang up Phil's purchase while they both blushed. "Sheriff went to fetch his daughter back home."

Eight

"IT'S TOO SMALL," ELSIE DECLARED, setting her small hands on her tiny hips, reminding Rey of his wife for the umpteenth time.

Seeing his daughter after being gone a couple of weeks had been surreal, since when he picked her up at her grandmother's home in San Francisco, he could have sworn Elsie had grown another foot and an even bigger attitude. Her opinions were certainly more decided than he remembered them ever being.

"The dress is the biggest size in a party dress that you have." Rey eyed both their reflections in the brass-framed mirror.

Elsie's strawberry-blonde hair, so much like her mother's, had been braided into two rows, courtesy of Barb. Her green-and-white-checkered dress with a ruffled collar might be a little tight around the torso, and the sleeves a little short, but as long as the dress buttoned and the girl could breathe all right . . .

Elsie biting her lip was never a good sign though. Usually, it was the precursor to tears. He had to think of something fast.

Leaning down, he said, "Tell you what, darlin'. On Monday we'll head into Cheyenne, and you can pick out a new dress or two."

Elsie's blue eyes lit up. "Ready-made?"

"Ready-made." Buying fabric and having Barb sew something up would be less money, but indulging his daughter wouldn't harm anything if done once in a while.

Elsie grinned, and Rey knew it would all be worth it because she pranced away. "I need to find ribbons to match this dress. Can you help tie them, Papa?"

"Of course." He followed after her as she crossed the room and opened a small drawer at the top of her bureau. It had been his wife's bureau, and although he'd packed many things away, Barb had helped him select items that Elsie could use now.

One of those was a box of various colored ribbons. Now Elsie opened the box and pulled out two green ribbons. She handed them over to Rey, and with a bit of fumbling at first, he managed to tie bows at the ends of her braids.

When Elsie next looked in the mirror, there was no pouting, only smiles.

As they headed out into the early evening light, Rey breathed in the fresh air. Much better than that of San Francisco. He understood why his mother wanted to live in a city with so much convenience, but for Rey, he planned on living out the rest of his life in Mayfair. He knew that the day might come when his daughter might make another choice, but for now, he'd be grateful for their time together.

"Are you going to dance with the ladies?" Elsie asked as she perched next to him in the driver's seat of the wagon.

"Hi-yah," Rey called to his trusty horse as he snapped the reins. The horse plodded forward. "I'm going to dance with you, Elsie. And you're a lady."

Elsie wrinkled her freckled nose at this. "I'm just a little girl, Papa. And you're too tall for me to dance with."

Rey chuckled. "How about you stand on my boots like we've done at home?"

"Maybe." Elsie lifted one of her small shoulders. "Barb says that a man gets lonely when he doesn't have a wife."

Rey's laughter died at that, and he peered at his daughter. "Barb said that, huh? Maybe Barb should mind her manners."

"One of my friends in San Francisco has a new mama." Elsie linked her arm through his. "Her mama died too, and her papa married another woman. She's very nice and let us try on makeup."

Rey didn't know what to focus on. The fact that his eight-year-old daughter had put on makeup or that she had a friend he didn't know about. His mother hadn't mentioned anything about new friends with new mothers. He'd definitely be writing a letter when he returned home tonight.

"I'm happy for your friend, and her, uh, step-mother sounds like a nice woman."

"She's very nice," Elsie said in a wistful tone.

Rey supposed he should have known this day would come sooner than later. Elsie didn't remember her mother, since she'd been only three when she died, but she still missed having a mother all the same.

It was just that . . . well, Rey didn't know if his heart could take another loss. Either for him or for his daughter. Besides, if he was set on staying in Mayfair, that narrowed any marrying options significantly. Women from Cheyenne might not want to move to such a tiny spot. Certainly no woman from San Francisco would ever consider moving into the wilds.

Now, why had he gone and connected that city of all

places to himself? Surely it was because he'd just returned there to pick up Elsie. No other reason.

"I'll tell you what, darlin'," Rey said. "If there's a woman you think I should ask to dance with tonight, then I will. Otherwise, I'm happy with just the two of us, all right?"

Her head bobbed in a brisk nod. "All right, Papa. I'll keep my eyes open."

Rey chuckled. "Don't make it too obvious though. I don't want anyone matchmaking for me."

"What does matchmaking mean?"

"Ah." Maybe he'd put his foot in his mouth. "Sometimes people think they know who a fella should marry, so they make introductions and so on."

"Like Barb?"

"What about Barb?"

"I heard her telling you about Miss Cannon's niece and how she's a pretty lady. Smart too."

Rey's throat felt like he'd swallowed a cup of dirt. "Uh . . . I didn't know you'd overheard that conversation."

"Oh, I did."

Rey might have laughed, but the last thing he needed was Elsie latching her sights onto Viola Delany. Out of all the women in all of Wyoming, she'd be the last one he'd ever court. Not because he didn't agree with Barb—Viola was a pretty lady and very smart . . . and other things like intriguing, easy to talk to, prim and proper, yet caring, even when she was being bossy . . .

But Viola Delany belonged in another place. San Francisco. Her checkered cotton dresses and flour-dusted aprons didn't fool him. The woman had dreams, and she should follow them. Even if it went against her parents' wishes.

"Miss Delany is a fine woman," Rey said, because he had

to say something to get Elsie's mind turned around. "She's only here for the summer though, to help out her aunt. She has a whole other life in San Francisco, and I'm afraid that even if I did ask her to dance, it wouldn't make her like me."

"She doesn't like you?"

All right, so he was mixing up all his words. "She likes me as anyone in town might like the sheriff who helps out. But she doesn't like me like a woman likes a man she might consider, uh, marrying."

He felt his daughter's penetrating gaze on him. "Did you ask her if she likes you?"

He looked down at her. "Hey, I thought you were eight. Not seventeen."

Elsie's cheeks dimpled—just like her mother's had. "You're funny, Papa."

Nudging her, he said, "I'll dance with a lady who is from town. You pick. Just don't choose someone who's going to disappear in a couple of months."

"All right, Papa."

So, it was that simple. Rey should be relieved, but he was far from relieved. He was thinking about Viola Delany at the barn dance. She'd be asked dozens of times, he was sure. All those men lined up at the bakery each day would be vying for her attention. She might not even notice him.

He tried to think of the other women in town. There were a couple of dozen women in their twenties and thirties, unmarried, or widowed . . . women his daughter could choose from. But none of them he was looking forward to seeing.

They joined other wagons and carts on the road leading to the Riley barn. It was the newest one in town, so it had been unofficially elected for the dance. Light spilled from the wide-open double doors, and it sounded like Old Jennings was already fiddlin' up a storm.

"There's Lucy and her brother!" Elsie suddenly said, pointing toward the family who was walking into the barn. "Can I go in with them?"

"Of course." Rey's heart stung a little. They hadn't even stopped their cart, yet Elsie was already wanting to spend the time with her friends. Not that he blamed her. She'd been gone for three weeks, and he'd become boring old dad.

And it wasn't like he was going to remind her that she'd been intent on matching him with a dance partner. No, he'd be happy if she clean forgot that part of their conversation.

"Hello, Sheriff!" Jana Hixon called out just as they climbed out of their cart. Jana was a woman in her sixties who rode horses more than she walked. Her swagger tonight was hidden by a wide-hemmed skirt that she probably only broke out once a year.

"Jana, a fine evening to you."

"Good to see you up and about," Jana continued as they walked toward the barn doors. Elsie skipped on ahead and joined her friends without even a glance back at him. "All healed up?"

"All healed up."

"Oh goodness." Jana stopped in her tracks. "What a spread. I'll be by the pie table if anyone needs me."

Rey looked over at the long tables set up on the far side of the barn. Tradition held that families brought their favorite pie, and everyone could try various kinds. Beth Cannon always brought a dozen or so from her bakery. She'd made it a habit of presiding over the pie table and serving up slices.

He scanned for signs of Beth but didn't see her. Another woman seemed to be arranging the pies this year. A blonde woman whom Rey recognized, even though her back was to him. His pulse did a strange sort of leap just knowing that Viola Delany had come to the barn dance after all.

He wasn't the only man who'd noticed her, of course. In fact, one was approaching her now.

Wallace.

Rey didn't know if he should be concerned or not. Certainly Wallace had learned his lesson from being kicked out of the bakery. To Rey's knowledge, the man hadn't been back since. So what was going through Wallace's mind now?

Rey began to thread his way to the other side of the barn, greeting others as he moved. Elsie was busy chattering and running around with her friends. When he was about halfway across the space, Wallace reached Viola, and she turned to face him.

Her smile was bright, but Rey didn't miss the way she gripped her hands tightly in front of her. Wallace said something, and Viola pointed to the rows of pies. Wallace stepped closer, sweeping off his hat. Viola stepped back. Wallace said something, and Viola shook her head. Then she moved around the table, putting the pies between her and Wallace.

Wallace frowned and gestured about something.

Viola's smile remained in place, but she shook her head again and folded her arms.

"Good evenin', Wallace," Rey said, arriving at his side. "Tried any of the pies yet?"

Wallace spun to face Rey, his expression going slack. "You sure seem to like pies as well, Sheriff."

"I don't think there's a soul in Mayfair who doesn't like a fine piece of pie," Rey said.

Wallace blinked, then nodded, as if he were trying to figure out if this was just a friendly conversation or something more.

Rey looked over at Viola. "Hello, Miss Delany. Fine evening."

Her mouth quirked, but she responded with a polite, "Hello, Sheriff. It is a fine evening."

Wallace seemed to hover. Rey remained by the table, scanning the pies as if each and every one was fascinating.

Finally, with an exaggerated huff, Wallace walked off, placing his hat firmly upon his head.

"Would you like to try a piece?" Viola asked, picking up the pie spatula.

"I would," Rey said. "But maybe in a few moments."

She set down the spatula. "Any excitement on your recent journey?"

"You mean like stopping a train robbery?"

Her smile was soft. And there went Rey's pulse leaping about again. "Something like that."

"Nothing so exciting." He nodded toward his daughter and her friends. "Unless you count Elsie spilling her ice cream on my hat."

"Oh goodness." Viola sounded like she was about to laugh. "That's quite the disaster."

"Quite."

She did laugh then, and Rey found himself grinning. He really should move on. Speak to other townsfolk. Make sure that any rabble-rousing was kept at minimum.

"Tell me about your daughter. Her name is Elsie, right?"

"Right. She's eight years old, going on about sixteen."

"Ah." Viola's smile was back. "I heard that quite a lot from my parents. But look at me now. Twenty-seven and perfectly respectable."

"You're twenty-seven?" Rey couldn't hide his surprise.

"Yep, I'm a spinster. A jaded spinster at that."

"Jaded? Did a man do you wrong?"

"You could say that, Sheriff Rey." Her gaze moved away from him. "Hello, Billy. Are you needing a slice of pie?"

Rey hid his scowl as he looked over at the man who'd interrupted.

Billy twisted a ratty hat in his hand as he held it against his heart. "I'd like to ask you to dance, miss."

"Oh, you are sweet for asking," Viola said. "I'm working the pie table this evening. Won't be dancing at all. Now, I'm sure there's several other ladies who'd be happy to dance with you. Bring her back here for a piece of pie after."

Rey wanted to shout in triumph. Apparently, Viola was quite smooth at turning away the fellas.

Nine

SHERIFF REY WAS DEFINITELY LINGERING, or was it loitering?

Whatever it was, Viola felt vastly amused. Butterflies were also making themselves busy in her stomach. Aunt Beth's words about the sheriff being "interested" in her wouldn't leave her mind. Still, she wondered if Rey was hanging around the pie table to watch over her because it was his civic duty, or because he wanted to get to know her better, or because he was bored?

It was honestly hard to tell. She really had nothing to lose by just asking him.

"Are you going to stand here all night and chase off every man who approaches me?" she said after his scowl and disapproving look sent away another cowboy.

Rey's green eyes landed on her. "I don't think you need my help in that corner, ma'am. Although I'm happy to oblige if necessary."

"You're calling me ma'am again."

"We're in a more formal setting."

He was teasing, she knew it. She made a studious assessment of the man. His height made him imposing to the average-sized man, she supposed. His profession added to that as well. But his kindness and frank-speaking made him appealing to women, not to mention those deep green eyes of his and his rugged features. Viola hadn't missed the stares of several women in the barn, including Della. At least Sidney had changed her focus to Phil, whom she currently danced with.

"I'll be fine, sir," Viola pronounced, returning his *ma'am* with her *sir.* "Now, you go find yourself a dance partner. The sheriff of the town can't always be on duty."

Interestingly enough, Rey hesitated, then murmured, "Just not looking forward to being cornered by my daughter again."

"Elsie? What hold does a child have on you?" Viola wasn't what she'd call a natural with children. But she'd been watching the eight-year-old Elsie off and on, and she seemed like a go-getter, and Viola liked that.

He chuckled at this and folded his arms. "Ah. Well. Elsie came home from San Francisco talking about her friend's new mother."

Viola did a quick scan of his sinewy forearms, then she averted her gaze before he noticed. "And?"

Rey took a step closer and lowered his voice, which wasn't too hard to hear over the energetic fiddler. "She doesn't remember her mother, and I knew it would only be a matter of time before she realizes what she's been missing."

Viola blinked. This was much more personal than she thought he might share with her, especially in a public setting. "And she's missing that now?"

Rey set his hands on his hips and looked down at the ground. "It seems that way, ma'am. On the drive over, she was determined to find me a woman to dance with." He raised his gaze to meet Viola's. "She's distracted now by her friends, but how long will that last? And even if I satisfy her and dance with someone tonight, then what about tomorrow, or next week? I just don't think I can abide living with a precocious matchmaker."

Against her will, Viola felt the edges of her mouth tug upward.

"Do you find that amusing, Miss Delany?"

"I might." Her smile grew.

Rey's eyes glimmered with humor. "It's not every day that a man confesses his life is secretly ruled by a child, whether he's a sheriff or not."

Viola laughed. "I'm impressed that you're at least willing to admit it. But don't worry, your secret is safe. I mean, who would I tell?"

Rey pushed up the brim of his hat and rubbed at his forehead. "Beth Cannon?"

"Oh, she'd be the last person I'd tell," Viola said. "She's already after me to give another man a chance. Says that one failed engagement isn't excuse enough to remain a spinster."

"You were engaged?" He looked quite surprised, which surprised her—it seemed that the town gossip hadn't reached him.

"I was, but he was caught in an indiscretion, and before marriage, that's unacceptable."

Rey frowned. "And it's acceptable during marriage?"

Viola shrugged a shoulder. "The unbreakable knot is already tied."

"That's hogwash," Rey said. "I know divorces can be tricky to get, but sometimes they're warranted."

Viola stared at him, then had to look away because her eyes were filling with tears.

"I'm sorry, Viola, for speaking of things not of my concern. But a man's got no business stepping out on his wife."

She nodded, swallowing hard as if it would hold back the threatening tears.

"I hope I didn't upset you."

"I'm fine." Viola exhaled slowly, then met his gaze. Could he tell her eyes were wet? "It's all in the past now anyway, and by the end of the summer, San Francisco will have forgotten about my troubles. I can return in peace and live happily ever after." She didn't mean for bitterness to seep through her voice.

Rey opened his mouth to reply, but they were interrupted by a slurred greeting.

"Well . . . hello there, pretty lady." Billy shoved his hands in his front pockets and rocked back on his heels. He wasn't wearing his usual hat. Instead, his hair hung in greasy strands about his face.

Even from across the pie table, Viola could smell the alcohol seeping from his pores.

"Hello, Billy," she said as primly as possible, pushing back all the emotions that had just been brewing. "What kind of pie slice can I get you?"

Billy shuffled closer, a slow grin spreading across his face. "I don't need any pie, pretty lady. I came to ask you to dance with me."

"That's kind of you," Viola began. "But I'm working the pie table tonight and not dancing with anyone."

Billy's palms thumped onto the table as he leaned toward her. "You gave that excuse to all the other fellas in here. But I'm different." He grabbed Viola's hand in a steel-trap grip. "I can make an honest woman of you and—"

Rey's fingers clamped around Billy's collar, and he tugged the man away from Viola. Next he drew Billy up to his face until they were nose-to-nose.

"I'm going to ask you once, Billy," the sheriff growled.

"Leave the barn and don't come back tonight." Rey held Billy in place for another several seconds, staring him down, then he let go of the man's collar.

Billy took a stumbling step back. He looked as if he were about to turn and walk away when suddenly he lunged at the sheriff.

Rey barely dodged the man's fist as the music around them faded, and people turned to watch what was happening.

"Settle down, Billy," Rey commanded, one hand held up and the other gripping his gun holster. "Nothing you're about to do right now will be worth it. Think before you act and before you sentence yourself to a night in jail."

"I'm tired of you thinking you're the boss of everyone in this town," Billy ground out, spittle flying from his mouth. "If I want to ask this lady to dance, then that's my business, not yours."

"She turned you down, Billy."

Billy sneered. "That's because you've been hovering over her all night. Someone needs to teach you a lesson."

Billy lunged again, and Rey simply sidestepped to avoid collision. Which was a good move on Rey's part, but a bad move for the pie table. Billy plowed into the table headfirst.

Viola leapt back as gasps and cries echoed about the room.

"He ruined the pies!"

"Get the man out of here!"

Men moved forward to pick up Billy, probably to finish throwing him out, but he wasn't moving.

"Wait," Viola cried. "He might need medical attention." She knelt next to the man who was lying face down and pressed two fingers against the side of his neck. His pulse beat steady and strong. "He has a pulse!"

Billy moaned and shifted as if he was going to try to turn over.

Viola scooted back, and Billy turned on his side, blinking at her like he wasn't sure how he'd ended up on the floor. Blood dripped from his nose, and he raised a trembling hand to gingerly touch his face.

"You've broken your nose, Billy." Viola's stomach lurched, but she refused to let the sight of blood do her in like it had with the sheriff. She swallowed and looked up at the gathering crowd. "Can someone hand me the ice bowl?"

She snatched a nearby cloth—most of the pies had been delivered with a pie cloth. A young girl knelt next to her. "Here's the ice. What are you going to do?"

Viola found herself staring into the eyes of Elsie. "I'm going to put the ice in this cloth, then hold it against this man's face."

All fire had faded from Billy's eyes, and now that he was dealing with a broken nose, the pain kept him mellow.

Viola worked quickly, and as she set the ice bundle on Billy's face, Rey knelt next to her.

"Here, I can hold this in place," he said. "I still don't trust this man."

Viola nodded and let him take over. She wasn't going to argue with the sheriff in front of all these people. They'd made enough of a spectacle as it was. Besides, Billy's temper had been disturbing to see—drunk or not.

"Well, let's get this mess cleaned up and see how many pies we can save," Viola ordered to the onlookers. She wasn't quite sure how she was feeling comfortable enough to boss everyone around, but she saw a need and wanted to do something about that.

"Help me out, Phil," Rey said. "Let's get this man to his feet."

"I got 'im." Deputy Thatcher appeared. He wasn't wearing any sort of uniform but was spruced up for the dance.

Between Phil and Thatcher and Rey, Billy was helped to his feet. His legs looked a bit wobbly, but he'd survive.

"I need a doctor," Billy complained.

"The doc will come visit you in jail," Thatcher said. "You're a fool for going after the sheriff. What were you thinking?"

Billy heaved a sigh and allowed the men to shuffle him forward.

"Elsie, stay with your friends," Rey barked at his daughter.

"Can I help the baker woman clean up the pies?" Elsie said.

Rey hesitated, his gaze shifting to Viola.

"I'd appreciate the help."

Rey nodded. "All right, then. I won't be long. Stay close to Viola. She's in charge of you until I return."

"Thank you, Papa."

Viola didn't know why she was smiling. Billy had nearly clobbered Rey, and now there was a massive mess to clean up, but a smile pushed through anyway.

"Set the pies that didn't turn upside down on the far table," Viola continued her orders. "The pies that are ruined can be put into this crate. The pigs won't be hungry for two days after tonight."

A few people chuckled. Several townspeople pitched in to help, and it wasn't long before the mess was cleaned up. The music began again and the dancing continued.

"You're really pretty," a little voice said next to Viola as she spaced out the remaining pies on the table.

Viola looked down at Elsie. Her bright blue eyes were curious. "Well, thank you. You're a pretty girl too."

Elsie grinned. She had a couple of teeth missing, but it only made her more adorable. "I'm going to tell Papa when he returns that you're the lady he should dance with tonight."

"Oh, uh . . ." Viola knew her cheeks were heating up. "He might be too busy with all that's gone on."

"They'll put Billy in jail and figure out what to do with him tomorrow," Elsie pronounced as if this was all a regular night of events. She'd probably seen a thing or two as the sheriff's daughter. "But Papa will be back here soon, and he promised that I could pick out a lady for him to dance with."

Viola didn't want to get in the middle of a father-daughter agreement, yet . . . "You know, Elsie, your father and I are friends. I'm only in Mayfair for a short while though. Maybe he should ask someone else to dance."

"No." Elsie gave her a huge smile. "I've made up my mind."

Ten

IF SOMEONE HAD TOLD REY a couple of hours ago that he'd be dodging a fistfight with Billy, then hauling him to jail, then dancing with Viola Delany, he would have laughed until his gut hurt.

But holding the real live, breathing Viola in his arms while they danced was no laughing matter. It might be a smiling matter, but it was also a nerve-racking event. Mostly because she was a much better dancer than he was, and also because she smelled like the peach pies she'd baked for the barn dance.

Oh, and her cheeks were definitely flushed, which only made her gray eyes sparkle and the color of her lips seem redder.

Viola was a beautiful, vivacious, and commanding woman. He'd seen that in her actions after Billy stumbled into the pie table. But Rey had to tell his brain that the woman was not a permanent resident of Mayfair. She'd be leaving at the end of the summer, and that would be that.

Still, dancing with her was something he couldn't very well turn down since Elsie had insisted on it.

"I know she's only a visitor, Papa," Elsie had said when

he'd returned to the barn that night. "But I chose Viola for you to dance with. I already told her too."

This had certainly caught his attention. "Oh, and what did she say when you told her?"

"She said you and she were friends, but I don't think that means you can't dance."

"It sure doesn't," Rey had answered.

So here he was. Taking a turn about the room with Viola as the fiddler played a slow melody. Rey could practically feel every single person's eyes upon him, but he decided not to care. He could dance with a woman and not make front-page headlines in the weekly *Mayfair Chronicle*, right?

"You seem to be deep in thought," Viola commented. "Did everything go well with Billy, or did he take another swing at you?"

Rey gazed into Viola's upturned face. "Oh, he was quite repentant. Most men get that way when they're facing jail time."

"Hmm." Viola looked away for a moment. "Well, thank you for attempting to throw him out, even though things went awry."

Rey chuckled. "You're welcome." He paused. "Did you think I was hovering over you like Billy accused?"

"Hmm," Viola said again.

Rey was beginning to think that maybe she was trying to torture him with all those mysterious *hmms*. "You can be honest with me, Viola. I'll take it like a man."

Her brows arched. "I've always been honest with you, but that doesn't mean I have to tell you all my thoughts and opinions. But if you really want to know, I can understand how Billy, or others, might have viewed their sheriff as hovering over the new lady in town. Or maybe it was just the pie table—I assume you're fond of pies like most people."

"I am fond of pies, but I was also enjoying my chat with you." Rey pulled her a half inch closer. "Is there something wrong with a little conversation?"

She lifted her chin a bit higher. "Nothing wrong with it at all. I just find it funny that we were both determined not to dance tonight, yet here we are."

"Here we are . . ." He knew he was smiling like a fool, but he found he didn't care. His little matchmaker daughter was probably going to read into this dance far more than she should, but again, Rey didn't care at the moment.

He thought about how wonderful it would be if everyone could leave the barn dance so that he could be alone with Viola. Why? He wasn't ready to put that into words, but there were too many potential interruptions. He felt like a giant clock was counting down, one tick at a time.

Viola's smaller hand was encased in his while her other hand rested on his shoulder. This brought him a measure of comfort that he'd forgotten about. How a woman's touch could bring him so much contentment.

"I'll bet word of this will reach my aunt before I return to her place," she said, "and then I'll never hear the end of it."

"Which will be?"

When her brow creased, he added, "What will your aunt pester you about?"

"Oh, she'll tell me what a fine man you are. She'll bemoan her arthritis and how she can't trust the other shopgirls as much as me. Then she'll finally add that you're the type of man who'd let me pursue my dreams. The type of man I could marry, have a family with, but still enjoy things outside the home."

"Am *I* that type of man?"

"Are you going to go back on your word, Reynold Christensen?"

281

"I've never gone back on my word, and I don't aim to now."

They weren't dancing anymore. They were simply standing in the middle of the floor, in each other's embrace, their words whispered between them.

"I've decided to do it," Viola suddenly said. "I don't know how my parents will react, but when I return home, I'm going to visit the nursing school in San Francisco and inquire about enrolling. If they won't have me, I'll look around at other cities."

Something twisted in Rey's heart, but he grinned. "Excellent. You're a natural, you know. Even tonight, with Billy being as rotten as he was, you still took care of his broken nose. And you didn't faint at all that blood."

"First of all, he wasn't you with a gunshot wound. Second, he deserved the broken nose for the way he acted. I guess seeing him face down on the ground showed that he was human after all."

Rey was very satisfied with her answer. Without a word, they both began to move again to the melody of the dance music.

"I'm proud of you, Viola," Rey murmured, ignoring his aching heart. "Making such a decision about nursing school must be hard. Especially when your parents might not support you."

Viola's hand seemed to tighten in his. "Knowing that not everyone believes as my parents do has made me see things differently and given me hope. Thank you, Rey. Between you and my aunt, I feel like I can follow my dream."

Rey had to ignore his own feelings about Viola's potential schooling three states away. "You'll be an excellent nurse, and maybe one day you'll want a family," he said, not knowing exactly where all of this advice was coming from.

"In a small town like Mayfair, you could do both. Doc could use someone to help out once in a while. Especially during times when he has to go on calls at one of the farms."

Viola tilted her head and studied him. He certainly hoped she couldn't read minds.

"Next thing you'll tell me is that there's a nursing school in Cheyenne."

"I think there is," Rey said with a wink. "But don't let me talk you into anything."

He was teasing, sort of, but what Viola did next would have leveled him if he hadn't been standing on firm ground.

"The dance is over, Sheriff." She rose up on her toes and kissed him on the cheek. "Thanks for asking me despite it being Elsie's idea."

Then Viola released him and walked away before he could tell her that even if Elsie hadn't been the instigator, he would have asked her to dance. But Viola was a half dozen feet away by the time his head stopped spinning. Now, why had she gone and kissed him on the cheek? Was that how things were done in the Delany family, or did it mean something more? Something that he didn't dare let his mind indulge in. Because every single person in the whole town would be talking about this before the hour was up.

Rey didn't speak directly to Viola the rest of the night. It was quite impossible since everyone seemed to want their dessert at the same time. The pie table remained populated while Viola cheerfully served up slice after slice. Rey guessed she'd been asked a few more times to dance, gauging by the men standing before her, hat in hand. But she never did dance again, and Rey took a bit of pride in that.

"Papa," Elsie said, appearing at his side while he was talking himself out of approaching the pie table and doing some of that "hovering." "Can I spend the night at Lucy's house?"

Rey looked down at his daughter. "How about another night? I've missed you too much to let you out of my sight."

Elsie giggled at this, and miraculously, she leaned against him. "All right, Papa. When you don't miss me so much, then can I spend the night?"

Rey bent and kissed the top of her head. "I think that can be negotiated."

"Sheriff, there's a couple of boys joyriding in one of the wagons outside. Folks are afraid someone will get hurt."

Rey turned to look at Phil. "Thanks for letting me know." Thatcher had remained at the jail, so Rey headed outside. It didn't take long to put the fear of the good Lord into the two teen boys.

When he returned to the barn, Old Jennings was packing up his fiddle, several townsfolk were putting away tables and chairs, and there was some negotiating over who was taking home the leftover pies.

Rey wondered if Viola would accept a ride home in his cart, but she was walking arm in arm with Della toward the entrance. He received a smile and a nod and then she was gone.

"Papa, are we staying here all night?" Elsie said, tugging at his arm, right before she gave a giant yawn.

"Nope. Heading out now." He grasped her hand. By the time they exited the barn, Viola Delany was nowhere in sight.

Eleven

HER SUMMER SPENT IN WYOMING turned out to be only three weeks, but Viola wasn't returning home to become mired in avoiding gossip about her broken engagement. She was returning home to have a frank conversation with her parents. Aunt Beth had hated to see her leave so soon, but she'd also encouraged it and promised that she'd let Della and Sidney take on more responsibilities at the bakery.

Which was why Viola was now walking up the steps to her family's large home and ringing the bell like she was a visitor. She didn't want to burst into the house and shock everyone.

She glanced back at the carriage she'd hired and left her luggage on. The driver had agreed to wait on the side of the road until she let him know if she'd be staying here or going someplace else.

The housekeeper, Macy, answered the door, and her eyes rounded to the size of saucers. "Miss Delany . . . you're back?"

"Yes." She gave a wide smile, but her stomach had cinched into knots. "Are Mother and Father home?"

"Of course, it's early yet. Come in. Let me help you with your luggage."

Viola had divvied up several of her nicer dresses and hats to Sidney and Della, who were both delighted with the gifts. So Viola only had one trunk and one carpetbag. "The driver can keep an eye on it until I speak to my parents."

She followed Macy into the house and looked about as if seeing it for the first time. Her three weeks' absence had made everything seem so different and foreign. The noise and traffic of downtown San Francisco. The boats upon the water, dotting the bay. The steep hills that her hired carriage had traversed. And now the polished floors and pillars of her home.

The click of heels came along the corridor leading to the library, and her mother walked into view. She stopped abruptly with a gasp. Her blonde hair was done up in an elegant twist, and diamonds graced her earlobes and neck. Her makeup was carefully and impeccably applied, and she wore a cream blouse and pale pink skirt.

"Viola . . . what in heaven's name? Has something happened? Why didn't you tell us you were returning so soon?"

The rush of words was like standing beneath a cold waterfall, because Viola knew her mother wouldn't like her answers.

"I have an urgent matter to discuss with you and Father, and I thought it would be better in person."

Her mother's brows dipped. "Has something happened to Beth? Or to you? Did my sister *mistreat* you?" Her voice went up an octave.

"Nothing like that. I'm perfectly well, and Aunt Beth is managing just fine in my absence. She was managing fine before—we all know why I really went to Wyoming."

"Well." Her mother crossed to her and kissed her on the cheek—a kiss that Viola barely felt. "You're just in time to attend the art gala tonight. It's black-tie, and your ex-fiancé is still not attending events, so you should be safe from seeing him. It might be good to show your proud face in public, after all."

"I won't be attending any galas, Mother."

"Why not?" Mother's eyes narrowed. "What is it that must be discussed so urgently? Is there a man in this story? Have you been . . . compromised?"

The look of horror and fear in her mother's eyes almost made Viola laugh. The lengths that Sheriff Rey had gone to stop even the mildest of flirting men had quite prevented any "compromising," as her mother might refer to it.

"No one has been compromised, Mother." Viola heaved a sigh. "Now, where is Father?"

"In the library." Mother's eyes narrowed once again. "I was just about to speak with him. He will certainly be surprised to see you."

Viola began to walk toward the library, and her mother's clicking heels caught up.

"What is this all about, Viola? You know your father doesn't like to be bothered with—"

Viola knocked on the closed library door, then, without waiting for any sort of inquiry, she opened the door and walked in.

The next few moments were filled with surprise on her father's part and fussing on her mother's part.

Father rose from his chair behind a large desk and walked around it to clasp both of Viola's arms. He wore a light gray suit and his shoes were shined to a high polish. His mustache twitched as he looked her over. "You've had too much sun, Viola. Sit and drink something. I knew sending you to your mother's sister's place was a mistake. We should have sent you to Philadelphia to spend the summer with my brother's family. It's farther away, but it's at least civilized and modern—"

"No, that's not what this is about," Viola cut in before her father's tangent could continue. She stepped away from both of her parents. "I've made a decision about my future, and I've returned to San Francisco to begin the inquiries."

"Inquiries into what?" Father asked, lines creasing his forehead.

"Nursing school." Viola paused as both of her parents frowned. "I'm twenty-seven and the survivor of a failed engagement. I've done things your way my entire life. I don't want another five or ten years to go by and not find out what I can really accomplish in life. Sitting around and hoping for another man to propose isn't my idea of fulfillment."

"You wouldn't be sitting around," Mother cut in. "Besides, the wait will be worth it. Marriage is wonderful, and you'll become a mother with beautiful children."

"Maybe," Viola said. "Maybe that will happen, but I'm not going to force it. I'm not going to court a man just because his father is a friend of our family's. I don't want a man who looks at me for an inheritance to pad his own pockets. I want to do something that matters. To me and to other people."

Father folded his arms. "And nursing school is going to bring you such fulfillment?"

Mother covered her mouth and sat on a chair. "You've been reading too many articles written by feminists. You're educated, Viola, and now it's time you use that education toward creating a marriage and raising a family. Nursing work is for spinsters who have no other options in life. You're beautiful and still young, and you come from a family of privilege and impeccable reputation."

"I don't have anything against the right marriage, and I'll be happy to have children if the situation presents itself," Viola said. Her father's face was reddening, and she knew his outburst was coming soon. "But I'm finished with high society. Whether or not you support me in nursing school won't change my mind. There are scholarships I can apply for, and most of these schools provide boarding."

Her father's mouth opened, then closed.

"Viola, you've had a long journey," her mother said. "Why don't you rest and then we can all discuss your time in Wyoming when you're feeling refreshed."

"That won't be necessary," Father cut in, his tone measured. "I don't need time to think this over, and it's clear that our daughter has done nothing but make plans without our consent." His gaze cut to his wife's, then back to Viola. "If you choose this course of action, Viola, after all we've done and provided for you . . . after all the protection we've offered you from this scandal, then you had better pray for a scholarship. Because no daughter of mine whom I'd ever claim will reduce herself to the job market."

When his fist slammed down onto the desk, Viola jumped.

Her father's anger was no surprise, yet to be standing here, after so many weeks away, and to hear his decisive words still cut deeply.

"All right, then," Viola said, her voice a scratch inside her throat. "I won't trouble you with this anymore. I will write to you of my progress, but don't feel obligated to write back." She recited the words she had practiced in her head during the long trip home. Otherwise, she would have melted like a puddle and broken into tears. She'd do that later.

Her eyes stung, and her neck muscles felt strained as she walked out of the library.

"Viola dear, stay and think this over. You've given us quite the shock. We have some time to work through things and maybe—"

Her mother's voice sounded like it was about to break, and Viola knew if she didn't keep moving, she'd give in and stay longer. But her father's words had been plain and final.

"Genevieve," Father's voice rumbled. "We aren't groveling to make her stay. She has made up her mind."

We can both be stubborn, Viola thought as a tear escaped anyway. She'd reached the door. With jerky movements, she tugged the door open. She was grateful she'd told the carriage driver to wait for her, even if that knowledge didn't make her happy.

What did she expect? This. Yet the ache was deep and painful.

"If they don't support your plan, you come back here," Aunt Beth had told her. "We'll send out applications to every nursing school you're interested in. There's no rush on anything, but there's no harm in getting started."

Viola swiped at the tears on her cheeks and approached the driver of the carriage. "Thanks for waiting. Can you take me to back to the hotel?"

The hotel was close to the nursing school on California Street and Maple. Viola didn't have unlimited funds, just what she'd earned at the bakery, plus the money she'd traveled with—which she'd spent on the return ticket.

"Sure thing, ma'am," the driver said.

Riding through the streets this time was a different feeling. Gone were the hope and anticipation of the hour before. Now those feelings were replaced by dejection . . . so she'd allow herself a few tears right now. Once she reached the nursing school, she'd need to push forward with the next part of her plan.

She was an independent woman now, no longer under the umbrella of her parents' control. This was what she wanted, right?

After the carriage pulled up to the hotel and Viola had checked into her room, she paused in front of the bedroom mirror. Her eyes were red-rimmed and her cheeks blotchy. But she didn't want to delay her visit to the nursing school. If they didn't have an opening, she'd have to make other plans.

The nursing school was a short walk from the hotel, and when Viola entered the front door of the building, she was surprised to see the place empty save for one woman sitting at a reception desk.

"Oh, hello," Viola said.

The woman rose to her feet and adjusted her spectacles. Viola guessed her to be in her mid-thirties. The nameplate on her desk said Miss Barnwell. "Did you have an appointment? I'm afraid that today is a field day, so the director isn't here."

Viola wasn't sure what a field day was. "I don't have an appointment. My name is Viola Delany, and I'm here to inquire about an application and possible availability to the school."

"Ah." Miss Barnwell's brown eyes narrowed. "Who sent you? We don't open enrollment until the beginning of next year."

"January?" It was the end of July, so that wasn't helpful at all. "I didn't realize. I . . ." Her voice quivered. That would not do at all. She drew in a steadying breath. "I should have done my research better."

Viola should have spent more time in her hotel room, working through her emotions, because to her horror, she began to cry. She tried to sniffle back the tears and keep her body from trembling, but it was no use.

"Oh, you poor woman, have a seat." Miss Barnwell came around her desk and offered Viola a chair.

She sank into it gratefully and pulled out a handkerchief to wipe at her face "I'm sorry. It's been a difficult couple of days. I guess I'm at the end of my rope."

"Where are you from?" Miss Barnwell asked, her voice gentle, as she sat across from Viola.

The entire story spilled out. From Viola's broken engagement to working at the bakery in Mayfair to the row with her parents.

Miss Barnwell listened to every word, offering sympathy as Viola talked.

"I'm so sorry to dump my life story on you," Viola said, wiping at her face again although it did little good. The tears kept coming.

"I knew there was a reason I stayed in the office today," Miss Barnwell said. "If you'd like, I can speak to the director tomorrow. Maybe there will be an exception. Once in a while a student has to drop out for one reason or another."

Viola felt a spark of hope ignite. "Are you sure? I don't want to be a burden to anyone."

"Oh, my dear, you won't be. In fact, you can take the assessment if you have time right now. It's about an hour-long test, and it would be good to have that in hand when I speak to the director."

Viola stared at Miss Barnwell. "I could do that right now?"

"If you have time?"

Viola gave a half laugh. "I have all the time in the world."

Twelve

REY STOOD IN LINE AT the bakery. Not because he was monitoring the crowds again—those had dwindled by half—but because he was purchasing a pie. Elsie's birthday was tomorrow, and he told Barb he'd provide the dessert. Not that Barb would expect him to bake a cake or anything.

Besides, Rey hoped to chat a moment or two with Beth Cannon. Find out how Miss Delany was doing back in San Francisco. Find out if she'd enrolled in nursing school. Find out what her parents had said.

It wasn't that he was expecting a letter—although he'd hoped she might write to him. Yet she didn't owe him any sort of chronicling of her life.

Rey moved up another few steps in line.

He missed seeing Viola at the pie counter. He missed the half smile on her face when their eyes connected. He missed her directness. He missed the gray of her eyes and contrast of her dark eyebrows to her golden hair.

And, of course, he'd had to field questions about Viola from his daughter. All these reminders of the woman were making her impossible to put out of his mind.

"Hello, Sheriff," Phil said.

"Hey there."

They shuffled forward another two steps.

The conversations around him were general "how-are-you's" and "sure-hot-today." It was August now, the hottest part of the year, and Viola Delany had been gone for longer than she'd been in Wyoming. Yet Rey remembered everything about her as if he'd seen her an hour ago.

"Next, please," Sidney said, manning the register today.

Rey glanced around for Beth but didn't see her.

"I'll have a peach pie," Rey said. "How are you doing, Sidney?"

"Fine as always." She cast a smile to Phil, who stood behind Rey, waiting his turn.

"And Miss Cannon? Is she up and about today?"

"Oh, she's next door at the mercantile picking up a few things." Sidney boxed up the pie and handed it over.

He paid, then tipped his hat. "Have a nice day." He'd turned to leave when Sidney's voice stopped him.

"Did you hear the latest about Viola?"

Rey froze, then slowly turned, calming his jumping pulse to say in a steady tone, "I did not. What's the latest?"

"She's going to school in Cheyenne. Wants to be a nurse, I guess." Sidney shrugged like she hadn't just turned Rey's world upside down. "Should be arriving any day now. Miss Cannon is hoping she'll stay here and commute, but there's boarding there too, so we don't know what she'll decide."

Rey swallowed once. Then twice. "Is that so? Well, good for her. She'll be a fine nurse."

Sidney flashed a smile, then turned her full attention on Phil. "What can I get you, Phil?"

Rey didn't hear one word between Phil and Sidney after that. He was trying to do the impossible. Walk while carrying a pie as his mind caught up to all that Sidney had packed into a few short sentences. He'd accepted the fact that Viola was in San Francisco. What had changed her mind?

Curiosity burned through him, and without even considering what he was doing, he headed to the mercantile. With a little luck, Beth Cannon would still be there and he could ask her himself. Maybe Sidney had some of her facts wrong? Rey's heart thumped a couple of extra beats. He hoped she didn't. He hoped to high heaven that Viola Delany was indeed returning to Wyoming.

That would be one step closer to . . . to what? Seeing her? Courting her? A lump pressed against his throat as his heart tried to escape his chest. Viola was coming back. Maybe not to Mayfair, but Cheyenne was thirty minutes by horse. And he couldn't wait to see her again. Because Rey was done kidding himself. He was halfway in love with the woman, if not all the way.

It was something he had to admit to himself. These past few weeks without her had made his life feel like the Sahara Desert—empty, vast, and uncomfortable.

His boots barely touched the ground as he strode into the mercantile. He never thought he'd feel this way about a woman again. Sure, he assumed he'd remarry someday . . . in the distant future . . . but to have all his thoughts and energy and desires once again center on a woman . . . This was unexpected.

The moment he spotted Beth Cannon examining ready-made aprons, Rey's steps faltered. Was he putting too much hope in the reasons for Viola's return? It might just be coincidence on her part—or a rift with her parents, and Rey didn't want that for her. Or it might be driven by the relationship between niece and aunt. All of this had nothing to do with *him*. He had to put himself firmly into place and not let his imagination get away with him.

"Hello, Miss Cannon." Rey approached the woman.

Beth looked up. She carried a basket that contained spice bottles. "Well, hello there, Sheriff. Nice day."

"If you like the heat of a thousand suns, it's a nice day."

Beth chuckled and folded the apron, setting it back on the shelf.

"How's your health?" Rey continued, apparently bent on making small talk before asking any of his dire questions.

"Today's a good day," Beth said. "I promised Viola that even on good days, I'd let one of the shopgirls run the register. We're still getting brisk business, even with Viola gone."

Rey nodded at this. "Your bakery has delicious food, so the good business is what you deserve."

"Why, thank you." She eyed the box in his hands. "I see you bought something?"

"A pie for Elsie," he explained. "Her birthday is tomorrow."

"Oh, what a sweet girl," Beth said. "Turning nine?"

"That's right." He cleared his throat. "Sidney mentioned something about your niece attending school in Cheyenne?"

Beth's eyes sparked, and her smile widened. "Sure is. Just received the letter today."

"Oh?"

Beth was grinning now. "I guess there's an opening." She lowered her voice as townspeople milled about the store. "She's been working in the nursing office at a school in San Francisco since there aren't openings. The school in Cheyenne is run by the sister of the director, and because Viola's parents are still against her decision, she decided there's no reason to stay in San Francisco for the time being. I know her parents will come around eventually, when they see how serious and dedicated she is. In fact, her mother paid her a visit the other day. Offered her money, which Viola refused."

"I'm sorry to hear about her parents' disapproval." And he *was* sorry. But he was also elated at the thought of seeing Viola once again . . .

Beth pursed her lips. "I'm not surprised, and that's all I'm going to say on the matter." She glanced down the aisle, then focused once again on Rey. "She asked about you."

Rey leaned against the nearby shelf, if only to have a bit of support. He mustered up a nonchalance that he didn't feel. "Oh?"

"I mean, not directly, but she asked me to catch her up on all the town's happenings."

Rey felt deflated. That was a far cry from mentioning *him*.

Beth gave him a wink. "Don't worry, Sheriff Rey. You'll have your Viola back soon." With that, she headed to the register, basket of spices in hand.

Beth Cannon was sure assuming a lot—on his part. Had he made his feelings obvious? Weren't his questions perfectly polite and conversational? As he headed out of the mercantile without buying a thing, he wondered, what had given him away? And did the rest of the town suspect the same thing?

"Papa," a young girl yelled from across the street.

Rey came to a stop. *Oh no.* Now Elsie would see what he'd bought. He'd wanted it to be a surprise.

She left Barb's side and ran across the street.

"You shouldn't run across the street," Rey said, wishing he could hide the pie box behind his back. It would be quite obvious though.

"There weren't any wagons or fast horses." Elsie's eyes zeroed in on the box. "You bought a cake?"

"A pie," he said. "I mean . . . it's a surprise."

"For my birthday?" Elsie practically squealed. She clapped her hands together.

"Sorry, Sheriff," Barb said, finally catching up to them after crossing the street much more slowly. Her gray hair was pulled into a tight bun beneath her straw hat, but perspiration gleamed on her face and neck despite the hat's shade. "I didn't expect to run into you so early in the afternoon. I thought we'd be safe doing a few errands now."

"It's all right." Rey tugged on his daughter's braid. "You'll find out soon enough, might as well be a day early."

Elsie jumped up and down a couple of times. "Can we have it tonight—like a birthday eve treat?"

It didn't take Rey long to decide. Peach pie on the day it was made was certainly better than the day after. "If it's all right with Barb."

Barb chuckled. "Oh, Sheriff, it's all right with me." She pulled out a fan from her shoulder bag and waved it vigorously in front of her face. "Now, who wants a cold lemonade from the mercantile before we head home?"

Elsie's hand shot straight up. "I do!"

"I'll have to meet you at home," Rey said. "I need to check in with Thatcher first."

As he strode to the sheriff's office, he decided that it was indeed a nice day—the nicest of days. He was very much looking forward to the peach pie tonight, as well as whenever Viola Delany swept back into town. He had no idea what he might say to her, or what the future might bring between them, but for now, he was enjoying the humming of his heart.

Thirteen

EVERYTHING ABOUT WYOMING REMINDED VIOLA of *him*.

Everywhere she looked, she thought she saw a tall cowboy, but each time it was someone else. It didn't help that so many men in Cheyenne wore cowboy hats and cowboy boots. Her heart had done more than one somersault, and her stomach wasn't in much better condition.

She should just take a carriage to Mayfair and see him, once and for all.

And then she'd know. She'd know if her constant thoughts about him had merit and if he returned those same thoughts.

"Excuse me, ma'am," a gentleman said as he moved past her toward the post office.

That's where Viola stood now, with three letters clutched in her hand. One to Aunt Beth, explaining that she'd try to visit each weekend, but she thought that living in Cheyenne would help her focus more on her training. The second letter was to Miss Barnwell and the director of the San Francisco nursing school, thanking them for the recommendation. And the third letter was to Sheriff Rey. She didn't know his address, but she assumed the title *Sheriff* would be directed to the right person.

His letter was very general, with a brief update on what had transpired the last several weeks. And at the end of it, she thanked him again for all of his help and protection in Mayfair. She'd been sure to add the return address to the envelope of the nursing school where she boarded.

That way he'd know where to find her, *if* he ever wanted to find her. Sure, she'd most likely see Rey when she visited Aunt Beth next week. But she didn't want the first time she saw him to be an awkward meeting—and she hoped that writing a letter explaining a few things would create a connection of friendship.

Was that really what she wanted? To have Sheriff Rey for a friend?

Yes, that's what she wanted. For now. Because she'd just committed to nursing school, and that needed to be her focus. She stepped into the post office and posted the letters. There. It was done.

Viola smiled to herself as she headed back to her rented room. In exchange for doing the laundry for other boarders, her rent would be covered. She needed to prepare for the church social tonight. She wouldn't let herself become a recluse, and despite all that had transpired with her parents, she wanted to honor her mother's original plea that she keep up on her singing. Surely the church in Cheyenne had a Sunday choir.

"There you are," Donna Dickson said as Viola walked into the back entrance by the rented rooms. "Are you coming to the church social still?"

"Yes, I just need to get ready," Viola told the brunette woman who had a ready smile and quick laugh. They'd become fast friends. "Give me ten minutes, maybe?"

"Of course." Donna flashed a smile and headed down the corridor.

Viola turned into her room and shifted through the bureau drawer to find her gloves. It was much too hot to wear them during the day, but an evening social might require more formal attire. She removed her bonnet and refreshed her hair arrangement.

Someone knocked on the door, startling Viola. It had only been a handful of minutes. Was Donna really that impatient?

"Yes?" Viola called.

"Someone's here to see you," Donna said through the door. "I told him you'd be a few minutes."

Him? Viola froze mid-motion adjusting her hair. Her heart began a slow pound. "Did he give his name?"

"Reynold Christensen."

Viola was glad there was a door between her and her new friend because she had to rest her hand on the wall next to the mirror. She didn't even know if she could get any words out to reply.

"Viola? Should I send him on his way?"

The curiosity in Donna's voice was plain.

"No, tell him I'll be out shortly." When she heard Donna's footsteps move away, Viola tried to resume fixing her hair, but her fingers were trembling.

Why was Rey here? In Cheyenne? At the nursing school? Maybe he had a message from Aunt Beth? Was everything all right with her? She gave up on her hair and sat on the edge of her bed.

She hadn't expected her pulse to jump around so much and for her stomach to erupt in anticipation. Donna was probably chatting with the sheriff—she was a friendly sort. And she'd be audience to their meeting.

It couldn't be helped. And she couldn't hide out in her room. Rey already knew she was here.

So she smoothed her hair over one shoulder and tied it with a ribbon. The hat and gloves could wait. Opening her door, she heard the rumble of a man's voice coming from the reception room. She headed down the corridor, following the sounds of conversation. As she neared, Rey's deeper tones separated from Donna's low laughter.

Envy pinched inside, surprising Viola. Rey was a free man, just as she was a free woman. She'd heard plenty of swoony comments over the sheriff when she was living in Mayfair. So why did Donna's laughter strike deeper?

Viola rounded the corner to find Donna sitting across from the cowboy. Rey looked over at Viola immediately, and her heart skipped more than one beat as his smile appeared. If he was smiling at her, he couldn't be delivering bad news, could he?

His cowboy hat rested on his knee, and he grabbed it, then rose to his full height so that she had to tilt her head upward to see him.

"Miss Delany."

"Mr. Christensen."

His green eyes flashed, and she knew he'd wanted her to call him Rey. But he'd been formal first, and they had an audience.

"Miss Dickson was just telling me all about the nursing program here. Sounds like you're in good hands."

"Oh, we're in good hands with Viola," Donna said. "She knows more than some of our current students."

Viola smiled politely because she was seriously resenting Donna's presence. Rey's gaze stayed on her, and she'd love to know what was going on inside his mind. "Is everything going well in Mayfair? How's Elsie doing?"

His smile reappeared. "Had a birthday this week, so I'm now living with a nine-year-old boss."

Viola couldn't hold back her laugh. "Well, tell her happy birthday for me."

Rey nodded. "Will do, ma'am."

Inwardly, Viola melted a little. He called her ma'am, no matter how many times she'd corrected him. It was his way of teasing her now.

"Who's Elsie?" Donna asked, which Viola found very impertinent of the woman to insert herself.

"My daughter."

"Ah, so you're married." Donna's voice held a note of disappointment. "Are you old friends with Viola, then?"

Rey finally turned his gaze fully to Donna. "I'm a widower, Miss Dickson. And Viola and I are new friends."

Donna's face flushed, but her eyes sparkled. "Well, you are welcome to visit any time. After class hours, of course."

"Thank you for the invitation," Rey said, a hint of amusement in his tone. His gaze shifted to Viola. "Your aunt sends her regards."

Not that Viola had forgotten about Aunt Beth, but seeing Rey so unexpectedly had made all commonsense questions flee from her mind. "How is she doing? I sent her a letter today." *And I sent one to you too.*

"She's doing very well," Rey said. "She gave me the location of this place."

"Who's your aunt?" Donna asked. "Is she the one who runs the bakery?"

"Yes, that's the one," Viola said, hoping that she'd kept the irritation out of her tone.

"Well, Miss Delany, I wondered if you might oblige me with a walk around the block."

"We were about to leave for the church social," Donna

said. "You should join us. We'd look good arriving with a new member."

"I—uh, don't live in this town, so I wouldn't exactly be considered a new member." Rey stumbled over his words. "Thank you for the invitation though, Miss Dickson." His gaze found Viola's again. "Pleased to see that you're settled in, Miss Delany. I'll give your best to Elsie and Beth."

"Thank you," Viola murmured, although inside she was screaming for him not to leave yet.

But that's exactly what happened. Reynold Christensen walked out of the reception room and onto the street, replacing his hat and striding away.

Viola's stomach dropped to her feet. Donna set in with the comments immediately, but Viola hardly paid attention. Ten minutes later, they headed to the church social, arm in arm, but Viola could only think about Rey walking out of the nursing school. His cowboy hat atop his head, his long strides taking him farther and farther away.

He hadn't come for any specific reason, which meant he'd come to see her. Was he doing other errands in Cheyenne, or was he heading back tonight?

Every word that Donna spoke now felt like cat claws scraping Viola's skin.

The church social didn't settle her heart or her mind. People milled about, and Viola introduced herself over and over. Finally, she told Donna she had a headache and would walk back alone.

"It's dark out," Donna protested.

"I'll keep to Main Street," Viola said. "Besides, there are plenty of people out walking. It's early yet."

She hurried along Main Street, keeping her eyes peeled. Maybe Rey hadn't left yet. Maybe he was loitering on the street, waiting for another chance to speak with her. But, of course, he wasn't loitering. She reached the nursing school without seeing him at all. He was truly gone.

She walked through the darkened building, her thoughts mulling over every word of their conversation. But mostly she thought of the way he'd looked at her. If she wasn't imagining things, the man was interested, just as Aunt Beth had stated.

Well, he'd get her letter tomorrow probably, and then maybe they could start some sort of correspondence.

Her step paused when she reached the reception room. In the light of the moon filtering through the windows, she saw an envelope on the floor by the door, as if someone had slipped something beneath it.

She crossed the room and picked it up. The envelope was sealed, and on the front, her name was scrawled across in bold penmanship.

Her breath shortened as she opened the envelope and tilted the letter toward the moon to read the words.

Dear Viola,

I should have expected our meeting to have an audience, but somehow I didn't plan for that. There are a few things I'd like to say to you, but they will have to wait until tomorrow. That is, if you can find time to get a way for a short walk? I'll be waiting across the street at 7:00 a.m., if that's not too early. I am happy to see you're doing well, and I'm sorry about the friction with your family. Your aunt told me a few things.

Take care,

Rey

She read the words more than once until she'd practically memorized them. He hadn't left after all. For some reason, she found that a very important detail. She'd find a way to meet him—a way that wouldn't be interrupted by Donna or anyone else.

Fourteen

WHEN 7:30 ROLLED AROUND, REY still didn't give up. Oh, he had all kinds of worries. Maybe Viola didn't get his letter. Or maybe she did but slept in. Or maybe she couldn't meet him after all. Or maybe she didn't want to.

He knew he'd surprised her the day before, but she didn't seem put-off by it. No, she was very agreeable and friendly. She'd hardly taken her eyes off of him, and he'd found that most gratifying.

Seeing her again had confirmed what he'd been feeling and what he could no longer deny.

He wanted to court Viola Delany. Well, he wanted to do more than court her, but courting would be the first step. She had just started nursing school, and that needed to run its course. Maybe she'd want to work in a bigger city versus a small town like Mayfair anyway. But should that prevent him from visiting her every so often? Taking her on walks? Going on rides? Sharing a meal or two?

He had hoped that this morning would be the start of their future . . . but if she didn't even show up, maybe he'd been mistaken. About everything.

The closer it grew to 8:00, the more his hopes seeped

out. Finally, he turned from the nursing establishment and began walking to the corral where he'd boarded his horse. The ride back to Mayfair would seem twice as long, that he was sure of.

"Rey!" someone called after him.

He thought he was imagining it at first, but when he heard his name a second time, he whirled around.

Viola was hurrying across the street, one hand on her hat, the other gripping a narrow book.

He stared as she closed the distance between them.

"You're still here."

Her gray eyes could have leveled him, but somehow he remained upright. "I'm still here."

And then she smiled, making her eyes sparkle. "Thanks for waiting. Sorry I'm so late. I live with a lot of nosy people." She looped her arm through his, about knocking him over with surprise, and tugged him along the boardwalk. "The sooner we're out of sight, the better. Donna is likely spying out the window."

"Donna?"

"Miss Dickson."

Ah. "She's a spy?"

Viola laughed, but it was a nervous laugh. "She's bored, is what I think. And nosy. But let's not talk about Donna Dickson."

"Let's not," he wholeheartedly agreed. He rather liked Viola's initiative to take his arm, and he rather liked the feel of her body pressing close to his, even if they were walking faster than he would have liked.

"I brought a pamphlet under the pretense of finding a quiet place to study." She held up said book. *Nurturing the Sick and the Training of Nurses.*

"Looks interesting."

Viola nudged him. "Now, tell me why you really came to see me yesterday, Mr. Sheriff."

They were near a garden that sat in front of a hotel. So Rey turned onto the garden path, which was a perfect place for some privacy and no prying eyes or ears of the likes of Donna Dickson.

"I wanted to see how you were faring," Rey admitted as they strolled along a garden path lined with bushes and spots of blooming flowers. The trees overhead offered enough shade that the flowers seemed to thrive. "Your aunt told me of your strife with your parents and that the nursing school in San Francisco didn't have any openings." He paused in his step and looked down at her. "Were your parents so very awful?"

Viola met his gaze, and in her eyes, he saw her distress. "My father was livid. My mother tried to give me money a few days ago, but I refused. I might be regretting that now."

Rey took off his hat and reached into the slot of the lining where he kept money like any cowboy did. "Here, I have some money. Can bring you more, too."

Viola took a step back. "I'm not taking your money, Rey. That's not what I intended when I told you about my parents. I want to do this on my own. It gives me a sense of accomplishment, more than I've ever had in my life."

"Are you sure?" Rey asked, even though he heard the conviction in her tone.

"I'm sure," she said in a soft voice. "Thank you for your offer. You're a good-hearted man."

"It's not a hard thing with a woman like you, Viola." He kept his hat in his hands. It was time for some serious talk. "I'm proud of all that you're doing. You'll be an excellent nurse."

He didn't expect her eyes to well with tears. No, that

wasn't his plan at all. "What is it? Did I say something wrong? Did you change your mind about the money?"

"No." Her voice came out shaky. "I don't want your money. I just . . . It's been a long few weeks. You and Aunt Beth have been my rock through everything. More than you can possibly know."

Her words completely stole his breath. She considered him a rock in her life? His heart galloped miles ahead of his thoughts, and he took a few slow breaths, trying to get his pulse under control. "I'll support you any way I can, Viola, I hope you know that." His own voice had turned raspy.

He hoped her tears would abate, but he wasn't sure of that fact because she suddenly closed the distance between them and wrapped her arms about his torso.

After he got over the initial shock, there was only one thing to do. Hold the woman who needed his support right now. Rey wrapped his arms about her and pulled her close. She nestled her face against his neck, and he rested his chin atop her head. She fit perfectly against him. He'd had a hint of that at the barn dance, but this . . . this was heavenly perfection.

"Thank you, Rey," she whispered.

"Anytime, sweetheart." He didn't plan the endearment; it just slipped out. And it fit. Viola Delany was a sweetheart through and through.

She drew away from him—not out of his arms, but enough that she could look him in the eyes. Her tears had dried, but there were traces along her cheeks. He lifted a hand and wiped away the moisture.

She didn't move, and her breaths came as rapid as his. Could she hear his heart thundering louder than a Wyoming storm?

"I have a confession, Viola Delany." If he didn't get it off his chest, it might well burst and keel him over here and now.

She was still in his arms, holding him close. "Then out with it, Mr. Sheriff."

Normally, he'd laugh, but he was too nervous for that. He drew in a breath, one filled with the scent of her, which happened to be peaches, even if she hadn't been baking a peach pie. The scent seemed to be her essence.

"I'd like to court you, ma'am." Another breath. "If you'll have me."

Viola's gray eyes stared into his own. He'd have given a right arm and possibly one of his legs to know what was going on in that brain of hers. "This is unexpected, Rey."

"Is it? In a good way, or a bad way?"

She smiled then, and his heart soared with hope. "In a good way. I don't know what you see in me, sir, but there's no other man in the world I'd rather be courted by than you."

Rey moved his hand to her face and ran his thumb along her jaw. "I see my future in you, dearest Viola."

Her eyelashes fluttered as he moved his hand behind her neck. "It looks like we're in agreement." She ran her hands up his chest, then looped her arms behind his neck, pulling him down.

He obliged.

"I think we should shake on our agreement," she whispered.

Their faces were only inches apart, and he could barely think beyond the words coming from her lips. "Shake hands? I have a much better idea."

"What's your idea?"

"This."

Rey kissed her then, because how could he not? He was

no greenhorn, and neither was Viola. He'd been married before, and she'd been engaged before. But none of that mattered now. The past slipped away, and only the present surrounded them.

Viola's mouth was soft, warm, and welcoming. Her fingers moved into his hair as she tugged him even closer. He smiled against her mouth, grateful for the privacy of this garden because he planned to give her a thorough kissing. None of that quick or furtive stuff.

Viola seemed in no hurry either. She smiled as well, then kissed him some more. He lifted her against him and wished they could skip the months of courting and go straight to the married part. But she needed time. He knew that.

"Put me down, Rey," she said with a laugh.

He chuckled and lowered her to the ground, then gathered her close, his mouth moving more slowly over hers this time. He settled his hands on her hips, the cotton of her dress warm and smooth beneath his fingers.

She sighed against his mouth, then drew back, her eyes a dreamy gray. "How long are you in Cheyenne?"

"I have to return this morning, but I can come back tonight or tomorrow. Whatever works for your schedule."

Her smile appeared. "You're going to wear your horse out."

"I have more than one horse, and besides, exercise is good for them."

Her fingers moved against his jaw, her thumb dragging against the stubble on his cheek. "Tomorrow morning, then. Same time, same place." She rose up on her feet and kissed the edge of his mouth.

Before he let Viola Delany get too carried away, he had to clarify something. "Wait. Does the same time mean seven o'clock or eight o'clock?"

She puffed out a breath. "Seven is a little too early, but maybe some days I can get out that early."

"Noted." He moved his hands behind her lower back and drew her flush with him. "I'll be here at seven o'clock tomorrow morning, and if I have to wait, I'll wait."

He loved the light in her eyes, the pink of her cheeks, and how her lips were swollen because of him. He didn't know how much time he had with Viola this morning—or in future mornings—so he decided to make the most of it. Slowly he lowered his mouth to hers again. He was in no hurry.

Epilogue

Five Months Later

VIOLA DELANY, SOON TO BE Viola Christensen, stood in the small living room of Aunt Beth's apartment. The upright mirror in the corner reflected a woman with blonde hair piled upon her head, wearing a white velvet dress. The pearl earrings and pearl necklace had been sent to her by her mother as a wedding gift.

But her parents weren't coming to the January wedding.

The cold wind whipped the bare trees outside along Main Street, but even the mournful howling didn't deflate Viola's heart. Parents or not, she was marrying Reynold Christensen this afternoon.

"You look like a beautiful winter rose," Aunt Beth said, coming into the front room. She wore her best dark blue dress with lace at the collar and cuffs. She beamed a smile and joined Viola in front of the mirror.

There were similarities between aunt and niece, but they only made Viola miss her mother more. This unexpected feeling had persisted all week—maybe it was because she and her mother had planned her last wedding together.

314

"I can't believe I'm really getting married." Viola gave a small laugh. "To a cowboy. And I'm going to be a step-mother, too."

Aunt Beth slipped an arm about her waist. "You'll find happiness every day of your life, dear. It's not every man who would agree with his wife about working as a nurse."

"Rey isn't every man." Viola tilted her head. "Besides, Elsie is excited to help me out after school. So it's two against one."

Aunt Beth chuckled. "You both have that man wrapped around your fingers. Now, let's get you hitched."

Viola turned away from the mirror and embraced her aunt. "Thank you for everything and for believing in me."

"None of the sappy talk. You'll make me cry off my makeup."

The two women headed downstairs where Deputy Thatcher waited for them with a carriage that would take them to the church.

Even though the wind was cold and blustery, and the sky hung with low, gray clouds, most of the town had turned up. Carriages and wagons lined the front of the church while horses stamped to keep warm.

"Here we are, ladies." Thatcher slowed the carriage in front of the church where someone had made sure there was room for the bride to arrive.

He handed both Viola and Aunt Beth down, then escorted them into the church. The organ music floated sweetly through the space, and everyone seated in the pews turned to look at Viola.

She grasped Thatcher's arm and forced a smile even though her heart was hammering in her throat. At the front of the chapel, Rey stood, wearing a full suit. She almost didn't recognize him with his slicked back hair and shaved face, but his smile was the same and those green eyes were the same.

The organ music changed to the wedding march, and Aunt Beth whispered, "It's your turn, dear. I'll see you after."

Suddenly Elsie appeared, wearing a white velvet dress, matching Viola's. Elsie held a basket of flower petals, and after grinning at Viola, she skipped down the aisle as she tossed petals. Most of them landed on the audience versus the floor, but no one seemed to mind.

Viola refocused on the man at the front of the church who watched her. She met his gaze, and even from a distance, she felt the warmth that was him.

"I'm ready," she told Thatcher, and the pair of them began to walk down the aisle.

The music soared around them, and Viola tried to smile at those in attendance, but her throat was so tight that it was hard to turn her head.

A gust of wind brushed the back of her head. Someone had arrived late, and Viola didn't think much of it until the music completely stopped. A man spoke in a rather loud voice behind her. "Is this the wedding of Viola Delany?"

"Are we too late?" a woman said.

Viola gripped Thatcher's arm and turned slowly around. She knew both of those voices.

Her parents had walked into the chapel, wearing long coats, heavy hats, their eyes bright, and their cheeks flushed red.

"Are you married yet?" her mother asked, her voice hitching. "Are we too late?"

Viola's mouth fell open. She couldn't have spoken if she wanted to.

The rest of the audience stared as if stunned. Not even Thatcher could form a word.

"We're not married yet, but if you'll take a seat, then you can watch the ceremony." Rey walked up the aisle. Tall and confident. He paused by Viola and bent to kiss her cheek. "You look beautiful, sweetheart."

"Rey . . ." she whispered.

"Yes?" He merely gazed at her, his green eyes calm, like an interrupted wedding was an everyday occurrence.

"My parents are here."

His gaze didn't leave hers, but his eyes sparked. "I can see that."

"Might I introduce you?"

"Of course."

Viola swallowed, then turned her head. Her parents were still standing just inside the entrance, although someone had mercifully shut the doors. "Mother, Father, I'd like you to meet Reynold Christensen. My fiancé."

Her mother moved forward. "Mr. Christensen, it's lovely to meet you." Her eyes brimmed with tears, and her lips trembled, but she was all smiles.

"Call me Rey." He extended his hand and shook Mother's hand. "Nice to meet you, Mrs. Delany."

Mother pulled a handkerchief from one of her pockets and dabbed her eyes.

"I'm Mr. Delany," a deeper voice said. "Viola's father."

Her father stepped up, his hand outstretched to Rey. The men shook hands, then Father's gaze was upon her.

"Viola, there's so much to say." A lump moved in his throat. "So much to apologize for." He looked around at the audience who was soaking up every word. "Might you do me the honor of allowing me to escort you up the aisle so you can marry this gentleman?"

"Oh, Father." Viola flew into his arms even though her dress was crushed and who knew what the result to her hairdo might be. When Father's arms hugged her tight, tears coursed down her cheeks. "Of course you can."

Next she stepped into her mother's arms. When they moved apart, Aunt Beth came forward, and the two sisters embraced for a long moment. Then Aunt Beth shook hands with Father and welcomed him to Mayfair.

"Beth, thank you for watching over our little girl," Father said, emotion edging his voice.

The confused audience, watching and avidly listening, began to clap as murmurs arose. Viola knew she owed many explanations, but for now the wedding must go on. She linked arms with her father.

"Now I'm truly ready."

Thatcher chuckled. "Everyone to their places. Let the wedding march begin again."

Viola's heart zoomed up and down with each step she and her father took toward Rey. He stood, hands behind his back, his gaze once again focused on her. The edges of his mouth lifted in an amused smile, and she could only guess at the thoughts behind his dancing eyes.

When her father released her arm, she took her place across from Rey, waiting for the reverend to begin the service. As he spoke, Viola's heart swelled at least another size or two. Her mother quietly sniffled in the front row, leaning her head on Father's shoulder, whose eyes were just as red.

"I love you," Rey whispered in the middle of the service.

"I love you too," Viola whispered back.

Her entire world had become this man and his daughter, but she was more than happy to add her own parents to the mix. She knew there was likely a lot of things to work out, a lot of things to understand, but they'd come to Mayfair. And that was the first and most important step.

After the reverend concluded, and after they exchanged their vows, Viola decided that the single gold band upon her ring finger was the most beautiful piece of jewelry she could ever wear. It was straight from Rey's heart, after all.

"May I kiss the bride?" Rey said as if they weren't being watched by a hundred people.

"You may," she whispered.

And then her cowboy leaned close, taking one of her hands in his. Before she closed her eyes, she saw him smile. Her eyes fluttered shut just as Rey made good on his promise and kissed his bride.

Heather B. Moore is a *USA Today* bestselling author of more than seventy publications. Her historical novels and thrillers are written under the pen name H.B. Moore. She writes women's fiction, romance, and inspirational nonfiction under Heather B. Moore. This can all be confusing so her kids just call her Mom. Heather attended Cairo American College in Egypt, the Anglican School of Jerusalem in Israel, and earned a Bachelor of Science degree from Brigham Young University. Heather is represented by Dystel, Goderich, and Bourret. Heather's latest books include *In the Shadow of a Queen, Under the Java Moon, A Seaside Summer, Until Vienna, The Healing Summer, The Slow March of Light,* and *The Paper Daughters of Chinatown.*

For book updates, sign up for Heather's email list:
hbmoore.com/contact
Website: HBMoore.com
Facebook: Fans of Heather B. Moore
Instagram: @authorhbmoore
Twitter: @HeatherBMoore
Blog: MyWritersLair.blogspot.com

Made in the USA
Columbia, SC
26 October 2023

24944815R00180